Whither Thou Goest

OTHER BOOKS BY AL LACY

Angel of Mercy series:

A Promise for Breanna (Book One)
Faithful Heart (Book Two)
Captive Set Free (Book Three)
A Dream Fulfilled (Book Four)
Suffer the Little Children (Book Five)
Whither Thou Goest (Book Six)
Final Justice (Book Seven)
Things Not Seen (Book Eight)
Not by Might (Book Nine)
Far Above Rubies (Book Ten)

Journeys of the Stranger series:

Legacy (Book One)
Silent Abduction (Book Two)
Blizzard (Book Three)
Tears of the Sun (Book Four)
Circle of Fire (Book Five)
Quiet Thunder (Book Six)
Snow Ghost (Book Seven)

Battles of Destiny (Civil War series):

Beloved Enemy (Battle of First Bull Run)
A Heart Divided (Battle of Mobile Bay)
A Promise Unbroken (Battle of Rich Mountain)
Shadowed Memories (Battle of Shiloh)
Joy from Ashes (Battle of Fredericksburg)
Season of Valor (Battle of Gettysburg)
Wings of the Wind (Battle of Antietam)
Turn of Glory (Battle of Chancellorsville)

Hannah of Fort Bridger series (coauthored with JoAnna Lacy):

Under the Distant Sky (Book One)
Consider the Lilies (Book Two)
No Place for Fear (Book Three)
Pillow of Stone (Book Four)
The Perfect Gift (Book Five)
Touch of Compassion (Book Six)
Beyond the Valley (Book Seven)

Mail Order Bride series (coauthored with JoAnna Lacy):

Secrets of the Heart (Book One)
A Time to Love (Book Two)
Tender Flame (Book Three)
Blessed Are the Merciful (Book Four)
Ransom of Love (Book Five)
Until the Daybreak (Book Six)
Sincerely Yours (Book Seven)

THE ANGEL OF MERCY SERIES

WHITHER THOU GOEST

BOOK SIX

AL LACY

MULTNOMAH BOOKS

This book is a work of fiction. With the exception of recognized historical figures, the characters in this novel are fictional. Any resemblance to actual persons, living or dead, is purely coincidental.

WHITHER THOU GOEST
published by Multnomah Books

© 1997 by ALJO PRODUCTIONS, INC.

Cover design by D² Designworks
Cover illustration by Vittorio Dangelico

International Standard Book Number: 978-1-60142-004-6

Published in the United States by WaterBrook Multnomah, an imprint of the Crown Publishing Group, a division of Random House Inc., New York.

MULTNOMAH and its mountain colophon are registered trademarks of Random House Inc.

ALL RIGHTS RESERVED
No part of this publication may be reproduced, stored in a retrieval system, or transmitted in any form or by any means—electronic, mechanical, photocopying, recording, or otherwise—without prior written permission.

For information:
Multnomah Books
12265 Oracle Boulevard, Suite 200
Colorado Springs, CO 80921

Library of congress Cataloging-in-Publication Data

Lacy, Al.
Whither thou goest/by Al Lacy.
p. cm.—(Angel of mercy series; bk. 6)
ISBN 1-57673-078-6
I. Title. II. Series: Lacy, Al. Angel of mercy series; bk. 6.
PS3562.A256W48 1997
813'.54—dc21 97-29863
CIP

146655433

For Kerry and Heidi McJunkins—
some people slowly ease into your heart,
but you charged into mine!
I love you.
I Thessalonians 5:28

PROLOGUE

AMERICA'S LATE NINETEENTH-CENTURY Wild West was well populated with outlaws and gunfighters, most of whom were spawned by the violence they experienced in the Civil War. It seemed that when the fighting was over in April 1865, great numbers of men who had worn blue or gray uniforms on bloody battlefields for four years still had a need for conflict and the smell of gunsmoke. Many of these men had gotten into trouble in their home states east of the Mississippi River, and had gone west to elude capture by the law.

The tame West slowly became the Wild West, as the wandering ex-soldiers sought adventure and excitement. Many turned to robbing banks, trains, and stagecoaches, while others found challenge in becoming feared for their prowess with a handgun. How fast a man could draw against an opponent, and how accurately he could shoot, made him a legend "in his own time." The more opponents he put down, the more feared he became.

Some of the most noted outlaws and gunfighters had been lawmen on the frontier who went bad for various reasons. Sometimes they went bad because of the low pay offered by towns, counties, or various territorial law agencies. They saw greater fortune in working the "other side" of the law. Others turned outlaw when those who had hired them, or voted them into office, complained about the way they were doing their jobs. In the minds of their critics, they were either too rough on lawbreakers or weren't rough enough. Often, these men got disgusted with the pressure and turned outlaw against a society they found impossible to please.

Other motivations sprang from being caught up in the quixotic phantasm born of mistaking outlaws, killers, and gunfighters as heroes. Many men died foolishly in fast-draw gunfights or in bloody shootouts with lawmen, often voicing their regret for having lived so violently, as they lay dying.

One infamous outlaw, who died as an old man, spoke of the depressive life he had lived. When Frank James—brother of Jesse—surrendered to Governor Thomas Crittenden at Jefferson City, Missouri, on October 5, 1882, he removed his revolver and gunbelt, handed them to the governor, and said, "I am your prisoner. I'm tired of running. Tired of waiting for a bullet in my back. Tired of looking into the faces of friends, and wondering if one of them is a Judas."

And, of course, there were always the good women of the Wild West who were left to stand weeping over the graves of husbands or sweethearts who had taken the wrong path in life.

There were also the men and women of the medical profession, who were called upon to use their skills on the men who lived violently and attempt to save their lives on the operating table.

Though it seems the Wild West is best remembered for its outlaws and gunfighters, there were good men who led decent lives and were excellent, loving husbands, including the lawmen who never tarnished their badges. When such a man stood at the marriage altar and took his vows, he meant every word he said, and proved it as time passed.

Just so the gallant bride, who lived in a rugged and unforgiving land that would not be settled and peaceful until after the turn of the twentieth century. She meant every word when she looked at her groom through her bridal veil and repeated after the preacher, "Whither thou goest, I will go; and where thou lodgest, I will lodge: thy people shall be my people, and thy God, my God."

1

THE MIDDAY SUN REFLECTED dully off the muddy Rio Grande wending its way past El Paso toward the Gulf of Mexico. It was a brisk December day in 1870, and a stiff wind swept down from the rugged Franklin Mountains, whose peaks took an uneven bite out of the blue Texas sky.

People stared as three teenage Mexican boys ran hard through El Paso's streets, ducking now and then into alleyways. Their pursuers wore wide-brimmed black Stetson hats and polished silver badges that bore the inscription: Texas Rangers.

The Rangers—Lieutenant Mark Gray and Corporal Jody Sleppy—were some ninety yards behind the boys when they saw them dash into a large barn on the north side of town. They had pursued the youths all the way from the bank of the Rio Grande, where the boys had attacked and robbed an elderly street vendor.

"We got 'em now Jody!" said Gray, between ragged breaths. As he spoke, he whipped out his Colt .45 and moved toward the barn.

Three months earlier, Mark Gray's wife, Mary, had been killed by Mexican bandits while riding in a stagecoach from Austin to El Paso. Ever since then, the lieutenant had shown hatred and a hair-trigger temper toward Mexicans. Twice, Jody had intervened to keep him from using excessive violence when they were capturing Mexican outlaws.

As they drew near the barn, Sleppy thought of the day less than a week ago when Captain Terrell Sears had warned Gray to get a grip on his temper and conduct himself as a lawman should, or he would have to turn in his badge.

"Mark," Jody said, "maybe you ought to wait here and let me go up close...see if I can coax them out."

The fiery excitement in Gray's eyes intensified as he said, "What's the matter, pal? You think I can't handle this?"

"I don't like what I see in you right now, is all. What those boys did was wrong, but the old vendor didn't look like he was hurt too bad. We need to arrest these boys and take them in. You look like you want to be both judge and jury."

Gray ignored Sleppy's words and cocked his revolver as he headed toward the barn. "Let's flush 'em out," he said.

"Don't forget, those boys aren't armed."

"And how do you know that? We were never close enough to 'em to see for sure."

"Eyewitnesses, Mark. The ones we talked to on the street. They said they didn't think the boys had guns or knives."

"You mean, they didn't *think* the boys were armed. But that doesn't mean they aren't! They've got to pay for what they did. If they have weapons and they try to use 'em, too bad for them!"

"Mark, listen to me!" Sleppy said. "You wait here. I'll go talk them out."

Gray ignored his partner's plea and stopped short of the open barn door. "All right, you lowdown scum, come out of there with your hands above your heads! If you don't do as I say, my partner and I will come in and get you! And you'll be plenty sorry if we have to do that!"

Immediately they heard a door open on the far side of the barn. When they ran around the corner, they saw the three boys heading across a field as fast as they could run.

Gray started after the boys, and Sleppy was close on his heels. Sleppy fired over the youths' heads and shouted, "Stop right now or I'll shoot lower!" The boys stopped in their tracks and raised empty hands above their heads.

Before they could turn around, Gray's revolver roared, and the boy in the middle fell facedown. The other boys wheeled about with their hands in the air and terror in their eyes. One of them cried out, "Please Señores Rangers! Please do not shoot us! We surrender!"

Sleppy looked at his partner in outrage and disbelief. "Mark, the kid stopped! Why'd you shoot him?"

"Don't you question me, mister!" Gray hissed. "I shot him because I thought he had a gun! I thought he was gonna shoot us!"

Sleppy knelt beside the fallen youth and scowled up at Gray. "With his back to us, Mark?"

Gray remained silent and watched Sleppy turn the boy over. "You saw his hands as well as I did," Sleppy said. "He wasn't carrying a weapon." He paused briefly to check the boy's pulse. "He's dead, Mark, and you killed him."

The two Mexican youths, who still held their hands above their heads, began to whimper.

"Shut up!" Gray said, glancing at the boys with hate-filled eyes. "If you no-goods hadn't robbed that old street vendor, your *amigo*, here, wouldn't be dead!"

Sleppy rose to his feet and fixed Gray with a cold stare. "Mark, Cap'n Sears will be furious when he learns you shot this kid in cold blood."

"Jody, you can't tell it that way to Sears! You're a fellow

Ranger. You've got to tell him it looked like the kid had a gun and was gonna open fire on us!"

Sleppy sighed as he slid his gun into leather. "Sure, Mark...with his back to us? Anyone can tell your bullet went straight in."

"Then you've got to tell the captain we couldn't get a clear view while we were chasin' 'em. It looked like he had a gun, and we couldn't take a chance. We had to shoot him."

"*We* didn't shoot him, Mark, *you* did. And the Captain will question these two prisoners. They'll tell him exactly how it happened."

"Not if they're dead, they won't!"

Sleppy squinted at his partner, who still held the cocked .45 on the Mexican youths. "Mark, get hold of yourself. What's the matter with you? You can't kill these kids. They're unarmed, and they've surrendered."

The lieutenant began to babble, and a wild look shone from his eyes. "Oh, yes I can. All Mexicans ought to be exterminated, but especially these two. They're not tellin' nobody nothin'! You gotta help me, Jody! We'll kill these two and tell Sears they were resistin' arrest. If they're left alive, I'll lose my badge and maybe even be prosecuted."

"You should've thought of that before you shot the kid, Mark. It's too late. You'll have to face the captain for what you did."

Mark Gray's body began to shake. He struggled to control his gun hand, forcing it to obey the warning message in his brain. In a flash, he wheeled, pointed his gun at Sleppy, and dropped the hammer.

The bullet's impact flopped Sleppy to his back. At the same instant, the two Mexican boys took off running. Gray turned and saw them heading for a thick mesquite patch on the edge of a shallow draw. He cocked his gun and fired, but the bullet plowed sod between the boys as they ran in a zigzag pattern. He fired repeatedly, but the boys disappeared into the draw.

"Drop it, Mark!" came a command from behind Gray. "Drop it, I said! You're under arrest for murder!" Sleppy was still on his back, but he held his gun trained on Gray without a tremor.

Mark Gray broke out in a cold sweat as he eyed the black bore of Sleppy's .45 and the cocked hammer behind it. He looked at Sleppy's wounded shoulder and then at his sweat-drenched face.

"I said drop it, Mark."

Gray watched his partner's pain-filled expression, then said, "You're a man of honor, Jody. You wouldn't shoot a man who wears a Texas Ranger badge on his chest." Even as he spoke, he snapped back the hammer of his own revolver and aimed between Jody's eyes. "See? I told you. It just isn't in you to shoot a fellow Ranger. What we have here, pal, is an old-fashioned Mexican standoff. And isn't that funny? I *hate* Mexicans!"

Sleppy's shoulder felt as if it were on fire. Strength was ebbing from his body along with his blood, and he knew he couldn't hold the gun steady for much longer.

"Now, let's see, Jody," Gray said, as he stood over him. "Since it isn't in you to pull that trigger, I guess I'll have to do it."

When Sleppy heard the hollow *click* of the hammer, his head bobbed in reaction, and his eyes fluttered.

Gray's face drew up in a puzzled frown as he looked at his empty gun. "Guess I lost count," he said in a tone he might have used if he'd just offered Sleppy a cup of coffee and found the pot empty.

Sleppy grimaced in pain, but he still held the gun steady on

Gray's face. "Like I said, Mark, you're under arrest for murder. And now, for the attempted murder of a Texas Ranger. Drop the gun."

Gray chuckled. "Like I said, it isn't in you to pull that trigger, Jody, especially if it means shooting me in the back. Now, I'm goin' over there to that farmer's corral and take one of his horses. All I want to do is make a clean getaway. Sorry I disappointed you. But I'm not sorry for the disappointment Sears will feel. I never did like him."

With that, Gray wheeled about and headed toward the barn at a fast pace.

Jody trained his gun on Mark's back and then dropped the barrel slightly. He couldn't do it. As he struggled to his feet, swaying unsteadily, he aimed at Gray again and shouted, "Stop! You're under arrest! If you don't stop, I'll have to shoot!"

Gray smiled to himself without looking back.

"Mark, I said stop! Don't make me do it!"

Just as Gray quickened his pace, he felt a burning sensation rip along his left side and heard the sharp report of Sleppy's gun. He staggered and grabbed at his side. "You dirty rat!" he hissed in disbelief.

Sleppy dropped to his knees and fired again, but the bullet missed Gray by three feet. He saw Gray stagger through the corral gate, and then Sleppy collapsed in a heap. His head was buzzing, and his strength was almost gone, but he struggled to get up. By the time he raised himself to his knees, he saw Mark Gray leading a bay mare through the corral gate. Gray had bridled her but hadn't attempted to throw on a saddle.

Sleppy watched his former partner swing aboard the animal and aim her northward at a full gallop. He lifted his gun and fired one more time, but the bullet went wild. Within seconds, Gray was out of sight.

Sleppy forced himself to a standing position, and the last thing he saw before collapsing unconscious was a wagon turning into the farmyard.

Captain Terrell Scars paced back and forth outside the operating room in El Paso's medical clinic. He was a tall man—six-foot-four, rawboned but muscular. Even though he was a captain, and not as likely to get into confrontations with outlaws and gunslingers as in his younger days, he still wore his gunbelt low and practiced his fast-draw daily. He had a reputation for being lightning quick on the draw and deadly as a rattler.

As he paced, he stroked his handlebar mustache nervously and muttered to himself. He looked down the hall and saw the farmer, Frank Clement, who had brought Corporal Jody Sleppy to the clinic and then gone to the Ranger office to notify him.

Clement approached Scars. "No word yet, Captain?"

"No. He's still in surgery."

"I just wanted to let you know that one of my horses is missing. You did say there was another Ranger with the corporal, and you were wondering what became of him."

"Yes."

"I think he took my bay mare, and he was bleeding. There was blood on the floor of the barn where I keep my bridles. Thought you ought to know."

"Thank you, Frank," said Sears. "I appreciate your telling me."

After Clement was gone, two nurses walked down the hall. One of them looked toward Sears. "Still no word, Captain?" she asked.

"No, ma'am. Could you go in there and see what's happening?"

"I'm sorry, sir, but anything that might interrupt Dr. Jeffries while he's doing surgery could prove unfavorable for your Ranger. I'm sure it won't be much longer."

Sears ran splayed fingers through his thick mop of salt and pepper hair, then nodded, and said, "I hope you're right. This is worse than waiting for a baby to be delivered."

"Your man will be all right, Captain," said the other nurse. "I was in the operating room when they brought him in. He did lose a lot of blood, but he looks strong and healthy. He'll pull through."

When the nurses were gone, Sears began to pace back and forth again, trying to make sense of what had happened. He was convinced that Jody Sleppy would never have shot anyone in the back. But Mark Gray had nurtured a hatred toward all Mexicans since Mary's death. If there was trouble between Jody and Mark about shooting the boy…

The door of the operating room opened, and Sears rushed forward. "How is he, Doc?"

Dr. Rayburn Jeffries smiled. "He's fine, Captain. I was able to get the slug out of his shoulder with no problem. He lost a lot of blood, but he'll build it back soon enough. We'll make him drink lots of water."

"No permanent damage?"

"No. He'll be good as new in a couple of months."

Sears's mouth turned down. "That long?"

"Mm-hmm."

"Is he conscious?"

"No, he's still out from the effects of the ether."

"I really need to talk to him, Doc. Will he be able to speak to me when he comes around?"

"He'll be groggy for a couple of hours after he wakes up. I'd say come back around seven o'clock tonight. He should be able to talk to you by then."

Corporal Jody Sleppy's first indication that he was still in the world of the living came at about four-thirty that afternoon. He was aware of people around him, but it took some time for him to realize he was in a place that smelled of medicine and antiseptic. By five-thirty, his mind was starting to clear. When he opened his eyes, he saw a nurse standing over him. He blinked until her face lost its blur. "Welcome back, Corporal," she said, as she smiled at him. "I'm Effie Muldoon. You're at the El Paso Clinic."

Jody noticed the sling holding his left arm and felt the pain in his shoulder. Suddenly it all came flooding back. He winced as he tried to move. "Am I in one piece, ma'am?"

"You sure are. Dr. Jeffries took the slug out of your shoulder and patched you up. You'll be fine in a couple of months."

"Months! Did you say *months?*"

"Indeed I did. It will take time for your wound to heal, but Doctor says you'll be fine eventually."

"Can I still be a Ranger?"

"Of course. Say, you Rangers have a sort of brotherhood, don't you?"

"I guess you could call it that. Why do you ask?"

"Because there've been eleven Rangers in here to check on you just since I came on duty at five o'clock."

Jody grinned. "Bless 'em," he said.

"For sure," Effie said, nodding. "Nurses on the other shift said your captain was here while you were in surgery. I think he'll be back later this evening. He must think a lot of you."

Three more Rangers came in to see about their friend. They had been gone a few minutes when Effie Muldoon brought in a tray with some chicken broth. Although Jody didn't care for chicken broth, he was hungry, and downed every drop Effie fed him.

At seven-thirty Terrell Sears appeared at Jody's open door.

"Hello, Cap'n," Jody said.

"Well, you're awake, I see," said Sears, smiling as he stepped into the room.

"I heard you were here when they had me in surgery, sir."

"Well, somebody had to play mother for you," the captain said with a chuckle. He picked up a chair and set it down beside the bed.

A crooked smile captured Jody's lips. "Somehow, Cap'n, you just don't look the part. At least, I never saw one with a mustache."

Sears barked out a laugh as he eased onto the chair. "I'm glad to see you still have your sense of humor."

"Yes, sir."

The captain's features turned serious. "I know bits and pieces of this robbery situation and the chase," he said, "but you'll have to fit it all together for me. First of all, I want to know who shot you, Jody."

Jody swallowed with difficulty and said softly, "Mark Gray."

"I figured as much. Unless I miss my guess, the whole thing centered around the fact that those boys were Mexicans, didn't it?"

"It did, Cap'n."

"Tell me about it. The whole story, starting from the moment you and Mark were called to the scene of the robbery."

Sleppy's weak body made the telling of the story slow, but when he finished, Captain Sears's expression was grim. He shook his head and said, "I'd hoped Mark was getting control of his hatred of Mexicans. Before Mary's death he was one of the best men that ever served under me. We didn't always get along, but I couldn't fault his work as a Ranger. Fast with a gun, too. He'd have been dead a dozen times if he wasn't."

Jody nodded. "I always wondered, sir, who was fastest, you or Mark?"

Sears pulled at his earlobe. "Well, you'll probably never have that question answered, son."

"Guess not. But I figure you've got the edge on him."

Sears grinned. "First thing tomorrow I'll have men out looking for him. Seems strange to consider him a fugitive. At least he'll be easier to catch since he's wounded."

Sleppy's lips pulled tightly in a grimace. "I wouldn't count on it, Cap'n. Mark's as tough as they come. And I don't think the wound is too bad, or he wouldn't have been able to get on that horse. Tell the Rangers to be careful. Mark would have killed me if there'd been one more live cartridge in his gun."

Sears smacked his fist into the palm of his hand. "I'd like to go after him myself. He's shamed the badge I pinned on him, and he's shamed the Texas Rangers."

2

ON THE SAME DAY CAPTAIN SEARS sent a team of Rangers on the trail of Mark Gray, two men rode toward Denver from the flat and frozen eastern plains.

Clear, cold sunshine touched the snow-laden earth, reflecting its bright glare all around. Max Richter and Hank Chatham squinted as they set their gaze on the Mile High city and the majestic Rocky Mountains beyond it, dressed in their snowy cloak.

As Richter and Chatham rode up Colfax Street, a biting wind made them turtle their heads into their upturned collars. The board sidewalks had been shoveled, and small piles of snow stood between the hitch rails and the edge of the boardwalks.

Richter's breath misted out as he spoke. "The town's grown a lot since I was here a year and a half ago." He raised a gloved hand and pointed toward the business district. "Well, lookee there. They've even got a hospital now."

"That's what the sign says," Chatham mumbled. "Mile High Hospital. Hey, maybe they got more banks, too."

"Well, if they do, we're still gonna pick the smallest one. Since our gang is down to just you and me, I ain't yearnin' to try one of the big ones. Too risky."

Chatham nodded. "A small one still oughtta get us enough cash to get through the winter in the mountains. Then come spring, we'll move on to California."

As the bank robbers rode past Mile High Hospital, Chatham said, "I sure miss Vic, Buddy, Ben, and Mort."

"Yeah, me too. Life ain't never gonna be the same without 'em."

"Our bank robbin' ain't either." Max sighed, and the icy wind carried the white plume away. "Course, we get to California, we just might find us some new boys who like gettin' cash our way. We're comin' up on the banks now," he said. "Looks like the same ones. See the Frontier down at the end of the block?"

"Yep."

"Looks like it's still the smallest."

"Well," Chatham said, "we'll just make us a small withdrawal."

"First things first, of course," Richter said, and winked.

"A drink?"

"Yep. Best saloon in town is the Big Buffalo—next block."

"Well, let's get to it."

Neither man turned his head when he rode past the Frontier Bank, and there was nothing about them to suggest their intentions. Max Richter had told his partner that not only did Denver have a sheriff's office, but the federal building on Tremont Street housed the district office of the United States Marshal. Deputy U.S. marshals often rode in and out of town, and the two outlaws had a good laugh over the possibility of being mistaken for the law.

The plan was that Max would enter the bank alone and make the tellers empty out their cash drawers at gunpoint, while Hank stayed just outside the door to stand watch. They would make a quick "withdrawal" and ride hard for the mountains. With a decent head start, they could find ample hiding places in the Rockies.

The two men dismounted and crunched through the snow up to the boardwalk and entered the Big Buffalo Saloon. They ordered only one drink each at the bar, then threaded their way around chairs and tables to a table in a back corner.

While they sipped their whiskey, they discussed the bank robbery in Burlington, Colorado, where their four partners had died. The bank had been robbed three times within ten days, and the marshal and the citizens of the town were ready for the next robbery attempt. Only Richter and Chatham made it to their horses and rode out of town.

A posse was soon on their trail, but the outlaws managed to escape and holed up in an old abandoned barn near the small town of Anton. They stayed there for nearly two months, then rode for Denver.

Richter polished off the contents of his shot glass, thumped it on the table, and said, "Let's do it."

Breanna Baylor walked along the boardwalk, holding the brim of her hat with one hand and clutching a small package with the other.

As she drew near Corrigan's Clothing Store, squinting against the glare of sunlight off the snow, she saw Sheriff Curt Langan and his deputy, Steve Ridgway, angling toward her as they crossed the snow-crusted street, timing their moves between wagons, buggies, and riders on horseback.

"Morning, Breanna," Langan said, touching the tip of his hat brim.

"Morning, ma'am," said Steve. "Cold enough for you?"

Breanna laughed. "I was thinking how nice it would be in Florida or southern California right now," she said. Then to Langan, "Stefanie and the children all right?"

"Mm-hmm. Stefanie's working at the hospital today. As you may know, one of the nurses is a patient there."

"Yes. Molly Simmons slipped on ice yesterday afternoon and hurt her back. So Stefanie's filling in for her?"

"Yes. Kathy Bayless will watch the children at the parsonage after school. The Bayless kids and our kids have a great time together."

"I've noticed that."

"So, is this a day off for you, Breanna?" asked Steve.

"No, I worked from eight till three o'clock at Dr. Goodwin's office yesterday, then did the four-to-midnight shift at the hospital. I'm scheduled to work the same shift this evening. I'm catching up on some shopping right now."

Langan turned to Steve. "There's a couple of rowdies to let out of jail after last night's trouble at the Rusty Gun Saloon. That is, if they've sobered up by now. Guess we'd better go check on them. And I've got a stack of paperwork to wade through while you sweep out the jail."

"How about *me* doing the wading, and *you* doing the sweeping?" Ridgway said with a laugh.

Langan clapped a hand on his deputy's shoulder. "That's the way it will be when I become the deputy and you become the sheriff, son."

Steve shrugged and winked at Breanna. "That day isn't far off. Next election, I'd say."

Langan snorted. "When rhinoceroses climb trees!"

Ridgway laughed. *"Rhinoceroses?* Boy, I should already be the sheriff of this county! Don't you know, Sheriff Langan, that the plural of rhinoceros is *rhinoceri?* How can you be the sheriff of Denver County and not know that?"

"It's not rhinoceri, kid. It's rhinoceroses. Right, Breanna?"

Breanna smiled and said, "I think you're both right. The plural of rhinoceros can be either rhinoceroses *or* rhinoceri."

"See there, smarty?" Langan said. "What do you think of that?"

Steve grinned impishly. "Maybe Breanna ought to be sheriff of Denver County."

"No, thanks," she said with a giggle. "Then I'd have to put up with *you* as my deputy!"

The three had a good laugh, then sheriff and deputy said good-bye to Breanna and headed toward the sheriff's office, still jabbing at each other.

Breanna watched them for a moment, grinning to herself, then moved on. She stopped in front of Corrigan's, and had just put her hand on the doorknob, when she heard a female voice say, "Yoo hoo! Breanna!"

She looked up to see elderly Maude Fleming, whom she had nursed back to health from a stroke a few months earlier and had led to the Lord in the process. Maude was about to enter the Frontier Bank, just three doors from Corrigan's.

Breanna waved. "Hello, Maude. How are you?"

"This cold weather bothers my arthritis some, but other than that, I'm fine. God bless you, honey!"

"You, too, dear."

Maude entered the bank, and Breanna stepped inside the clothing store. The little bell above the door jingled. The heat from the potbellied stove near the counter kept the store comfortably warm.

"Well, if it isn't the most beautiful woman in all the world!"

came the voice of Breanna's sister, Dottie.

She was standing near the counter with store owner Bertha Corrigan and three other women.

Breanna batted her eyes and said, "You only say that because you and I look so much alike, Dottie, dear."

Dottie laughed, sounding just like Breanna. "How else can I get such a compliment, except from my husband?"

Breanna turned her gaze to the other women. "Hello, Bertha...René...Maggie...Janet."

The ladies chorused a greeting as she walked up to the group.

She glanced around as she laid down her package and slipped off her gloves. "You ladies run poor Harry out of the store?"

Bertha snickered. "I think we might have. Harry doesn't like girl talk. He remembered something he needed to do in the storeroom."

Breanna smiled. "Did those two blouses I ordered come in yet, Bertha?"

"Yes. I have them ready for you." The store owner turned and pulled a small package from a shelf behind her, laying it on the counter.

While Breanna was paying for the blouses, Maggie Stroud said, "Breanna, have you heard from your handsome John Stranger lately?"

"Yes, I—"

Her words were interrupted as the front door opened and the little bell jingled.

Pastor Robert Bayless held open the door for his wife and then stepped in behind her. Kathy's cheeks were rosy from the cold. As greetings were exchanged all around, Breanna placed the change from her purchase inside her purse.

"We're here to buy me a new pair of gloves," Kathy announced, heading for the table that displayed men's and women's gloves, and mittens for children. "My old ones are about to come apart."

Pastor Bayless turned to Breanna. "Heard anything from John?"

"To answer your question, and Maggie's, yes...I received a telegram from him yesterday. He's finished the work in Butte City, Montana, and will be home day after tomorrow on the morning train from Cheyenne City. He sent the wire from Billings."

"Did he say how it went in Butte City? That snow ghost thing, I mean?"

"No details. Just that the killer is dead. John said he's fine—not even a scratch."

"Praise the Lord for that," spoke up Dottie. "Matt and the kids and I sure prayed hard enough for him."

Breanna nodded. "I'm so thankful to God for His protective hand on John."

"Ah...Breanna..." said Bertha Corrigan

"Yes?"

"I haven't heard anything about wedding bells. Are they in the offing?"

Breanna's face tinted. "Well..." she began, clearing her throat and glancing at the pastor, "wedding bells definitely are in the offing, but there won't be an official announcement until John returns. But we've agreed that upon his return, we will ask our pastor for an appointment to discuss the wedding."

Bayless chuckled and looked at his wife. "Honey, I told you it was getting close," he said.

Dottie hugged her sister. "Oh, sweetie, I'm so happy for you!"

"Thank you, little sister."

René Allen, who was in her early twenties and yet unmarried, said, "Oh, Breanna, you are so fortunate to have a man like the rugged John Stranger in love with you!"

Breanna smiled. "And don't I know it!"

Harry Corrigan came from the back room in time to add his two cents. "Well, he's mighty fortunate to have such a lovely and charming lady in love with *him!*"

"You're so right, Harry," Dottie said, and slipped an arm around her sister's waist.

"You two embarrass me," Breanna said, picking up her packages. "It's time yours truly finished her shopping. Two more stops to make."

Breanna stepped outside into the nippy air and listened to the sound of hooves and wheels crunching on hard-packed snow. She pulled her coat collar around her neck and turned right on the boardwalk. Halfway to her next stop she realized she'd forgotten to put on her gloves after leaving Corrigan's. Oh, well, it wasn't that far to the general store on the corner.

Inside the Frontier Bank, Max Richter swiveled the muzzle of his revolver between the two frightened tellers, telling them to hurry up.

He flicked a glance at two men—the bank president and another officer—who sat at desks behind a gated railing with their hands above their heads. Richter warned them that if they let down their hands, he would shoot a teller.

There were seven customers in the bank—four men and three women. They had been given the same warning, and they stood like statues with their hands above their heads.

Richter glanced toward the door where his partner stood

just outside on the boardwalk. He noticed that Hank had opened the door a little too wide. No matter; they were almost done here anyway.

As Breanna walked toward the corner, her attention was drawn to the rough-looking man standing outside Frontier Bank looking in. She slowed her pace and studied the man's back, then looked straight ahead when he glanced over his shoulder. She was still two stores away from him. From the corner of her eye, she saw him glance at her, then look down the street from one end to the other before putting his attention back inside the bank.

Breanna looked past him through the partially open door, and saw a husky man holding a gun. Her pulse quickened, and there was a prickling all over her body.

She glanced at the man at the door. At least his gun was still holstered. She looked around to see if there was any sign of sheriff, deputy, or any of the deputy U.S. marshals, who were often seen on Denver's streets.

Although there were many vehicles and saddle horses at the hitch rails, the street was almost devoid of people. She saw three men entering a saloon a half-block away, but to call out for help would endanger the people inside the bank, as well as herself. A woman and a small child were climbing into a buggy in front of the general store, but there was no one else in sight for over two blocks in either direction.

The man continued to look inside the bank as if he'd dismissed the harmless woman walking toward him.

Compulsion overrode Breanna's better judgment. With pounding heart, she laid her packages down and tiptoed up behind Hank Chatham. In one smooth move, she yanked his revolver from its holster, cocked the hammer, and took two steps back, holding the gun on him with both hands.

Chatham whirled and slapped at his empty holster. His face went gray with shock as he found himself looking down the muzzle of his own gun.

"Down on your face, mister! Now!" Breanna said in a low voice.

Chatham's face turned beet-red, and he gave her a hot stubborn look.

"Now!" Breanna said, pointing the gun directly between his eyes.

Her hands began to tremble, and Hank swallowed hard. His gun had a hair trigger. One tiny jerk of her forefinger would put a .45 slug in him. "Okay, okay," he said, dropping to his knees. "Just point that thing away from me."

Breanna followed his movements with the muzzle of the gun as he dropped to his knees, then lay facedown on the boardwalk.

Suddenly the man inside the bank was backing out the door, carrying a moneybag in one hand and his gun in the other. He glanced over his shoulder and hissed, "Hank where are y—"

Max Richter stopped short when he saw his partner in such a helpless position and a woman holding Hank's own gun on him. He hissed at Breanna, "I'll kill you, woman!" and started to swing his gun around.

Breanna knew it was shoot or get shot, and the breath gushed from Richter's mouth as he jackknifed from the impact of the .45 slug to his midsection and keeled over headfirst.

Chatham started to get up.

"Stay right there, buster!" Breanna said, swinging the muzzle in his direction.

Suddenly there were men pouring out of the bank and from stores and shops up and down the street. A deputy U.S. marshal who was riding by pulled rein and slid from his saddle.

"Get the sheriff, deputy!" the bank president shouted. "We've got a man to arrest, and one to take to the hospital!"

The federal man nodded, vaulted into the saddle, and galloped away.

Harry Corrigan and Pastor Bayless came running from the clothing store, with Dottie Carroll and Kathy Bayless right behind. Bertha and the other women stood on the boardwalk, looking on. Dottie reached her sister just as she handed Chatham's gun to one of the men who had come from the bank.

Breanna then dropped to her knees beside the outlaw she had shot. He was bleeding profusely and only half-conscious.

"What happened, Breanna?" asked Pastor Bayless.

"Bank robbery. The big one was inside, and the other one was at the door as a lookout. I got his gun just before his partner came out. Made him lie facedown, as you see him now. The other one cursed me, saying he was going to kill me. He was bringing his gun around to do just that, and I didn't have any choice but to shoot him."

"Are you all right, Breanna?"

"Yes. But this man isn't. We've got to get him to the hospital."

3

Hank Chatham's countenance sagged as Sheriff Langan and Deputy Ridgway ushered him down the short hall to the cell block. A barred door stood open, waiting for him. The other five cells were empty.

Chatham stiffened as he neared the cell door, and Langan gave him a not-so-gentle shove, propelling him into the eight-by-ten cubicle.

"Lock it, Steve," Langan said, as he slammed the door.

The outlaw whirled around and moved to the barred door as Ridgway turned the key. "Stinkin' woman," he said.

Langan pressed close to the bars. "Watch your mouth, Chatham. You're talking about a dear friend of mine."

"Mine, too," Ridgway said. "No more talk like that about Breanna. Bothers you that a little lady took your gun away from you and foiled the robbery, does it?"

"She'll get hers," Chatham said.

"Not by your hand, she won't," Langan said. "I told you, I've got a drawer full of wanted posters on you and your pal. Both of you are wanted for murder in three states and two territories. Your next stop will be at the end of a rope. And so will your partner's, unless he dies from that bullet in his stomach. *Your* bullet."

"If it hadn't been for that woman—"

"You've got it wrong," Langan said. "Don't blame her. You and Richter chose to rob that bank."

"Yeah, but how many women would do a thing like that? Take a man's gun from him, and make him lie down on his face?"

Ridgway chortled. "Not many. But there aren't many women like Breanna."

The lawmen left Hank Chatham with his angry thoughts and returned to the office.

"Steve, I've got this endless stack of paperwork to attack," said Langan. "You go on over to the hospital and see how they're coming with Richter. If he pulls through, we'll have to handcuff him to the bed till he's ready for his own private cell."

"Okay. Too bad about that paperwork...I already got my sweeping job done."

"Get outta here!" Langan said in mock anger.

Mile High Hospital's head nurse, Mary Donelson, began administering ether to the man on the operating table.

"Don't put him under too deep, Mary. This shouldn't take long," said Dr. Matthew Carroll, Denver's top-notch surgeon and chief administrator of the hospital.

Mary had already laid the surgical instruments on a small cart and wheeled it to the head of the operating table. She left the folded, ether-soaked cloth over the patient's nose and mouth and stepped to the nearby cupboard where Carroll waited to wash his hands.

"All right, Mary, let's get the surgeon ready," he said, holding his hands over a porcelain basin.

She picked up the water bucket. "Running water, like the Bible—"

A tap on the door interrupted her words.

"I'll see who it is, Doctor."

Nurse Rhonda Lampley stood at the door. "Dr. Gleason sent me, Mary," she said in a half-whisper. "Has Dr. Carroll started the surgery on Mr. Gaylord?"

"No, but he's about to. What is it?"

"Doctor Gleason's going to take over in here. There's a man with a bullet in his stomach who needs Dr. Carroll's expert hands. That's how Dr. Gleason put it. Can Dr. Carroll come right now?"

"What is it, Rhonda?" came Dr. Carroll's voice when he saw who was at the door.

"Well, sir, your sister-in-law just shot a bank robber. She's here to help you with the surgery."

Carroll's blond eyebrows arched in disbelief. *"Breanna* shot a bank robber?"

"Yes, sir. She'll tell you all about it later, but Dr. Gleason says you're the one to do the surgery, and asks that you come quickly."

"All right." He turned to Mary. "Dr. Gleason is already familiar with Mr. Gaylord's problem. He'll be able to proceed here without delay."

"Yes, sir."

Dr. Carroll walked toward the other operating room, where Dr. Gleason met him at the door and made a couple of remarks before heading toward the other surgery room.

As Gleason entered, he said, "All right, Mary, let's get to work on Mr. Gaylord. His operation will be child's play compared to what Dr. Carroll faces."

Max Richter was barely conscious as two nurses worked over him, sponging away blood from his wound and cutting away his shirt. Louisa Birkin and Shirley Maxwell were both new in Denver and had only casually met Breanna Baylor, but felt a little in awe of her excellent reputation as a nurse. They looked up expectantly when the door opened.

Rhonda Lampley preceded Dr. Carroll into the room and headed for the cupboard to prepare the ether.

"Where's Nurse Baylor?" asked Carroll, looking around.

"Right here, Doctor," Breanna said as she entered the room, tying the surgical gown behind her narrow waist.

Dr. Carroll stepped up beside Shirley and looked at the wound, then turned his gaze on Breanna. "Rhonda tells me this man robbed the Frontier Bank, and you shot him."

"Yes," Breanna said, as she moved toward the cupboard. "Shirley can pour water for us while we wash our hands...as soon as you're ready, Doctor."

Carroll examined the wound more closely. "And you asked to help with the surgery, Breanna?"

"Yes, I did. The man was going to kill me, Doctor. I shot him in self-defense. But I...I want to help save his life if I can."

Louisa, who continued to prepare the patient for surgery, said, "Miss Baylor, why would you want to help save this outlaw's life?"

As soon as Shirley lifted the water bucket, Breanna poured lye soap on her hands and held them over a basin so Shirley could rinse them. "As a Certified Medical Nurse, Louisa, you should understand. We took an oath to save lives."

"I know, but if I'd shot a man to keep him from killing me—especially when I was single-handedly foiling a bank robbery—I think I'd let some other nurse help save his life."

Breanna rubbed her hands briskly while Shirley poured a slow, steady stream of water over them. "It was my duty as a citizen of Denver to stop the bank robbery, if possible," she replied. "And as a Christian and a Certified Medical Nurse, I must make every effort to keep Max Richter alive."

"Well, you're made of better mettle than I am," said Shirley. "If the man had tried to kill me, I wouldn't have the same attitude you do."

Breanna shook the water from her hands and dried them with a sterilized towel. "I'm ready, Doctor."

Mary Donelson's office was directly across the hall from the operating room. A large glassed-in window gave her a good view of the hall.

Nearly four hours had passed since the surgery began, and Mary's daughter, Stefanie Langan, and Deputy Sheriff Steve Ridgway, waited with Mary in her office, discussing the particulars of Breanna's involvement in the foiled robbery.

The door across the hall opened, and Rhonda Lampley emerged, looking tired. Breanna and Dr. Carroll followed. As the trio moved toward Mary's office door, she rose from her desk to meet them. "How did it go?" she asked.

"He's alive at the moment," Carroll said. "The next twenty-four hours will tell the story."

Mary nodded. "I've assigned Stefanie to watch over him till her shift is up."

"Anything special I need to know, Doctor?" asked Stefanie.

"Just check for hemorrhaging. I closed all the severed arteries, of course, but they could open up again."

"Yes, sir."

"He still might not make it. That slug really tore up his insides."

"I'll keep a close eye on him, Doctor," Stefanie said, "and I'll advise the same to the nurse who takes my place when the shift changes. How long will you be here, Doctor?"

Carroll glanced at the clock above the surgery door. "At least until six. Call me if you need me. I'll check on the patient before I go home."

"Yes, sir." Stefanie then crossed the hall and entered the surgery room to check on Max Richter.

Mary embraced Breanna while Deputy Steve Ridgway and Dr. Carroll looked on, grinning.

"I'm so proud of you," Mary breathed into her ear.

Breanna's lips curved in a soft smile. "I just did what had to be done."

"And worked for nearly four hours, along with Dr. Carroll, to save that man's life."

Steve Ridgway sighed. "Saved his life so we can hang him. He's wanted for murder in three states and two territories."

"Well, at least it will be the law that ends his life, and not me," Breanna said.

"If he makes it at all," said Carroll. "He's got a long way to go."

Ridgway nodded. "If he survives, Doctor, the sheriff wants me to handcuff him to the bed. I'll stay in touch with you so I'll know when that's necessary."

Carroll nodded. "And if I don't happen to be here when you come in, or I'm unavailable, Mrs. Donelson can tell you what you need to know."

"All right. Thank you, sir."

Breanna looked at Steve. "Is Chatham a wanted murderer, too?"

"Yes, and he's really got it in for you. It's your fault he's going to hang, you know."

"My fault?"

"Sure. You're the one who captured him."

"And I'm the one who made him murder people?"

"All he knows is that a woman took his gun away from him and made him lie facedown on the boardwalk while she shot his partner. And now his partner may die, and Chatham for sure is going to hang. So you see...it's all your fault."

"Maybe I'll have a better day tomorrow," Breanna said, rolling her eyes. "Well, I've got to clean up and get out of here. I didn't finish my shopping."

When Breanna reached the lobby of the hospital, she found a reporter and a photographer from the *Denver Sentinel* waiting for her, along with Denver's mayor, Jess Collins, and Edgar Turnquist, president of the Frontier Bank.

Mark Gray clutched his bleeding side as he rode toward Guadalupe Springs, a small village at the foot of the Guadalupe Mountains, nearly a hundred miles from where he'd stolen the horse.

An ex-Texas Ranger named Cecil Yates lived there. He had worked as a partner with Gray many times in Gray's early years as a Ranger, and they had maintained their friendship, even when Yates was transferred from El Paso to Fort Worth.

Shortly after Cecil was transferred, he was wounded in a gun battle with outlaws. The bullet shattered his right knee and left him with a stiff leg and a decided limp. He was forced to retire from the Rangers, even though he believed he could still do the job. When the chief Ranger of his district pronounced him unqualified, and no Ranger office anywhere would let him back on the force, Yates became embittered.

Now Gray thought about how he would use that to his advantage and get Yates to hide him and find medical help.

He found a small creek and bathed his wound in the cool water, then drank his fill. When the flow of blood had stopped, he ripped up his shirt to make a bandage, then led the mare to a large rock that jutted out of the ground, and mounted. It would be a long ride to Guadalupe Springs, but once he got there he had no doubt Cecil would help him, even if Captain Sears put a team of Rangers on his trail.

Gray stopped a few times, whenever he came to water, but pressed on all night long.

Late in the afternoon of the next day, he reached the village, which was populated with a mixture of Caucasians, Mexicans, and Indians. He was exhausted and could no longer hold himself erect in the saddle. About an hour before, he had begun to bleed again. Now he bent low over the mare's neck while the blood trickled through his fingers as he pressed his hand to his side.

Adults and children alike gawked at him as he painfully guided the bay down narrow streets past mud hovels and ramshackle frame huts, turning at one corner then another.

Cecil's shack was at the end of a dead-end street. None of the tumbledown shacks in Cecil's block were occupied, and beyond his house were rock-strewn fields of sagebrush and cactus that ran some two hundred yards to the base of the barren Guadalupes. The twin summits, Guadalupe Peak and El Capitan Peak, loomed over the village like giant sentinels.

Gray saw a shadow at the front window of Cecil's shack as he guided the mare into the yard between two gnarled and twisted piñon trees. The shadow moved, and the squeaky front door opened.

"Mark!" Cecil called, limping across the porch and small yard as fast as he could. "What's happened to you?"

Gray let go of the reins and spoke through gritted teeth. "I've...been shot."

Yates reached up. "Just ease on down, ol' pard. Let's get you into the house and see what we can do."

Moments later, Gray was stretched out on a rickety old bed. Yates did a quick examination of the wound and said, "Bullet went on through, Mark. You can be mighty glad for that."

"I am."

"You're losin' blood, though. You need doctorin'. Tell you what. There's an old Comanche woman who lives on the north side of the mountains. Not far. She's our local physician, sort of. She's good at usin' herbs and plants and that kind of stuff, and she's real good with gunshots. I'll go get Nana. Be back in about half an hour or so. She'll clean the wound, stitch it up, and get the bleedin' stopped. You just rest."

Thirty minutes later, Yates returned with Nana, whom Mark Gray figured must be at least ninety years old. Her long hair was totally silver. She had deep wrinkles in her neck and face. Her dark eyes shone and she gave him a toothless smile when Yates introduced her to his friend.

Nana carried a well-worn leather bag, which she set on the table next to the bed. She pulled Mark's hand away from the wound and bent over it, squinting. "Mmm," she said. "Nana stop bleed. Mark Gray hold again."

Gray pressed his palm to his side once more, and Nana lowered the leather bag to the floor and opened it. She began taking out supplies and laying them on the small table.

The old Comanche woman used liquid from a dark bottle to wash the wound. It burned fiercely, but Gray endured it without uttering a sound. She then used a crude needle and something that resembled thread to suture the wound. Then she covered the wound with a strong-smelling salve and used old but clean cloth as a bandage.

When she was finished, Mark tried to pay her, but she wouldn't accept the money.

"No, no," she said, waving a palm at him. "Nana help Mark Gray because he friend of Cecil Yates. Cecil Yates go hunting much. Bring meat to Nana. We friends. Mark Gray friend."

Nana said she would come back to look at the wound in two moons if Cecil would bring her. He agreed to do so, and then he and the old woman left.

Yates returned a half-hour later and sat down beside his wounded friend on a beat-up wooden chair. "Okay, pard, let's hear it. You chasin' outlaws somewhere around here and get yourself shot?"

"No," Gray said, gritting his teeth in pain. "But it's a long story."

"Well, before you get started, how's Mary doin'?"

"Mary's dead, Cecil."

"What? How…when?"

"October. She went up to Austin to visit her sister. Stagecoach. On the way back, Mexican bandits stopped the stage to rob it. A passenger pulled a gun and shot one of the Mexicans when the bandit took his gold pocket watch. The other bandits filled him full of lead. Just kept shootin' after he was already down and probably dead. Mary screamed at them to stop, and they turned their guns on her. Dirty Mexicans took money and jewelry, and rode away with their dead companion draped over his horse. I was in town when the stage came in. The fool passenger's body was layin' in the rack up top. They had Mary's body inside. When I saw her—"

Gray's voice failed him, and he bit his lip to keep the tears at bay.

Yates leaned forward and squeezed his friend's arm. "I'm so sorry about Mary, Mark. Don't say anymore. I know it's hard to talk about it. My Martha was killed two weeks after we were married."

Gray nodded.

Yates eased back on the chair. "So tell me about this gunshot."

Gray gained control of his emotions, then told his friend how he and Jody Sleppy had been walking toward the Ranger office the day before, after placing their horses at the livery, when they were summoned to the scene of a robbery.

"Those Mexican kids left that poor old vendor lyin' there on the ground with his head bleedin', and took off. Jody and I caught a glimpse of 'em runnin' away, and we went after 'em. Chased 'em quite a ways...to the north side of town. We were gettin' closer when we saw 'em run into a farmer's barn. Kids were probably no more than fifteen or sixteen. Weren't armed."

Gray's face looked sad as he said, "It was then that Jody started actin' strange, Cecil. It was like those three kids had done somethin' personal to him. He wanted to go in there and kill all three."

Cecil Yates shook his head knowingly. "Sometimes lawmen go off the deep end like that," he said.

"Yeah, that's just what he did. I saw the wicked look in his eye and told him to stay back and let me handle it. I was gonna talk the boys out and arrest 'em, but Jody wanted to kill 'em. He started shoutin' toward the barn, tellin' those Mexicans to come out right now or we were comin' in. I knew he was gonna shoot 'em down if they came out that door."

Gray raised his arm in agitation, and a pain shot through his side, making him gasp. When he began speaking again, he said, "Suddenly those boys went out a back door and started runnin' across the field. I tried to stop him, but Jody opened fire. He hit one boy in the back. Kid went down dead. I grappled with Jody, at least givin' the other two a chance to get away. When they were gone, I let go of him, and he started cussin' me.

"I told him to cool down, Cecil, and I headed for that poor dead boy's body. Jody shot me—right in the back. I went down to my knees, but I was able to return a shot. Jody went down, screamin' that he was gonna tell Captain Sears it was me who killed the kid. Crazy as he was actin', I knew he'd do it too. I didn't want to kill Jody, even though he was gonna lie about who killed the kid. It was either kill my fellow Ranger—which I just couldn't do—or run. So I ran. I took that mare out of the farmer's corral and took off with my side bleedin'."

"Well, of all the rotten things..." said Cecil. "He probably lied about the whole thing to Sears."

Gray nodded. "Oh, I'm sure he did. You know I've been on the captain's blacklist for a couple years. We just haven't been hittin' it off too good. Now that he's heard Sleppy's lies, there's no way I could get treated fairly if I went back. They'd want to string me up. Sears will have his boys after me. All I can do now is hide while I'm recuperatin', then head for Arizona."

"I'll help you hide," said Yates, "but why Arizona?"

"Well, you know it would be dangerous for me to hide around here for long. Sears knows where you live, and he knows we're friends. He'll have his bloodhounds around here shortly."

"Yep. That's why I'm gonna put you with Nana. She's got a shed out behind her house. Fella could stay there for a while without bein' too uncomfortable. She'll take you in if I explain that you're in trouble. When you're ready to go, you can hightail it out of here. Now, tell me about Arizona."

"You ever hear of a Ranger name of Jim Carter?"

Yates rubbed his chin. "Yeah. He was up in Austin, wasn't he?"

"Right."

"And had some kind of problem. Got out of the Rangers. Come to think of it, weren't you and he pretty close friends?"

"That's right. I worked that district for a while. Saved Jim's life in a gun battle with a gang of rustlers."

"So what you're tellin' me is that Carter's in Arizona."

"Sure enough. And maybe you remember hearin' that Jim was real bitter when he left the Rangers, and he went bad."

"Rings a bell."

"He's as bitter toward the Rangers as you are, Cecil."

"That's *real* bitter, then."

"He's got reason to be, just like you do. Another Ranger named Clete Fishman was a lieutenant, and he wanted Carter's position as captain in the Austin office. He framed Jim, makin' it look like he'd done a misdeed. Jim got fired, and Fishman got the position."

"There're crooks everywhere," Yates muttered.

Gray nodded. "So anyway, Jim disappeared, and I lost all track of him. I found out from another ex-Ranger that Jim's been in Arizona almost since he got fired. Goes by the name of Jock Hood now. His wife's dead, but his four sons are all with him. The sons go by the name Hood, too. Well, this other ex-Ranger told me Jim's got a ranch near Phoenix, called the *Bar-H.* He's done quite well in the cattle business and has become the richest and most powerful rancher in the Phoenix area."

"Good for him," Yates said.

"Somethin' else, Cecil. Jim's also into helpin' outlaws who

are on the dodge find hidin' places. For a price, of course."

Yates grinned. "Naturally."

"Jim owes me. I'm sure he'll give me a hidin' place for free. Captain Sears is like a hungry wolf when he wants a fella bad enough. I've got to lay low for quite a while."

Yates rose to his feet. "Guess it's about supper time. I'll fix us somethin' to eat. Before first light in the mornin', I'll take you over to Nana's. I suppose some of the village people saw you ride in?"

"Yeah."

"Well, when Sears's bloodhounds come nosin' around, I'll tell 'em you might've been here, but I must've been gone when you knocked on my door, 'cause I never saw you."

BREANNA HOVERED BESIDE HER BROTHER-IN-LAW as he examined Max Richter, who had not regained consciousness after surgery the day before. Stefanie Langan and her mother stood close by, looking on.

"What do you think, Doctor?" Breanna asked.

Matt Carroll's features looked glum as he pulled back Richter's eyelids and studied his pupils. "I don't know, Breanna. The crucial first twenty-four hours have passed, but I'm not sure he's going to make it."

Richter's color was pasty, and his breathing was so shallow that the rise and fall of his chest was barely perceptible.

Dr. Carroll checked Richter's pulse and listened to his heart for the second time in as many minutes. When he dropped the stethoscope and straightened, he sighed. "Signs here aren't too bad, but his pupils don't look good. If he'd just regain consciousness..."

In her heart, Breanna prayed, *Dear Lord, please don't let him die from the bullet I put in him.*

On a nearby table lay the morning edition of the *Denver Sentinel.* Bold headlines told the story of Breanna Baylor's heroic act that foiled the bank robbery and resulted in the capture of the robbers. Beneath the headlines was a large photograph of

Breanna in the lobby of Mile High Hospital with Frontier Bank president, Edgar Turnquist. Jess Collins, Denver's mayor, stood with them. Collins had just given Breanna a written commendation from the people of Denver for her courage and quick thinking.

A smaller article on the front page told how Breanna had saved the life of President Ulysses S. Grant, earlier in the year, at the railroad station in Abilene, Kansas.

When Dr. Carroll palpated the area of the wound to make sure no infection had set in, Max Richter began to jerk and groan, then his eyelids fluttered, and he looked around with glassy eyes.

"That's better!" Dr. Carroll said, and gave Breanna a smile.

Richter blinked, attempting to focus on the doctor's face.

"Mr. Richter, I'm Dr. Matthew Carroll. You're in Denver's Mile High Hospital. Do you remember what happened yesterday?"

The outlaw swallowed hard and blinked. "Yeah. Gutshot."

Carroll nodded. "Nurse Baylor and I removed the slug from your midsection."

Mary and Stefanie watched Richter's eyes widen when he finally focused on Breanna.

"Yes, Mr. Richter," Breanna said softly, "I'm the one who shot you."

"She's also the one who helped me save your life, Mr. Richter," Carroll said. "At her own request, I might add. You were hemorrhaging profusely, and without her help I couldn't have closed off all the arteries in time to keep you from bleeding to death. You have Miss Baylor to thank that you're still alive."

The outlaw turned his head away.

Dr. Carroll smiled at Breanna and said, "He's going to make it, Sis."

When Breanna heard Stefanie say to Mary, "Praise the Lord, Mom. She won't have to bear the burden," she turned around and embraced them both.

"I know it's a relief to you, Breanna," said Stefanie. "Now you can put your mind on the big event tomorrow."

"Oh, yes!" Breanna said. "Tomorrow morning at nine-thirty, my John will be home!"

John Stranger sat alone in the rocking, swaying railway coach as the train rolled southward toward Cheyenne City. The stars shone like tiny crystals against black velvet in the moonless night sky.

Lanterns burned low at each end of the coach, and the rest of the passengers were asleep. Several were snoring, and could be heard above the clicking of the wheels.

John couldn't sleep for thinking about seeing Breanna the next day. His mind went back to the night three weeks before, when he and Breanna were having dinner at the Carroll home…

The meal was over, and the adults were sipping a final cup of coffee at the kitchen table. Seven-year-old Molly Kate sat on "Uncle" John's lap. James, her nine-year-old brother, looked across the table, eyes flashing, and said, "Okay, Uncle John, I wanna know all about how you captured that Leo Tupa!"

"James," Dottie, his mother, said, "you heard Uncle John and Aunt Breanna say they had things to talk about tonight. Uncle John is leaving town early tomorrow morning. He can tell you about it another time."

"I think we've got time to tell the Tupa story, Dottie," John said.

Molly Kate stayed in his lap while he told about his pursuit and capture of the outlaw high in the Rocky Mountains. When he finished, James said, "I can't wait till I grow up, Uncle John! I'm gonna be fast with a gun, just like you, and chase bad guys! Only I'm gonna wear a badge."

Molly Kate looked up into John's cool gray eyes. "How come you don't wear a badge, Uncle John? You always chase bad guys."

"I'll have to explain it later, honey," he said, kissing the top of her head. "Right now, your Aunt Breanna and I have to go."

"Not till I help with the dishes," Breanna said.

The two sisters argued about it good-naturedly, with Dottie insisting that she and the children would do the dishes. As usual, Breanna won. Matt and John stayed at the table while the others worked around them.

"So where are you going tomorrow, John?" Matt asked.

"When I stopped by Chief Solomon Duvall's office this morning to tell him about Tupa, he said he'd received a telegram from Sheriff Johnson of Silver Bow County, Montana, a few days ago, asking me to come up there. Seems that a murderer I helped send to the gallows is back from the grave."

"What?"

"It can't be the same man, but I'm going to help Sheriff Johnson get to the bottom of it. I wired him that I'll leave for Montana tomorrow morning. I haven't yet had a chance to tell Breanna."

At mention of her name, Breanna's ears pricked up. She listened for what John would say next as she continued to help Dottie clean up.

"I'll take the six-thirty train for Cheyenne City in the morning, then catch the afternoon train to Billings. Union Pacific finished laying track between Cheyenne City and Billings just about a month ago."

"I did read something in the paper about that," Matt said.

"Then I'll take a stagecoach from Billings to Butte City."

"Butte City…isn't that where you were last summer when you almost got caught in that forest fire?"

"Billings. The fire was in the forest country northwest of there."

"But you've been to Butte City before. Seems like you mentioned chasing down an outlaw up there."

"I went up there a couple of years ago to help Sheriff Johnson trap a killer."

"You did trap him, and he hanged," Breanna said, moving toward the table. "You told me all about it. What was the killer's name? Something like Sturgman, wasn't it?"

"Sturgis. Payton Sturgis."

"So now what's the problem in Butte City?" Dottie asked, as she wiped off the table with a damp cloth.

"Wel-l-l, they, ah…have another killer on the loose in the area. Sheriff Johnson seems to think that since I helped stop Sturgis, I might be able to help with this guy."

Dottie chuckled. "Come on now, John. I know why you're really going back to that part of Montana. You want to see if you can get a glimpse of that big black horse that saved your life last summer. What did you call him?"

"He called him Chance, Mom," James said. "Didn't you, Uncle John? 'Cause he was your last chance to make it out of that fire!"

John looked at the small boy and smiled. "That's right, James. However, sweet sister of my loving Breanna, when I go to Butte City, I won't have time to beat the forests looking for Chance, much as I'd like to."

John smiled to himself as he remembered how the rest of that evening had gone when he and Breanna were finally alone...

It was nearly eight-thirty when John guided the rented buggy around the big house belonging to Dr. and Mrs. Lyle Goodwin, and halted in front of the little cottage that was Breanna's home.

He built a fire in the potbellied stove, while Breanna started one in the kitchen stove and put on the coffeepot.

They sat down in the parlor as the room began to grow warm, and by the soft lantern light Breanna looked into John's eyes and said, "All right, Mr. Stranger, out with it."

He blinked, letting an innocent look capture his face. "Out with what?"

"Butte City. Sheriff Lake Johnson. Some killer on the loose. What else is it?"

"Well, Miss Baylor, just how do you know there is something else?"

Breanna leaned close, touched her lips to his lightly, and said, "I just know you, darling. You were holding back something when you answered Dottie's question about the problem in Butte City."

A slow grin worked its way across his handsome face. "You're acting like a wife."

"Well, dear man, I have news for you. I'll *really* learn to read you when I am your wife!"

John's features changed, taking on a serious cast.

"Sweetheart," he said softly, "I told you at the hospital this morning that there was something very important I wanted to talk to you about. Let me do that first, then I'll explain about Butte City."

Breanna was surprised to see him rise from the couch and drop to one knee in front of her.

She blinked in puzzlement. "What is this, John?"

He took her hands in his own. "We've been asking the Lord to guide us as to when we should marry. You said you believed the Lord would show me, and that you were ready whenever I got the go-ahead from Him. Well, Miss Breanna Baylor, I have absolute peace in my heart about a date." He swallowed hard. "Miss Breanna Baylor, will you marry me on the first Sunday of next June, at our church, in an afternoon ceremony?"

Tears welled in Breanna's eyes and spilled down her cheeks. She threw her arms around his neck and said, "Yes! Oh, yes!"

They embraced for a long moment, then John kissed her tenderly, sealing their agreement.

When he was once again sitting beside her on the couch, he took her hand and said, "The date, darling, is June fourth."

"It'll be the third most marvelous day of my life," she replied. "The first most marvelous day of my life was when I met my precious Jesus, and He saved my soul. And the second most marvelous day of my life was when I met a tall, dark, handsome man on the Kansas plains in a thunderstorm, and he saved me from being trampled by a herd of stampeding cattle."

John smiled.

"And on the third most marvelous day, you will save me from being an old maid!"

They laughed heartily and kissed again.

Breanna squeezed John's hand as she said, "When we talked in the past about getting married, you said we would both have to cut our travels quite a bit in order to have a married life. I can always work at the hospital or at Dr. Goodwin's office, but what will you do? I realize money is no object, but knowing my John, I know you'll have to be busy."

"The Lord hasn't revealed all the details to me yet," he said. "All I know is that I have perfect peace about us getting married in June. I have no doubt He'll show me His will about my occupation sometime between now and when we get married."

"Of course He will," Breanna said.

John smiled at her again. "So when I get back from Montana, we'll talk to Pastor Bayless and set up that Sunday afternoon for the wedding."

Breanna flung her arms around his neck again. "Oh, darling, I'm so happy!"

As he held her close, John half-whispered in her ear, "You couldn't be as happy as I am. The Lord has given me the most beautiful and wonderful woman in the world to be my wife!"

After several minutes, Breanna settled back against the couch and looked at John expectantly. "Now, what about the Butte City business?"

He took a deep breath and said, "You recall the story of when I was up there two years ago, some maniac was murdering people at random in the town. Turned out that maniac was Payton Sturgis."

"Yes, I remember."

"Well, it's starting all over again, except the killings are not random this time. The killer has named his intended victims, and he's killing them one at a time."

"Is there some pattern to it? I mean, some reason he's picked his victims?"

John scrubbed a hand over his mouth. "Yes, and this is the bizarre thing about it. Apparently he left a written list with the first body. The fifteen men on the list are the same men who had a hand in putting Sturgis's neck in the noose. You know—the judge, the jury, and the like."

"'And the like.' You mean like John Stranger, who tracked him and caught him. And probably like Sheriff Lake Johnson. If it was a twelve-man jury, then the judge, the sheriff, and you would make fifteen."

"Yes, Breanna. That's about the way it stacks up."

"I don't want you to go."

"I have to. I've got to help Sheriff Johnson stop this man before he kills every man he's marked. He's killed three men already."

Breanna sat silently, studying his eyes for a moment. "John, I love you, and I don't want anything to happen to you. But I also know you, and I understand why you have to go. And that's one of the reasons why I love you so much. I won't try to stand in your way, darling, because I know you believe you owe it to those people to go back up there and stop this killer. But I *will* be praying for God's hand on you."

John looked at her tenderly and said, "I appreciate that. And don't worry. The Lord will bring me back to you, alive and kicking. After all, He made us for each other, and we've got a wedding coming up."

As John listened to the clicking wheels taking him south, he sighed and thanked the Lord that the Butte City killer, known as the "snow ghost," was dead, and he was returning to Breanna just as he said he would.

He glanced out the window for a few moments at the sparks flying by and the stars twinkling in the night sky. Then he tried to find a position on the hard coach seat to get some sleep.

WHILE JOHN STRANGER STUDIED THE STARS over Wyoming through the coach window, Breanna Baylor was on her knees beside her bed. When she'd finished praying, she slipped between the covers, weary in mind and body, and soon fell asleep.

It was near dawn when her often repeated dream recurred…

The pump organ was playing "Here Comes the Bride," and Breanna held Dr. Lyle Goodwin's arm as they walked down the aisle of Denver's First Baptist Church. In her free hand, she carried her bride's bouquet, which was tied to a small white Bible with a white ribbon. A delicate veil covered her face.

The building was packed to capacity. The crowd was standing, and everyone was turned so they could see the bride. Breanna could sense every eye on her.

She felt her heart thumping in her chest. This was the day she had dreamed of for so long. She felt elegant in her shimmering white gown, and was honored that Dr. Goodwin would be the one to give her away.

At the head of the procession were the bridesmaids, all

young ladies from the church. They were followed by Breanna's sister, Dottie, her matron of honor. On the right side of the aisle stood Dottie's husband, Dr. Matthew Carroll, smiling first at Dottie, then at his adopted children, James and Molly Kate. James was the ringbearer, and he walked just ahead of Molly Kate, carrying both the bride's and groom's rings, which were tied with ribbons to a small white satin pillow. Molly Kate walked just ahead of the bride and Dr. Goodwin, carefully dropping rose petals on the floor from a little basket with a hooped handle.

Atop four steps from the floor, in the center of the platform, stood Pastor Robert Bayless, Bible in hand.

Martha Goodwin, who was like a mother to Breanna, stood at the aisle on the second row on the bride's side, smiling and dabbing at her eyes with a hanky.

Breanna had not yet focused her eyes on the groom. She would wait until she was a little closer. She felt a touch of sadness that her parents had not lived to see this day and had not met John.

The sadness faded, however, when she set her gaze on the groomsmen who stood in a fan shape, waiting for the bridesmaids and matron of honor. Inside their lines stood Chief U.S. Marshal Solomon Duvall, John's long-time friend and best man. And next to him…

Like a magnet, the tall, dark, handsome man attracted her gaze. She smiled through the veil, and felt tears well up in her eyes. John smiled back, love beaming from him.

The organist let the music fade as Breanna and Dr. Goodwin drew up. From the platform, the pastor said, "Who gives this woman to be married to this man?"

"In place of her deceased father and mother, my wife, Martha, and I do," said Goodwin.

Bayless smiled. "Will you please, sir, place the bride's hand in that of the groom."

Goodwin did so, then Breanna raised up on her tiptoes and, through her veil, kissed the good doctor's cheek.

Breanna turned to a teary-eyed Dottie, handed her the Bible and bouquet, then looked up at the groom who towered over her and slipped her hand into the crook of his arm. John's eyes were drinking in her beauty, and then he mouthed the words, *I love you.*

The bride blinked, and the tears that filled her eyes spilled warmly down her cheeks...

When Breanna woke, she touched her cheek and her hand came away wet. "Oh, dear Lord Jesus," she said, "thank You for my wonderful John. Thank You for the love You have given us for each other. Help me to be the wife he needs and deserves."

She lay back peacefully and soon was fast asleep.

At six-fifteen the next morning, John Stranger was snatched from a deep sleep when the train whistle blew and the bell began to clang as the train chugged into Cheyenne City.

He sat up and covered a yawn, then rubbed his eyes and stretched. It would be another hour before the train bound for Denver left the station. He took his two bags from the overhead rack and stepped out of the coach, then walked back to the stock car he'd rented.

Chance whinnied as John rolled back the latticed door and entered. The entire car was built with walls of lateral slats four inches apart to let air and light in.

"Good morning, big guy," John said, stroking the stallion's long face. "I hope you got more sleep than I did."

Chance nickered softly.

"Oh, you did, eh? Well, if you knew how gorgeous your new owner is, you wouldn't be able to sleep, either. She's going to love you, ol' boy, I'll tell you that. And if you're like me, you'll fall in love with her the first time you see her, just like I did."

Chance bobbed his head.

John opened the grain bin and dipped a load of oats into the feed trough. "There you go, big guy."

Chance began munching while John opened the compartment where the hay was stored and forked some into the trough next to the oats.

Next, he removed the lid from a large water barrel, took a bucket from a wire hanger on the back wall, and filled the metal water trough next to the feed trough.

"Okay, pal," John said, patting the stallion's muscled rump. "Hope you enjoy your breakfast. Before you eat lunch, you'll feast your eyes on some real beauty, I guarantee you."

Chance nickered again as John moved to the sliding door and started to close it from the outside.

"My, oh, my! What a horse!" a voice said.

John turned and saw a short, ruddy-faced man in a conductor's uniform standing on the platform.

"Like him?" John asked.

"Who wouldn't? Where'd you buy him, mister?"

"I won him."

"You *won* him? In a poker game?"

"No, no. I was up in Billings, Montana. Horse trader up there had brought him in wild, off the range. Seems nobody could ride him. Many men tried, and every one of them got bucked off. Horse trader finally offered him to the first man who could ride him."

"And you were the one?"

"Yep."

"How's come you could ride him and nobody else could do it? You a professional horse breaker?"

"No, sir."

"Didn't think so, the way you wear that Colt low on your hip. Gunfighter, huh?"

"Nope."

"Well, what do you do?"

"I answer questions for inquisitive conductors."

The man laughed. "Okay, that's what I get for bein' so nosy. So you won him because you were the first man who could ride him."

"That's what I said."

"Well, mister, I'm here to see that this stock car gets hooked up to my train. So I guess you must be going to Denver."

"Yes, Denver's our destination."

"Guess I'll see you in one of the coaches."

"Sure will."

"Marvelous animal," said the conductor, shaking his head. "Marvelous animal."

John stood on the platform and watched as a small engine chugged up. A man jumped out and hooked it to the caboose, then went to the front and unhooked the caboose from the stock car.

Soon, the stock car was between the caboose and the last coach of the train bound for Denver. Stranger found a seat in the coach, placed his hand luggage overhead, and went back outside to check on Chance one more time.

The train chugged out of Cheyenne City on schedule at seven-fifteen.

✣

At eight o'clock, Breanna Baylor entered the lobby of Mile High Hospital. Receptionist Peggy Walters had just sat down at her desk, and she flashed a winsome smile and said, "Good morning, Breanna. I didn't expect to see you this early. Isn't John getting home later this morning?"

"His train's supposed to arrive at nine-thirty, and am I excited! When we're apart, there's a big hole in my heart. I'll be in to finish my shift after he and I have had a few minutes together. But right now I've got a little missionary work to do."

Peggy's eyes flicked to the Bible Breanna carried in her hand. "Who's getting the sermon?"

"Well, it's not exactly a sermon, Peggy, but I'm concerned about Max Richter."

"Richter! You're going to preach to *him?*"

"Not preach, honey. I'm going to witness to him. Like all sinners, he needs the Lord."

"Yesterday you shot him with a gun; today you're going to stab him with the Sword."

"How about that!" Breanna said. She chuckled to herself and gave Peggy a little wave as she headed for Richter's room.

When she entered the hall, two nurses carrying breakfast trays greeted her. One of them asked what time John would arrive. When Breanna answered her, the other nurse said, "How about you do my work, and I go meet John?"

Breanna moved toward the stairs. "Not on your life, honey."

The nurses went on their way, laughing.

At the top of the stairs, Breanna met Mary Donelson, who had just left her office.

"Good morning," Breanna said, smiling.

"Good morning, Breanna," Mary said. "You're not due in

till later—after John arrives. Why are you here so early?"

"Is Max Richter awake, Mary?"

"Yes. He's had his breakfast. Didn't eat much, but he looks pretty good this morning compared to the way he looked this time yesterday." She nodded at Breanna's Bible. "Be interesting to see how far you get. He's pretty hardheaded *and* hardhearted."

"I'll give it a shot, anyway."

Mary giggled. "Isn't that what you did day before yesterday?"

"Hmm?"

"Gave it a shot..."

"Oh. Yes. That *is* what I did, didn't I?" She began to walk down the hall, then said over her shoulder, "As Peggy put it a moment ago, this time I'm going to stab him with the Sword."

When Breanna stepped into Richter's room, he was lying on his back, eyes closed. At the sound of footsteps he opened his eyes and scowled when he saw who it was and noticed what was in her hand.

"How are you feeling today, Mr. Richter?" Breanna asked.

"What do you care? If it wasn't for you, I wouldn't be layin' here."

"Shouldn't you say, if it wasn't for you robbing the bank, you wouldn't be here?"

Richter glared at the Bible in her hand. "What's that for?"

"Mr. Richter, I care about you. That's why I asked to assist Dr. Carroll with your surgery. I'm glad the bullet I put in you didn't take your life."

"So what difference does it make? I'm gonna hang, anyway."

"That's why I'm here this morning. I'd like to share with you what Jesus Christ, God's Son, did for me many years ago.

He saved my soul, washed all my sins away in His blood, and put me on the road to heaven."

Richter's eyes grew cold. "I don't believe in God."

"You don't believe there's a God who created this universe and gave you life?"

"There ain't no God."

"Oh, but there is. And you can know Him, even as I do, Mr. Richter. He loves you. Jesus loves you. He went to the cross and paid the penalty for your sins. You can be forgiven and cleansed, and go to heaven when you die, if you'll put your faith in Jesus to save you. Otherwise, you'll spend eternity in hell."

"Hogwash! There ain't no God. There ain't no heaven, and there ain't no hell."

Breanna opened her Bible, flipped a few pages, and said, "Listen to this. Psalm 14:1 says, 'The fool hath said in his heart, There is no God.' The God you say doesn't exist says that you're a fool, Mr. Richter. You can deny His existence all you want, but one day in eternity you will stand before that very God at the judgment."

As she spoke, Breanna flipped to the book of Revelation. "Listen to this, Mr. Richter. The Apostle John was allowed by God to look into the future. He wrote down what he saw. 'And I saw a great white throne, and him that sat on it, from whose face the earth and the heaven fled away; and there was found no place for them. And I saw the dead, small and great, stand before God…'

"You will be in that throng who stands before God, Mr. Richter. It says in this same passage that God will open the Book of Life. Your name won't be there if you die without being saved. Listen to the last verse in this chapter: 'And whosoever was not found written in the book of life was cast into the lake of fire.' That's hell in its final state, Mr. Richter. But you don't have to go there. Let me read to you about Calvary."

"I'm not interested, lady," Richter said. "I don't believe any of that stuff, 'cause like I told you, I don't believe in God. Call me a fool if you want to, but I say there is no God."

"*I* didn't call you a fool. *God* calls you a fool. All you have to do is look around you. When you see an effect, that effect had a cause. Creation is the effect; *God* is the cause."

Richter's lips made a bloodless line beneath his heavy mustache, and the muscles of his jaws bunched. "Get outta here," he said.

"Mr. Richter, I—"

"I said get outta here! I'm through talkin' to you! Get out!"

Mary Donelson appeared at the door. When Richter saw her, he bawled, "I want her outta here! Now!"

Mary hastened into the room. "Mr. Richter! You'll pull your stitches loose! Calm down."

"I'll calm down when you get this female fanatic outta my room!"

Breanna turned toward the door. "Jesus loves you, Mr. Richter. I just wanted to—"

"Out! Out! Out!"

At precisely nine-twenty, Breanna entered Denver's Union Station and went to the platform where the train from Cheyenne City would arrive. People were gathering all around her to meet friends and family members.

When the distant sound of a whistle met Breanna's ears, her heart leaped. The whistle sounded again, and soon the train came into view. Breanna's heart began to hammer against her ribs.

The big engine rolled into the station amidst clanging bell and hissing steam. The three coach cars halted directly in front of Breanna and the rest of the group waiting to greet passengers.

Breanna noticed the stock car with its lateral slats, and the large dark form inside, but quickly ran her gaze to the small platforms of the three coaches, eager to see the man she loved.

Suddenly the tall, handsome man with the twin scars on his right cheek stepped out of the last coach, carrying the familiar pieces of hand luggage. Breanna darted toward him.

John dropped his luggage, took three long strides, and opened his arms. "Hello, sweetheart," he said, as she ran to him and he embraced her.

They kissed, and Breanna said, "I've missed you so much, John!" Then she backed away to look him over.

"What's this?" he asked.

"I just want to make sure you're unscathed, as you said in your wire."

He grinned at her. "I'm fine. No cuts or bruises. You're acting like a wife again."

Breanna laughed. "Well, big fella, it's only going to get worse when I actually *am* your wife!"

She embraced him again, then turned toward the exit, expecting him to pick up his luggage so they could head for the buggy she'd borrowed from Dr. Goodwin. "While we ride to your hotel, John, I want to hear all about this 'snow ghost' you brought to justice. Did they hang him?"

"No. He and I were at a standoff inside a barn. I shot him off the hayloft. He was dead when he hit the floor."

"Well, I'm glad he won't be killing anyone else."

"So's the town of Butte City."

Still John made no move to pick up his luggage. Breanna

gave him a quizzical look and said, "Aren't we going?"

His gaze moved to the stock car behind her where the railroad workers were pulling a heavy gangplank toward the platform from underneath the floor. He had given instructions to the conductor, and they were being carried out to the letter.

"Not quite yet, sweetheart," he said, with a cat-who-ate-the-canary grin. "There's something I need to do."

Breanna cocked her head to one side. "John, what are you up to?"

He took her in his arms, looked deep into her sky-blue eyes, and said, "We're still getting married June fourth, right?"

"Of course. Why ask such a question?"

"Just wanted to make sure you hadn't changed your mind."

"John," she giggled, "what's going on?"

"I've brought you a wedding present."

Tiny lines penciled themselves on her brow. "It's six months till we get married."

"This is an early wedding present. I want you to stand right here and wait for me to come back."

"Where are you going?"

"You'll see."

Breanna watched him walk toward the stock car.

The workers had been instructed only to put the gangplank in place. Now they stood back, along with the conductor, and looked on with curiosity.

John stepped across the gangplank and slid back the door just enough to enter the car. Breanna's gaze was riveted on the sliding door. What could be in there, except a horse? But why would he give her a horse for a wedding present?

"Are you ready?" he called from inside.

"As I'll ever be!"

The door slid open, and Breanna's eyes popped as John led

out the largest stallion she had ever seen. He was so black that even his winter coat shone in the sunlight. She'd never seen such a magnificent horse.

"Sweetheart," John said, leading the big stallion across the gangplank toward her, "I want you to meet Chance."

BREANNA COULD HARDLY CATCH HER BREATH. "Oh, John! How did you—?" Where did you—? When—?"

One question at a time, please," he said, laughing. "I'll tell you about it later. At lunch, maybe?"

"Oh, darling, I have to be at the hospital. We're a little short-handed, or I wouldn't have consented to work today. Matt gave me time off to come and meet you and to spend a little time together, but I'll need to get back shortly."

Chance nickered in a low voice and bobbed his head at Breanna.

John glanced at him and grinned. Then to Breanna, "How about dinner?"

"I'm wide open for that!"

"All right. I'll tell you the whole story over dinner at the Crystal Palace."

People who passed by eyed the big stallion. One man paused, looked at John, and said, "That your horse, mister?"

"No. He belongs to the lady."

The man looked Chance up and down, glanced at Breanna, and said, "How does she get on him?"

"Well, she hasn't yet. But she will."

The man shook his head and walked away, muttering something that sounded like, "Maybe if she gets a good run at him."

The big black bobbed his head again and nickered softly, then moved a little closer to Breanna. She reached out and patted the side of his face. "You're a nice boy, Chance," she said.

Another soft nicker.

John stroked the horse's long neck. "Chance, ol' boy, this is your new boss. As I've already told you, her name is Breanna."

Chance moved his ears back and forth, bobbing his head.

"Yep, ol' boy. Just as I thought. You *are* just like me."

Breanna rubbed the horse's muzzle and looked at John inquiringly. "What do you mean, just like you?"

"I told him if he was like me, he'd fall in love with you at first sight. Look at him."

Breanna laughed and stroked Chance's face and rubbed his muzzle. "Well, Chance," she said, "I feel the same about you."

Chance's size and beauty had people collecting by the minute to admire him.

Breanna looked Chance in the eye and rubbed his muzzle some more, then said, "John…remember what I said I wanted to do if I ever met Chance?"

"Yes…"

"Do you think he'd let me do it?"

"Are you kidding? Just look at him. You've got him wrapped around your little finger, just like me. I'm sure he'd love a hug…just like me."

"Oh, John, you're impossible!"

Breanna moved closer to the huge animal and wrapped her arms around his neck. There were some "oohs" and "ahs" among the crowd as they looked on. They didn't see the tears in her eyes as she squeezed the horse's neck and said, "I owe you so much, Chance! There you were in the wild, running free as the wind. You could have just taken your herd and run away when that fire came. But you let my John ride you to safety. You saved his life, you big wonderful boy! Thank you!"

Chance whinnied shrilly and bobbed his head.

When Breanna finally let go of the sleek neck, she said, "Oh, John, I love him! Thank you! I can't wait to hear how you found him, darling, and how you were able to get the saddle on him…and how you got him into the railroad car."

"We'll save all of that for tonight."

Breanna began measuring the horse with her eye and then said, "That man was right, John. How am I ever going to get onto Chance's back? He must be eighteen hands."

"Well, not quite, but a good healthy seventeen, I'd say."

"So how am I going to get on him?"

"I'll train him to kneel down so you can mount."

"Can you do that?"

"Sure. Smart as Chance is, he'll pick it up in a hurry. Especially since he's in love with you. Well, we'd better get going."

John loaded his luggage in the buggy and tied Chance to the rear. He helped Breanna in and climbed in beside her, taking up the reins. She scooted as close to him as possible and slipped a hand under his arm.

"Do you need to go home and change before you go to the hospital?" John asked.

"No. I have a change of clothes there."

"All right. I'll take Chance to the livery stable and get reacquainted with Ebony, after I let you off at the hospital. We'll keep Chance at the livery, too. I'll take the horse and buggy back to the Goodwins' and pick you up at seven tonight. That sound all right?"

"You know it does."

John clucked to the horse pulling the buggy, and the big black followed like a veteran.

Breanna was quiet for a moment, then said, "John, what's Ebony going to think when he sees you with Chance?"

"I'll tell him that Chance is *your* horse. He'll understand."

Breanna laughed. "All right. But what will you do if the two of them don't get along?"

"They'll get along. Now, if they were both stallions, they probably wouldn't, but since Ebony's a gelding, there won't be a problem. Chance will be the high and mighty mogul, and Ebony won't even care."

When they reached the hospital, John guided the buggy to the front of the main entrance, set the brake, and hopped out. Breanna slid to the same side, and John helped her to the ground.

"Excuse me," she said, and walked back to the big black stallion. She put her arms around his neck and hugged him tenderly.

John walked Breanna to the door and held it open for her. He waved at Peggy Walters, who sat at the receptionist's desk, told Breanna he loved her, and then headed back for the buggy.

Hostler Willy Sparks's eyes bulged when he saw John Stranger leading the massive stallion through the livery gate.

He hurried out to meet Stranger and ejected a low whistle. "Well, lookee what Mr. Stranger's done come up with! Where'd you come by him, John?"

"Montana."

"Oh, yeah. When you left here three weeks ago, you did tell me you were goin' up to Montaner. Big, ain't he?"

"Yep."

"And beautiful."

"That he is. Do you remember when I left Ebony with you last summer and went to Montana?"

"Shore."

"And when I came back, I told you about the big wild stallion that saved me from a forest fire?"

"Shore do. Remember what you called him, too. Chance. 'Cause he was your last chance to make it to safety."

"Good memory, Willy. This is Chance."

"Well, I'll be! And you went back up there and caught him, eh?"

"Not exactly, but I did break him to the saddle, so to speak. I gave him to Breanna."

"I imagine she likes him."

"Oh, yes. How's my Ebony?"

"I sold him to a slick-talkin' horse trader for five dollars."

"You did, and your name's worse than mud, I'll tell you that."

Willy laughed. "He's back there in the corral. Other side of the barn."

"I'll go see him in a minute. You need to know, Willy, that Chance hasn't been ridden by anybody but me. He's still got some wild in him and isn't used to being around humans. Be careful not to spook him when you feed and water him. And I'd say be careful when you brush him. He's never been brushed before."

"Gotcha. Horses is my business, John. Ol' Chance and I will get along fine."

"Good. Might watch other people around him, though. I don't want anyone getting hurt."

"Will do. I'll partition off a part of the corral for him, and I'll put him in one of the back stalls where there's less traffic."

"Thanks, Willy. I'll come by every day when I'm home, to exercise him and train him. Well, let's see how he takes to you."

Willy moved toward Chance slowly, holding out an open palm, and soon was rubbing his muzzle.

John was pleased. "Okay, my friend. You take him, and I'll go see Ebony."

John passed through the barn and stepped out into the corral. More than a dozen horses looked his way, but there was a shrill whinny when the big black spotted his master.

Like a loving dog, Ebony trotted to John, neighing his hello. They had a sweet reunion, then Stranger bridled and saddled him and took him out for a good ride.

That evening at the restaurant, John and Breanna chatted animatedly until their food came, then gave thanks to the Lord and started eating.

Halfway through the meal, Breanna said, "All right, Mr. John Stranger, I want to hear how you found Chance and brought him home to me."

"It was the Lord's hand, honey. Everything was timed so perfectly."

"I can believe that," she said, smiling. "When our God does something, He does it with precision. I can't wait to hear the details."

"Well, sweetheart, it was like this. When I left Butte City, the stagecoach passed through the canyons toward Billings, and my thoughts ran to you and our wedding." John relived the entire episode as he told it to Breanna…

⁂

The tall Rocky Mountain canyon walls dully reflected the wintry sun as the stagecoach descended from the mountains. Suddenly John's eye caught movement on the windswept, snow-covered prairie. A small herd of wild horses stood on a rise, watching the stage, and a white stallion reared, pawed the air, and whinnied.

John smiled as he beheld the animal's beauty. So you're the leader of the pack, are you, big boy? he thought. His mind naturally went to Chance, the black stallion who had saved his life the previous summer. Where are you this morning, Chance, ol' boy? he wondered. Running wild and free somewhere north of here, and leading your herd in God's Big Sky country?

The stage changed horses at Bozeman, and the fresh team quickly put miles behind them as they galloped across the rolling Montana prairie.

It was midafternoon when the stage rolled into Billings. John took his luggage from the shotgunner's hands and headed along the east edge of town toward the railroad station. The train from Cheyenne City wouldn't arrive in Billings until almost five o'clock, and it wouldn't pull out until six-thirty. Nearly four hours to wait.

He strolled about the town and occasionally greeted people. He was still a ways from the depot when he saw the Billings Cattle and Horse Trading Company's corrals and barns across the road to the east. There were about fifty cowboys lined up along the fence at the largest corral. They were shouting and cheering as one of their own rode a bucking horse.

John crossed the road and walked toward the corral. As he drew near, he saw a smaller corral, where some twenty mares were penned up. He blinked in surprise when he recognized one of the mares. She had run with Chance! Her markings were too unique to mistake. He hastened toward the corral and saw another mare who had followed Chance, then another, and another.

When a cowboy came out of the small log cabin that served as the office and nodded a greeting, John hurried toward him and said, "Do you work for this company?"

"Sure do, pardner. You look to be afoot. You in the market for a horse?"

"No, I'm taking the evening train to Cheyenne City, then going on to Denver. But I'd like to ask you something."

The cheers of the cowboys filled the air.

"These mares…I saw them last summer, running wild with a big black stallion up north of here. Fella couldn't mistake them."

"That's for sure," the cowboy said. "My boss and some of the men were up in the north country a couple weeks ago and rounded up this herd." He paused and extended his hand. "I'm Lefty Durham."

Stranger set down his bags and shook the cowboy's hand. "Just call me John. Your boss didn't happen to bring in their leader, did he, Lefty?"

Durham grinned. "He sure did."

"Is he still here?"

"I'll say he is. All these mares have been broken to the saddle. But not their leader. That big black beast is meaner'n a snake. Nobody's been able to break him. They can't stay on his back long enough."

"Is that so?"

"Yeah. Twenty-two men have tried to ride him. In fact, number twenty-three is over there tryin' to ride him now. That's what all the hollerin' is about."

Lefty could tell by the shouts that the rider had just been thrown. He laughed. "Well, there'll be another poor sucker try here in a minute or two. He'll get throwed, too. That black devil ain't never gonna let nobody stay on his back."

Stranger grinned. "I'd say that must be some kind of horse if twenty-three men can't break him."

"That he is. In fact, the contest now is for ownership."

"What do you mean, contest?"

"The big black has become somewhat of a legend around here. My boss, Biff Symonds, announced that he'll flat give that horse to the first man who rides and tames him."

The cheers picked up again.

"I want to see this," John said.

Lefty chuckled and motioned for John to follow him. As they drew up to the large corral, John looked over the fence and his blood warmed at the sight of the big stallion.

Chance! he thought. *You big beautiful piece of God's creation!*

The stallion bucked savagely as he bounded across the corral. Suddenly the rider went sailing through the air and landed hard on the ground. Chance snorted, pawed earth, and trotted away, dragging the reins through the dirt.

Suddenly the cowboy stood to his feet as his friends kidded him from behind the fence. His face was purple with anger. He ran to Chance and picked up the reins, cursing him.

Chance laid back his ears and whinnied as the cowboy held the reins and jerked off his belt. All the cowboys went quiet as the angry rider began striking the horse across the face with his belt.

"Hey!" Stranger shouted, dropping his bags and vaulting the fence.

Biff Symonds had opened the gate to charge in and stop the

rider, too, but John was ahead of him. When Stranger reached the cowboy, he jerked the belt out of the man's hand and sent a punch to his jaw that laid him flat on his back.

Chance wheeled, trotted to the farthest side of the corral, and stood there, pawing the ground.

Symonds drew up to Stranger. "I don't know who you are, mister, but thanks for knockin' that cowboy's block off. He had it comin'." Then he looked toward the crowd of cowboys and said, "Couple of you boys come and drag this guy outta here!"

When Symonds turned back to John, he saw him staring at the stallion. "Some animal, eh?"

Stranger nodded. "Yes, sir. Your man Lefty Durham just told me you've offered to give him to the man who rides and breaks him."

"That's for sure. The man who can do that deserves to own him."

"How many more are standing in line?"

"None. You want to try?"

"Yes, I do."

"Well, it's your life and limbs. What's your name, stranger?"

"That's good enough."

"What?"

"Just call me Stranger. John Stranger."

"Okay, John Stranger, you want to be the next victim?"

"Sure."

Symonds looked toward the men at the fence. "We've got another taker, guys! This fella wants to see if he can ride the big black!"

Cheers went up.

John headed toward Chance, who was still on the far side of the corral, and Symonds headed for the gate.

"Well, boys," Symonds said, "that guy says his name is John

Stranger. He'll be victim number twenty-five!"

Chance was breathing hard and nickering as John drew near. The horse had not looked directly at him until that moment. Now his ears pricked up, and his whinny came out deep and low.

John smiled as Chance began bobbing his head. "Hey, big guy, you *do* remember me, don't you?"

The stallion moved toward John, and when they came together, Chance whinnied soft and low again. The cowboys watched, awestruck, as the man in black stroked the stallion's face while speaking to him in soft tones.

"Well, ol' boy," John said, patting the horse's muscular neck, "once you let me ride you to save my life. How about a second time, so I can take you home with me?"

The crowd of horsemen watched spellbound as the tall stranger placed his foot in the stirrup and swung aboard. The stallion remained calm and obeyed Stranger's touch as he trotted toward the gate and the bunched-up cowboys.

Stranger reined in at the gate and said to Biff Symonds, "If you'll open the gate for me and my horse, Mr. Symonds, I'd appreciate it."

A wide-eyed Symonds obeyed and said, "Mister, you can have the bridle and saddle, too."

Stranger smiled broadly as he nudged Chance out of the corral and drew rein where he'd left his two bags. As he started to dismount under the admiring gaze of the crowd, Symonds hurried to him with Lefty at his side, and said, "Stay in the saddle, Mr. John Stranger. Lefty and I will carry your bags to the depot for you."

The two men followed as John slowly rode Chance to the depot. When they arrived, Biff and Lefty wished John well, told him good-bye, and headed back for the corrals.

John went to the ticket office, paid to have a stock car attached to the train, then rode Chance around town for a while.

The train arrived on schedule, and after the stock car had been coupled to it, Stranger led Chance into the car, which was equipped with both feed and water troughs.

While the big black stallion munched on hay, Stranger patted his neck and said, "Just wait, ol' pal. Breanna's wanted to meet you ever since last summer. She's going to be so excited when I give you to her for an early wedding present!"

John looked at Breanna across the dinner table and finished his story by saying, "And, honey, when I said that, Chance nickered and said, 'Yes, sir, John. I can't wait to be Breanna's horse!'"

"Sure he did!" Breanna said, laughing in delight.

"Well, he *did!* He sure showed it, didn't he?"

"He did that, all right." She laid down her fork and reached across the table to touch John's hand. "Thank you again, darling, for bringing Chance home and giving him to me. I really do love him."

The waiter drew up with a steaming coffeepot in his hand. "More coffee, ma'am? Sir?"

When their cups were full and the waiter had gone, John set his gaze on the woman who had so captured his heart. "Miss Baylor," he said, "why didn't you tell me about the bank robbery incident?"

Breanna blushed. "Well-l-l-l…it was no big thing. How did you find out?"

"Only nine or eleven people told me. That was a mighty brave thing to do."

"Really, it wasn't. I did it almost without thinking. The

opportunity to grab the man's gun was there, so I just took it."

"So how's the man you shot getting along?"

"He'll make it...so he can hang."

"Mm-hmm. I heard about how you asked Matt to let you help save his life. You're some lady, Miss Breanna, do you know that?"

"Just a sinner saved by the grace of God," she replied.

"I suppose this—what's the guy's name you shot?"

"Max Richter."

"I suppose this Richter was pretty surprised to see the gal who shot him working over him on the operating table."

"He didn't recognize me until it was all over. I tried to witness to him, John. But he calls himself an atheist and wouldn't listen. He ordered me out of his room. That was yesterday. I tried to talk to him again this afternoon, but he raised a fuss, swore at me, and told me to leave him alone. Curt's got him handcuffed to the bed now."

"Well, honey," said John, "you can't shove salvation down his throat. You've done all you can."

"I know," she said, sighing. "It must be a horrible thing to go into eternity to face a holy God whose existence you've denied."

"That's for sure."

They ate quietly for a few minutes, then John said, "Let's talk to Pastor Bayless after the service in the morning about setting up an appointment to discuss the wedding."

"Sounds good to me. But John...when will you tell the pastor your real name? He'll need to know before the wedding."

"Might as well tell him when we have our appointment. In fact, the rest of the town might as well know, since those who attend the wedding are going to hear it anyway."

Breanna nodded, then said, "I'm glad. I know you've had

your reasons for keeping your name a secret, but as you said a few months ago, those reasons are no longer valid. And I certainly wouldn't want to be called Mrs. Stranger. And if the Lord gives us children, they couldn't be called little Strangers."

John laughed. "You're right, sweetheart. It's time to quit going by *Stranger,* and reveal my name."

They finished the meal and walked out into the cold night air.

When John drove the buggy past the Goodwin house and pulled up in front of Breanna's small cottage, she said, "How about another cup of coffee?"

Two kerosene lanterns—one on each side of the cottage door—lighted the porch and surrounding area.

"I think I could handle that," he said.

John set the brake, wrapped the reins around the tube that held the buggy whip, and stepped out. He turned to Breanna with a smile and said, "May I help you out, Miss Baylor?"

"Why, yes," she said, scooting to his side of the seat and extending her hand. "Thank you, Mr. Brockman."

When she touched the ground, John kissed her hand. "You're welcome, Mrs. Brockman-to-be."

They laughed together, and Breanna said, "I like the sound of that name, darling. *Brockman.* It has such a solid sound."

"You do, eh? Well, I think Breanna Baylor Brockman sounds good."

"So do I. And for short, you could just call me B. B. B."

She reached into her purse and pulled out one of many silver medallions John had given her in the first few months after they met. She angled the medallion toward the lantern light so he could see the lettering that circled the five-point star: *THE STRANGER THAT SHALL COME FROM A FAR LAND—Deuteronomy 29:22.*

With her other hand, she inserted the key in the door lock, and said, "John Brockman, don't you think it's time to clear up another mystery for me?"

He eyed the medallion. "You want to know about the far country?"

"Yes. Don't you think it's time to tell me where you're from? I mean, after all, a wife should know where her husband comes from, and something about his people."

John smiled and reached past her, pushing the door open. "Yes, my sweet. You're right. It's time you know."

Breanna stepped inside, where lanterns already illuminated the parlor, and John followed, giving the door a push to close it. "You'll have a hard time believing this, darlin', but the far country I'm from is—"

The door closed, and the stars above Denver twinkled silently in the heavens.

CECIL YATES WAS CLEANING up after breakfast when he heard the sound of several horses thundering into his small yard.

"Took 'em long enough to get here," he muttered, and wiped his hands on the dish towel.

He glanced out the kitchen window and saw three Rangers enter the barn with their guns drawn. At the same time, there was a loud knock at the front door.

He draped the towel over the edge of the cupboard and ambled to the door. He didn't recognize either of the two men whose faces were set in harsh lines.

"What can I do for you, Rangers?" Yates asked pleasantly.

"Are you Cecil Yates, the ex-Texas Ranger?" the taller one asked.

"Yes." Yates noted other Rangers standing close by.

"I'm Lieutenant Croft Hammett, and this is Sergeant Wade Simmons. We're from the El Paso office."

"Do you want to come in?"

"I'd like to ask you a question," Hammett said bluntly. "Are you harboring Mark Gray?"

Yates frowned. "You mean *Lieutenant* Mark Gray, the Texas Ranger?"

"Yes, only he's not a Ranger anymore."

"What? Mark's not a Ranger? What happened?"

"You haven't answered my question," said Hammett. "Are you harboring him?"

"Well, pardon me, but what's he hidin' for?"

"You still haven't answered my question."

"No, I'm not harborin' Mark."

"Lieutenant," came the voice of a Ranger who was approaching the front porch.

Hammett turned to look at him.

"He's not in the barn, and there isn't any sign of him. He's not in the privy either."

Hammett nodded. "All right." He turned back to Yates. "We'll accept that invitation to come in now. We want to search the house."

"Now hold on a minute," said Yates. "Are you callin' me a liar?"

"No. Just doing my job. I have to make sure Gray isn't hiding in here."

"Then why'd you ask, if you weren't gonna believe me?"

"Just Ranger procedure. You ought to know that."

Yates glowered at him, then took a step back. "Okay. Look your eyeballs out, if you want. I told you he ain't here. I haven't seen Mark in prob'ly four years."

Hammett and Simmons made a quick search of the shack and returned to the front door where Yates waited. As they holstered their guns, he said, "Told you."

Hammett gave him a bland look. "So you haven't seen Gray in four years?"

"Somethin' like that. You gonna tell me what Mark's done, and why he ain't a Ranger anymore?"

"He killed an unarmed Mexican teenage boy. Shot him in the back. Then he tried to kill another Ranger. Shot him down, then took off on a stolen horse. He's on the dodge. Captain Terrell Sears sent us here. Said you and Gray used to be pals. Figured he might come to you for help. The Ranger he meant to kill got a shot off and wounded him."

"Well, I ain't see him," Yates said.

"If he shows up, you'd better not hide him," said Hammett.

"Why would I do that?"

"Friendship. And the fact that you're holding a grudge against the Texas Rangers. Captain Sears told us about that."

A frown hardened Yates's gaze. "You fellas through checkin' out my place?"

"Looks like it."

"Fine. I've got better things to do."

He watched the Rangers mount up and ride away. He would wait a day or so, in case they left a man behind to watch him, then ride over to Nana's place under cover of darkness. Mark would be interested to know the Rangers had finally shown up.

Captain Sears looked up from the letter he was writing when he heard horses blowing outside. He went to the window and saw his ten-man unit. Only Croft Hammett and Wade Simmons dismounted.

Hammett and Simmons talked to the other men for a few moments, then the Rangers rode away, while the lieutenant and the sergeant crossed the boardwalk and entered the office. Sears knew what to expect by the look on their faces.

He adjusted his position in his chair and said, "Don't tell me..."

"Captain," Hammett said, "we couldn't find hide nor hair of Gray. It's like he's disappeared off the face of the earth."

Sears's face looked grim. "If we don't track him down right away, we'll lose him for good. You go to Yates's place?"

"Yes, sir. Yesterday morning. He says he hasn't seen Gray in four years."

"You believe him?"

"No reason not to. There was no sign of Gray in or around his shack. We talked to people in the town, and they haven't seen anybody looks like Gray."

Sears slammed his fist on the desk. "You've got to catch him, men! Get on it again tomorrow. Find his trail, track him down, and bring him in! If he's heading north, he'll be harder to catch. Winter will set in up in snow country and make it impossible to stay after him. Don't let that dirty turncoat get away!"

On Sunday after the morning service, John "Stranger" Brockman and Breanna Baylor waited until everyone else had shaken the preacher's hand and passed out the door, then they approached him. Kathy stood beside her husband, and the Bayless children were quietly sitting on a pew in the auditorium.

Kathy embraced Breanna, and the preacher shook John's hand.

"Pastor," John said, "Breanna and I want to set an appointment to talk to you."

Bayless winked at his wife. "Honey, I wonder what this is about?"

John chuckled. "You know exactly what it's about."

"And I'm very glad for the two of you," Bayless said, clapping a hand on John's shoulder. "Let's see. I'm sure I could see you tomorrow. How's early afternoon?"

"I have a better idea," spoke up Kathy. "How about if John

and Breanna come for a snack at our house after church tonight? You could talk about the wedding then."

The pastor grinned and nodded. "How about it, folks?"

John and Breanna exchanged glances.

"Sure," said John.

"Can we bring anything?" asked Breanna.

"Only yourselves," Kathy said.

That evening, the Bayless children were having a snack in their room while the adults sat at the kitchen table. Kathy had baked a spice cake, and its sweet scent along with the aroma of hot coffee filled the room.

The pastor asked John to lead them in prayer as they thanked God for the food.

When the "Amen" came quickly, Breanna smiled and ran her gaze across the table to the Baylesses. "You can tell when John's hungry. He prays real short."

Breanna watched Kathy cut the cake and place it on small plates. "What delicate china, Kathy. It's beautiful!"

"It was a wedding present from Robert's parents. I only use it for very special guests."

"We're honored," said John.

Soon they were eating, and Bayless said, "So, how soon are the nuptials?"

"June the fourth," said John. "That's a Sunday. We'd like to have an afternoon wedding."

"June the fourth. I see. Somehow I figured it would be sooner."

"It's the date the Lord put on my heart," John told him. "Breanna and I have prayed about getting married for quite some time. We both feel that June fourth is right."

"Well, we'll just set it for that day then. Are you thinking of an outdoor wedding?"

"Probably not," said Breanna. "If it rained, it would ruin everything. So we'll just plan to have the wedding in the church building."

"Then so be it. We'll get together on the details as the time draws closer."

"That'll be fine," said John.

"I assume Dottie will be your matron of honor, Breanna," said Kathy, eyeing the way John was politely devouring his piece of cake.

"Yes."

"That's wonderful. If I can help you in any way at all, please let me know."

"I was going to ask you if you would be our coordinator. You know, make sure everybody who's coming down the aisle is in place and leaves the back of the auditorium at the right time."

"I'd consider it an honor," said Kathy.

"And we'll be honored to have you do it," John said, swallowing his last bite of spice cake.

Kathy smiled. "Another piece, John?"

"Well-l-l-l…"

"Go ahead, John," the preacher said, chuckling. "Then I won't be so conspicuous when I eat my second piece."

"What about the third, dear?" Kathy said, smiling impishly.

"Hush, wife. I won't eat that one till they're gone."

"If there's any left when John gets through," Breanna said, and laughed.

Kathy cut pieces of cake for both men, and the women watched them eat it for a minute, then Breanna said, "John…"

"Yes?"

"The name."

"The name? Oh! The name!"

The Baylesses exchanged glances.

"She means my real last name," said John.

Pastor Bayless smiled. "You mean it's not Stranger?"

"You know it's not."

"Of course I do, but I never worked up the courage to ask. When you've preached at church, I've always introduced you as the stranger named John."

"So, what is it?" asked Kathy.

"Brockman, Mrs. Bayless. B-R-O-C-K-M-A-N."

"Well, that's a nice name. And it'll leave Breanna's initials the same. Just like when I married Robert."

"Okay, John, I want to know where you're from," said the preacher. "Is Brockman an English name?"

John chuckled. "Sometimes, but not always."

"Why do I get the feeling we're not going to find out which country this 'far country' is?"

When John grinned but said nothing, Bayless looked at Breanna. "Do you know what the 'far country' is?"

"Yes, but I'm sworn to secrecy."

The preacher threw up his hands. "Well, I guess life always has its little mysteries."

"And that's one of them," John said.

"How about if I made a whole spice cake just for you, John?" said Kathy. "Would you tell me?"

He looked at her with a pained expression and said, "Don't put me in a position like that! I can resist anything but spice cake!"

Breanna laughed. "I'll remember that when we're married and I'm trying to coerce you into doing something you don't want to do."

John threw back his head in mock chagrin and said, "I can't believe I just gave away one of my secrets!"

Breanna poked him in the ribs. "I'm listening, if you want to give away some more."

He winced and gently pulled her hand away. "Not tonight."

"Ah, but you just gave away another one!"

"What's that?"

"You're ticklish!" She pulled her hand from his grasp and poked his ribs again.

John grabbed her hand and said, "Look, little girl. It is written in the law of the Medes and the Persians: Thou shalt not tickle thy fiancé in the ribs!"

"Oh, it is, eh? And how about when he's my husband?"

"It says that, too!"

The foursome had a good laugh together, then Robert Bayless said, "John...Breanna...Kathy and I want to congratulate you on your decision to become husband and wife. We can see God's hand in your lives, and it's quite obvious He made you for each other. It will be my privilege to officiate your wedding ceremony."

"Thank you, Pastor," said John.

"Are you still going to do a lot of the visiting nurse work after you're married, Breanna?" asked Kathy.

"My plans are to cut back on travel. I'll take the visiting nurse jobs as the Lord leads, but in order to be the wife I should be, I'll need to be home more. I'll work more at the hospital and at Dr. Goodwin's office."

"Which means you will also be traveling less, John?" Bayless asked.

"I think so. I'm really not sure right now what God's plan is. I'm absolutely sure it's His will that Breanna and I marry, and

I'm confident He'll reveal His plan for my work before we do."

"We'll be praying about that," said the pastor. "In fact, I'd like to pray with you right now and ask the Lord to bless and guide the two of you as you move toward your wedding day."

John took Breanna's hand as they bowed before the Lord and joined the pastor in prayer.

When John and Breanna were in the buggy, driving home, she cuddled close, enjoying the crisp, cold air.

"Tell you what," said John. "If you have time tomorrow, we'll go by the livery stable and let you see Chance. I've been riding him every day to give him a good workout, and Ebony, too."

"I'm glad you're doing that, and yes, I'd love to see Chance tomorrow. Late afternoon all right?"

"Sure. A few more weeks, and Chance will be ready for you to ride him."

"I'm a little nervous about that."

John chuckled. "Once you're in the saddle, his size won't be a problem. I'm training him to kneel, and he's doing well."

"Is he as fast as he looks?"

"Faster. That big guy can flat run. Ebony's fast, but I'm sure Chance can outrun him. Good thing he's as fast as he is. He had to outrun that wind-driven fire last summer. When he was charging toward that last small opening in the circle of fire, it felt like we were flying."

"So you don't think you and Ebony will want to race Chance and me?"

"Nope. But we sure are looking forward to riding with the two of you."

"Me, too." Breanna's warm breath made little puffs of vapor

as she spoke. She squeezed his arm in a sudden wave of affection and said, "I love you, darling."

"I love you, too, sweetheart."

Cecil Yates rode into Nana's small yard about an hour after darkness fell. He looked at the shed out back. When he saw lantern light, he dismounted and limped toward the door. "Mark! It's Cecil! You in there?"

He heard a rustling sound, followed by the click of the latch, and the door squeaked open.

He could see Nana's small form silhouetted against the light of the lantern. Mark lay on the cot with blankets heaped on him.

"Come inside, Cecil Yates," said the old Comanche woman. "Your friend is very sick."

Cecil latched the door behind them and set his gaze on Gray, whose eyes were closed. "What's the matter with him?"

"His wound infected," said Nana, bending over to wipe perspiration from the sick man's brow. "Nana feared it would happen. She is treating it with garlic clove. Will take time, but will heal infection."

Gray opened his eyes. His teeth were chattering, and his body shook beneath the covers.

"Mark, can you hear me?" Yates asked, bending close.

"Y-yeah."

"I came to tell you that Sears's boys showed up day before yesterday."

"F-figured they would. Glad you put me here with Nana. Y-you convince 'em you hadn't s-seen me?"

"I think so. I waited this long just in case they stuck around to keep an eye on me."

"Who'd Sears s-send?"

"A Lieutenant Hammett, Sergeant Simmons, and a whole bunch of other ones."

"I know Hammett and Simmons. Th-they might come back. You be careful."

"Yeah."

"Sears is a bloodhound. He won't g-give up."

"I know. Don't worry, I ain't gonna let him find you."

"You're a real friend."

"Nana friend, too," said the old woman.

"Ycah," nodded Gray. "You sure are."

"She'll make you well, Mark. You just hang in there."

Gray gritted his teeth and nodded.

"It was just like you said, Mark."

"What's that?"

"You said Sleppy would turn the story around and make you the bad guy. That's exactly what he did."

"S-so, who's surprised? I knew he'd lie about it."

Yates leaned low. "I'll go now, Mark. Let you rest. Be back in a few days to see how you're doin'."

"Thanks, Cecil," said Gray through chattering teeth. He watched his friend until the door closed behind him.

A week passed, and when the Ranger unit returned to El Paso, Captain Sears was extremely frustrated when they reported no trace of Mark Gray. Over the next few days, the baffled captain sent telegrams to lawmen all over the West, advising them of Gray's crimes and telling them to be on the lookout for the ex-Texas Ranger who had turned killer.

⁂

Christmas came and went, as did New Year's Day, 1871.

In the weeks that followed, John Brockman worked with Chance every day, taking him for rides and training him to obey every sign that came from his rider. People around town admired the beautiful animal and thought it was wonderful that John had given him to Breanna Baylor.

In mid-January, Brockman walked into Chief U.S. Marshal Duvall's office on a bright, cold morning.

Duvall smiled and rose to his feet behind the desk. "Good morning, John."

Brockman reached across the desk to shake his hand. "I know you're busy," he said, "so I'll be brief."

"Always have time for you, my friend. Besides, I was wanting to talk to you anyway. We'll just kill two birds with one stone today."

"Whatever you say," John said, easing onto a chair in front of the desk.

Duvall sat down. "You first."

"Okay. You were in the church service when Pastor Bayless announced that Breanna and I are getting married in June."

"Yes. June 4, I believe."

"Right. I'd have talked to you about this before, but we've both been so busy."

"Don't I know it!"

"Sol, we've been close friends for some time. I want you to be best man in our wedding."

Surprise showed on Duvall's weathered features. "Me?"

"You."

"Why, John, I'm overwhelmed. You've got other friends who would love to have that privilege."

"But I want you. And Breanna does, too."

A smile broke across the older man's face. "I'm deeply honored, John. Yes, of course I'll be best man in your wedding."

"Okay, that's a sealed matter. Now, what can I do for you?"

"I need help."

"Name it."

"Training new deputy U.S. marshals. Are you going to be in town for a while?"

"Unless that Chief United States Marshal of the Western District comes up with some outlaw for me to chase down."

"Oh, him. Well, if he does, I'll have to let you go after the outlaw," he said with a wry grin.

John gave him a knowing look. "So you want me to train some new men in handling guns, is that it?"

"That's it. I've got four new men coming in. They're all in their twenties and are experienced lawmen—deputy town marshals or sheriff's deputies. As you know, they'll be facing outlaws of all kinds. Many of those outlaws are plenty fast on the draw. I need you to teach these men the art of fast-draw. They may already fancy themselves fast, but I need you to convince them they need to sharpen up on their speed and accuracy in order to survive."

"Okay, Sol. When do we start?"

"They arrive in Denver day after tomorrow. You set the time of the sessions, and I'll let you tell me when they're ready to go out and keep the peace."

The new federal deputies Nelson McGinnis, Ken Murdock, Kyle Henderson, and Wes Howard arrived as scheduled, and began their training with John Brockman the next day in a field east of Denver.

"Okay, gentlemen," John said. "One at a time, I want to see you draw and fire at that dead tree over there. Who wants to go first?"

Kyle Henderson rubbed his jaw, and said, "I really don't need this training, Mr. Brockman. I'm plenty fast as it is...and accurate, too."

"Where have you been a lawman, Kyle?" asked the tall man, who towered over the others.

"Scott City, Kansas. I went up against three hotshot gunfighters while wearing the deputy's badge, and you see me standing before you, so you know who was fastest."

"I'm glad for that," said Brockman. "But there are lots more hotshots out there, just itching to outdraw a deputy U.S. marshal. Makes them look good to the outlaw world."

"I can handle whoever comes along," Henderson said coolly.

"You're the fastest gun in the West, are you?"

McGinnis, Murdock, and Howard looked at each other and grinned.

"Well, I don't know that I'd go so far as to say that," Henderson said.

"So there are men out there faster than you?"

"Probably a few."

"Tell you what," said Brockman. "Let's empty our guns and draw against each other. This won't prove accuracy, but the fella who's got his gun in hand and cocked before his opponent does is usually the one who walks away. Okay?"

"Sure," said Henderson, a cocky look on his face.

Brockman and Henderson removed the cartridges from their guns, snapped the empty cylinders in place, and put about forty feet of ground between them. Both men hooked their greatcoats behind their holsters.

"Let me see you draw, Kyle," said the tall man.

"Oh, no you don't," Kyle said. "A man doesn't get a chance to see the other guy draw before he faces him in a real gunfight."

John shrugged.

Henderson planted his feet apart on the tawny winter grass, and said, "Okay, teacher. Whenever you're ready."

Brockman grinned. "Tell you what, Kyle. I'm going to give you the advantage. Your hand is hovering over your gun. I'm going to raise my hand as far as I can reach."

As he spoke, John raised his gun hand above his head.

Henderson looked at him askance. "You're really going to start your draw against me with your hand up there?"

"Yep."

"Why?"

"To prove a point. Okay, Kyle, go for it whenever you're ready."

Henderson's hand snaked downward. Before he could get his fingers wrapped around the butt of his revolver, he was looking down the muzzle of Brockman's Colt .45 Peacemaker with the hammer cocked.

Henderson's face blanched, and his eyes bulged in disbelief.

McGinnis, Murdock, and Howard grinned smugly at each other.

"Think you're ready for the big boys, Kyle?" asked Brockman, holding his gun level on Henderson's midsection.

Kyle blinked and licked his lips. "I get your point, sir."

"Good!" said John. "Now we can get down to business."

ON FRIDAY, MARCH 3, John Brockman reported to Chief U.S. Marshal Duvall that his four students were ready to fulfill their duty as deputy United States marshals.

On Sunday, John preached in the morning service at the invitation of Pastor Bayless. During the weeks he had schooled the four young deputies, John had given them the gospel of Jesus Christ. Though none had turned to Christ, two of them—Wes Howard and Kyle Henderson—were in attendance that day to hear John preach.

At the close of the service, both Howard and Henderson responded to the invitation and received the Lord. There was great joy among the people at seeing these men come to Christ.

After the service, Dottie and Matt Carroll came up to John and Breanna. "We were wondering if the two of you have plans for dinner," Matt said.

John glanced at Breanna. "Well, we were going to a restaurant."

"How about the Carroll Restaurant?" asked Dottie.

John's eyes twinkled as he said, "There are two things I really like about that place."

Dottie grinned. "And just what might those two things be?"

"The food and the hugs I get from Molly Kate, and not necessarily in that order."

Molly Kate, who was standing close by, giggled. She ran to him and raised her arms. "I'll give you an early hug, Uncle John!"

"And I'll take it, sweetie!" He swept her up in his arms and held her tight.

As the group moved outside the church, James drew up on John's other side and said, "When we're havin' dinner at our house, will you tell me some more stories about gunfightin' and catchin' outlaws, Uncle John?"

"Sure, James. I've always got more stories than you've heard."

"Even if he has to make them up," said Breanna, laughing.

"Oh, Aunt Breanna, Uncle John doesn't make those stories up. Do you, Uncle John?"

"Of course not. But if you really want to hear some exciting stories, ask your aunt to tell you about her own adventures. You know, stopping bank robberies, tackling presidents, and that kind of thing."

Breanna opened her mouth to retort but was interrupted when a gray-haired man left his buggy and stepped toward John.

"Mr. Brockman, you don't know me," the man said. "My name's Gerald Coffey. Could I have a few minutes with you?"

John looked at Dottie. "Do I have time to talk to this gentleman?"

"Sure. We'll take Breanna home with us, and you get there as soon as you can."

As the Carrolls and Breanna climbed into their buggy, John turned to the man, who looked to be in his late sixties, and said, "Now, what can I do for you, Mr. Coffey?"

"I was in the service this morning, Mr. Brockman. You're a powerful preacher."

John waited for him to proceed.

"I just moved to Denver from St. Louis, Missouri. I'm going to open up a new hotel here."

"The way this town's growing, I'm sure it will be needed," John said.

Coffey nodded. "I'm a widower, Mr. Brockman, and I came to First Baptist Church hoping to meet some nice older women."

"Well, I know there are some fine Christian widows in the church, sir. How long have you been a Christian?"

"All my life."

"You mean, since you were a boy?"

"No, since I was a tiny baby. And that's why I wanted to talk to you. I disagree with something you said this morning from the pulpit. You made it sound like I'm not a Christian."

"What was it, Mr. Coffey, that made you a Christian when you were a baby?"

"Why, I was baptized."

"You're telling me that as a tiny baby, you repented of your sin, called on Jesus Christ to save you, and received Him into your heart as personal Saviour when the water was poured on your head?"

"What? I don't understand."

"Jesus said, 'Except ye repent, ye shall all likewise perish.' Repentance is a change of mind about your unbelief toward Jesus Christ, a sorrow for your sins, and a turning to Jesus by faith to save you from going to hell. Paul said plainly that he preached 'repentance toward God and faith toward our Lord Jesus Christ.' Repentance and faith are like Siamese twins and cannot be separated. With true repentance, there is a turning *to*

God *from* whatever has held you in your unbelief. For it is your unbelief that condemns you before God."

Gerald Coffey blinked, and a new light began to shine in his eyes. He leaned forward as if he didn't want to miss a word of what John was saying.

"Mr. Coffey, John 1:12 says, 'As many as received him, to them gave he power to become the sons of God, even to them that believe on his name.' When a lost sinner is sorrowful for having sinned against God and turns in repentance from his unbelief, calling upon Jesus to come into his heart and save him…that's when he becomes a Christian.

"Mr. Coffey, when you were a tiny baby, did you turn to Jesus Christ from your sin of unbelief, acknowledge to Him that you were a guilty lost sinner, and receive Him into your heart by calling on Him?"

Gerald Coffey looked down. "Well, ah…no."

"So when did you become a Christian?"

The silver-haired man rubbed his chin. "I guess I didn't. But I want to. Will you help me?"

"Sure. Let's go inside where it's warmer. I want to show you some more Scripture, and you can settle this thing here and now."

"Thank you, Mr. Brockman. I appreciate you taking the time."

"The pleasure is mine, sir," said John, leading him toward the door of the church building.

James Carroll hurried to open the front door when the knocker sounded. "Hi, Uncle John!"

"Have you started eating yet?" asked the tall man, stepping inside.

"We were just about to go ahead, but you made it."

When John entered the dining room with James at his side, Molly Kate came from the kitchen and pointed to a dining-room chair. "This is where you'll sit, Uncle John. 'Tween me and James."

He smiled at the little girl and then turned to Breanna as she set the last of the hot dishes on the table.

"Hello, darling," she said. "Who was that man? I heard him say his name is Gerald Coffey, but who is he?"

"He said he's going to open a new hotel in town. He's a widower from St. Louis. Said he came to church today to see if he could meet some women his age."

"What did he want to talk to you about?"

"My sermon."

Matt, who was just coming through the kitchen door, heard John's last words. "Did the man take issue with something you preached, John?"

"He questioned something I said that indicated he wasn't a Christian. Turned out, he wasn't."

"Did he get saved, Uncle John?" asked James.

"He sure did, praise the Lord."

"Another brand plucked from the burning," Breanna said happily.

"Sure enough. I'll tell Pastor Bayless about him so he can follow up."

"Well, everybody," said Dottie, "let's sit down to the table."

Matt led in prayer, thanked the Lord for the food, and for saving Gerald Coffey. They had barely begun to eat when James said, "Let's hear some stories, Uncle John."

"James," said Matt, "Uncle John might like to eat a meal in this house just once without having to tell you stories."

John smiled. "I don't mind, Matt. I'll just tell a couple of them, then everybody can talk about whatever they want."

John's stories seemed awfully short to James, but he didn't complain.

Soon Molly Kate looked up at the tall man, and said, "Uncle John, when you and Aunt Breanna get married, then you'll be my *real* uncle, won't you? Right now, you're my *pretend* uncle."

"That's right, sweetie," he said, leaning over to kiss her on the cheek.

Molly Kate blushed and looked at her aunt.

Breanna smiled. "You know, Molly Kate, you're a very fortunate little girl. You're one of very few females I'll allow your Uncle John to kiss."

Molly Kate looked pleased, and there was laughter around the table, then Dottie said, "Breanna, do you have any plans yet about having your wedding dress made?"

"Not yet. I know how I want it to look, but I haven't decided which seamstress to hire."

Dottie paused for a moment, then said, "I know I've never been a professional seamstress, but I make a lot of my own dresses, and Molly Kate's. We can afford to buy them, but I just enjoy making them."

"And you do a marvelous job," said Breanna.

Dottie looked at her sister with eager eyes. "Would...would you let *me* make your wedding dress?"

Breanna's eyes widened in surprise, then immediately filled with pleasure. "Why, of course, Dottie. It never even crossed my mind to ask you to do it. I'd be thrilled and honored to have you make my dress."

Dottie lit up with excitement. "Good! Let's get together soon, and you draw me a sketch of what you have in mind. We'll pick out the material, and I'll get started!"

❖

While John was driving Breanna home that night, he said to her, "I think Chance is ready to be ridden by his owner."

"Really?"

"Mm-hmm."

"Well, I planned to take tomorrow off to give my house a good cleaning. Dottie and I are going to shop for my dress material in the afternoon. But I can have the house cleaned by nine and then ride Chance between nine and noon."

"Sounds good to me," said John. "Tomorrow morning between nine and noon it is."

The sun was at the midway point in the morning sky when Breanna stood in the livery office talking to hostler Willy Sparks, while John visited Ebony and gave him a rubdown.

A brisk March wind was blowing, but the temperature was mildly warm.

After a while, John stepped through the office door and said, "All right, Breanna, Ebony's in his stall and I have Chance saddled and ready to go. You wait at the gate in front, and I'll lead him through the barn to you."

"Wonderful horse, Miss Breanna," said Willy. "I'm eager to see you on his back."

"Me, too," she said, nervously wiping her moist palms on the sides of her split riding skirt.

Breanna walked to the gate that opened to the street and waited. Moments later, she saw the barn door open. The other corral came into view, showing her some of the horses. Then John appeared, leading the imposing black stallion. Breanna thought he looked gigantic silhouetted against the sunlit rectangle of the door as John led him through the barn's deep shadows.

When they emerged, and the wind caught Chance's mane, it looked like whipping black flame. He pranced into the sunlight, his head held high, and every line of him spoke of wildness. Yet when he spotted Breanna, he whistled shrill and clear, pressing John to hurry him to her.

Breanna smiled, pleased with her horse's reaction at seeing her. She thought she had never seen so much muscle on a horse, yet his body lines were graceful and beautiful, and suggested speed. His head was like a savage war charger's and splendidly noble.

As Chance drew up to his owner, he snorted and nickered softly, bobbing his head.

"Good morning, big boy," Breanna said, as she stroked his long face and patted his neck. "It's been several days. Miss me?"

"Ready to ride him around the corral?" asked John.

"Ready as I'll ever be."

"I'll keep a good hold on the reins while you mount, just in case he fools us."

Breanna eyed the stirrup. "John, I can't lift my foot that high."

John laughed. "All right, try this. Step up real close to his left side, tap his shoulder three times, and say, 'Chance…down.'"

"That's it?"

"Mm-hmm."

Breanna tapped the horse's muscular left shoulder and said, "Chance…down."

The big black dropped down on the knees of his forelegs.

"He did it!" Breanna said, smiling at John.

"Tell him how good he did, and step aboard."

"That's a good boy, Chance," she said, as she put her left

foot in the stirrup and swung her leg over his back.

John still held the reins, making sure Breanna was settled in the saddle, then said, "Okay, tap his shoulder three times and say, 'Chance…up.'"

Breanna did as he said, and the massive animal gently stood up on all fours.

"Good boy, Chance!" Breanna said, patting his neck. "That's a very good boy!"

Chance stood there calm and composed, moving his ears back and forth.

"Looks like you're safe in the saddle, sweetie," said John, swinging the reins over the horse's majestic head. "Here you go. Just give him a slight nudge with your knees as you've done with your rental horses, and walk him around the corral. When you're comfortable with him, trot him some."

For twenty minutes, John and Willy watched with pleasure as Breanna walked and trotted her horse around the small corral.

Finally Breanna guided Chance at a walk toward the two men and said, "You've trained him well, John. He obeys the reins and my vocal commands perfectly. Are you ready to go for a ride?"

"Let's do it. Ebony's saddled and bridled. I'll be right back."

Moments later, John led his own black horse toward Breanna. The stallion and the gelding nickered at each other as John swung into the saddle.

"You two have a nice ride," Willy said, opening the gate.

Ebony showed no animosity toward Chance, and the two moved alongside each other like old friends.

When they angled into the street, John said, "So, where do we ride today?"

"You know where," Breanna said, and smiled.

They put their mounts to a steady gait and headed south out of town. When they were past the residential area, they turned southwest and rode for some three or four miles until they were near the foothills to the Rockies.

Soon they were riding along a small creek lined with bare-limbed cottonwoods. Spring was still a few weeks away in Colorado.

The creek had a trail alongside it that ran all the way into the mountains. They had taken this trail—Breanna's favorite—many times before.

Soon they drew near a beautiful white two-story house Breanna had admired since she first saw it over a year before. It stood in a grove of cottonwood and weeping willow trees.

"There it is, darling," Breanna said with a sigh. "My dream house. Someday maybe we can build one like it out here somewhere."

John chuckled. "It may be ugly on the inside. Maybe you wouldn't like it at all."

"Are you kidding? A house that attractive on the outside has to be equally so on the inside."

"Did you ever find out who owns this place?"

"Yes...just last Friday. I happened to mention it to one of the tellers at our bank—Elmer Ferguson. He told me Foster Maddox had the house built."

"Oh. Owner of the Denver Stockyards Company."

"Yes. Elmer told me Mrs. Maddox died over a year ago. I never met either one of them."

Breanna grew quiet as she pulled rein some seventy yards from the road. John drew up beside her and watched her gaze at the house.

It was white frame with large front windows, upstairs and down, adorned with black shutters. It had a wide wraparound front porch. Once Breanna had driven into the yard, so she knew the back porch was screened in. Four wide steps led up to the front porch.

A white picket fence ran across the front of the property, down the sides, and all the way to the rear property line and across the back. The place sat on six acres. There were plenty of towering cottonwood trees scattered around the property and on all four sides of the house, along with weeping willows and a great deal of brush. A small barn and other outbuildings were visible from the road, all painted white.

The large front windows sparkled in the sunlight, and Breanna could just make out delicate lace curtains.

The house looked to be about ten years old, but the paint was relatively fresh. It was obvious the place had been well taken care of.

A trace of sadness showed on Breanna's face. John noticed it, and asked, "What's the matter, honey?"

Her voice was low as she said, "I didn't tell you something else I learned from Elmer on Friday."

"What's that?"

"He said that Mr. Maddox sold the stockyards company to Jess Cline about three weeks ago."

"Jess Cline who owns the Broadway Bank?"

"Yes. And Elmer told me Maddox sold this place just last week."

"Did he say who bought it?"

"He didn't know. Somebody with money…they paid cash for it."

"I see. So why the sad face?"

"Oh, it's silly." Breanna hesitated. Then her words came out in a rush. "Well, you told me that we'd buy a piece of land and have a house built on it. And I know we're about ready to proceed with that plan, since winter's almost over. But ever since I first saw this place, I've had a secret wish that if it ever sold, somehow I could buy it. I mean, even before you asked me to marry you. I've thought about this place even more since we set our wedding date. While you were in Butte City, I drove out here in Dr. Goodwin's buggy a couple of times to just look at it and wonder if I could talk you into building a house like it. That's…ah…sort of why I wanted to ride out here today."

"I see," John said quietly.

Breanna sighed and looked back at the house. "Oh, if only I'd known it was for sale!"

"Do I detect that you'd rather have this house and the ground around it than another piece of property and a house like it?"

"Well-l-l-l, it's just that the way the trees—John, darling, of course I'll love whatever land we buy. And you don't have to build a house like it. As long as I have you, I could live in a shack on a rock and be perfectly happy."

John leaned from his saddle and took her hand. "I appreciate that, sweetheart, but the wife of John Brockman isn't going to live in a shack on a rock."

Breanna smiled and squeezed his hand, then set her gaze on the house once more. "If only I'd known it was for sale…" She took a deep breath. "Oh, well, it's sold, so that's that. Poor Mr. Maddox. It must've been hard to give up the house where he and his wife had lived. Elmer said he didn't know if Mr. Maddox would buy a small house in town or leave Denver."

"He left for Wisconsin the day after he sold the house last week," John said. "Moved back there to be near his children and grandchildren."

It took a few seconds for John's words to sink in. Then Breanna turned her head slowly and looked into his eyes with a direct and focused gaze. "How did you know that? I thought you didn't know who owned this place."

"I never said I didn't know who owned it. I simply asked if *you* had ever found out who owned it."

Breanna cocked her head and studied him, but didn't say anything.

He kept his features impassive as he said, "I know who owns the place *now.*"

Her eyebrows arched. "You do?"

"Mm-hmm."

"Well, who?"

"I'm looking at her."

FOR A BRIEF MOMENT, Breanna's tongue seemed glued to the roof of her mouth, and her voice had left her.

John waited in silence and let a slow smile work its way over his face.

Breanna finally found her voice. "John, what are you telling me?"

"The answer to your question," he replied, still smiling. "You asked me who owns this place, and I said I'm looking at the owner. Well, *co-owner,* anyhow. I'm the other half. You're looking at our new home, darlin'."

Tears welled up in Breanna's eyes. "Oh, John…you…you bought this place from Foster Maddox?"

"Yes. Last week."

She leaned from the saddle and he lifted her from Chance's back and held her tightly as she wept for joy, saying, "Oh, John, I love you! Thank you!"

After a moment, he lowered her to the ground and dismounted, then took her into his arms. "Would you like to see inside?"

"Oh, could I, John?"

"I don't know why not. It's your house. I bought all the furniture, but if there's something you don't like, we'll replace it."

They tied the horses to the hitching posts near the porch and moved up the steps. Breanna paused and let her gaze run over the wide wraparound porch. Mrs. Maddox had decked it with attractive outdoor furniture, and it had a large porch swing.

Breanna rushed to the swing and sat down, giving it a push. She looked up at John like a delighted child. "Oh, darling! Isn't it wonderful? We'll sit out here on summer evenings together!"

"We sure will," he said, grinning, then turned and placed a key in the lock.

Breanna left the swing and hurried to him. When the door swung open, he bowed and gestured toward the interior. "Your palace, your majesty."

The sun shining through the windows, illuminating the dainty lace curtains and the beautiful wood of the floor, took Breanna's breath. "Oh, John! I love it!"

To the right of the door was a parlor; to the left a large dining room, separated beyond the vestibule by a spacious hall. Directly ahead was a wide staircase leading to the second floor. The gleaming banister and handrail were handcarved, and there was a faint odor of beeswax in the air.

They entered the parlor first. It had a lovely carpet with muted colors of dark red, green, and beige. Breanna ran her gaze over the ornate sofa and two wing-backed chairs, in a pattern of dark red roses and a green and ivory design, and told herself they might take getting used to. Later, if they still seemed too dark, she would replace them. Exquisitely carved tables, covered with lace and embroidered scarves, stood next to the sofa and chairs. Fancy kerosene lamps adorned each table.

In the center of the outside wall was a magnificent stone fireplace with two beige overstuffed chairs in front of it. There were lamp tables beside each chair.

On the back wall was a beautiful upright piano and stool.

There were paintings of snow-covered mountains, seascapes, and autumn forests on the walls.

Overall, the room had a warm, inviting look to it, and Breanna envisioned cozy evenings spent in it with John.

Next was the dining room. Breanna loved the large table that was covered with a beautiful cloth. Candlesticks reflected the soft sunlight filtering through the lace-curtained windows. Breanna gazed in wonder at a china cupboard filled with beautiful china. There was also a fireplace in this room.

Down the hall behind the staircase was a well-stocked library and sitting room. The walls were lined with mahogany bookshelves, and the mantle over the fireplace was of the same wood. There was a rolltop desk and comfortable overstuffed chairs. The draperies were patterned with flowers, and creamy sheers covered the windows. As with the parlor, there was an abundance of lamps.

"Oh, John, it truly is a dream house!" said Breanna, as they moved across the hall from the library into a bright, airy kitchen. The tall man's heart was thrilled to see his bride-to-be so happy.

In the kitchen the cupboards were plentiful, and there was a round pedestal table and six matching chairs. A lantern hung over the table, and beneath it on the shiny hardwood floor was a braided blue and white rug. There was also a matching rug by the back door. Crisp white tieback curtains adorned each of the four windows.

Breanna looked around in delight. "What a cheery kitchen! We'll have many happy times in here, won't we, darling?"

"We sure will," John said, grinning.

Breanna caressed the shiny black cookstove as they passed it to go out the back door. They stood on the screened-in porch and surveyed the massive backyard. There was a large cottonwood tree close to the porch, and Breanna envisioned a child playing in a rope swing that hung from one of its low limbs.

They reentered the house and ascended the staircase that opened onto a wide hall with several doors down each side.

Breanna stopped and took John's hand. "Darling, it truly is a palace!"

They kissed, and then he gently pulled her forward, urging her to look inside each room.

In addition to the master bedroom, there was a sewing room and three bedrooms, all furnished exquisitely. Breanna pictured these bedrooms occupied by little Brockmans and could almost hear their happy chatter. Each bedroom had a washstand with a flowered pitcher, and the floors were adorned with colorful braided rugs.

The master bedroom was at the front of the house, and covered the breadth of it. Breanna was speechless as she beheld the beauty of it. There was a huge four-poster bed with a snow-white bedspread trimmed in dark green. All the curtains matched the spread, and the wallpaper was vine-covered. A soft green rug covered most of the hardwood floor.

There were two tall chiffoniers on either side of the bed, and a matching pair of intricately carved armoires next to the closest windows.

Breanna quickly formed plans for how she would make some decorative changes to personalize the room and make it theirs.

Against a side wall was a fireplace with a gilt-framed mirror above it. In front of the fireplace were two soft easy chairs covered in white and dark green.

Breanna slipped her hand into the crook of John's arm and

sighed. "Darling, this is much more beautiful than I ever dreamed. You are the most thoughtful and wonderful man in the whole world."

John smiled and said teasingly, "You don't *always* know what's going on in my mind, do you?"

Breanna shook her head and laughed. "You sure fooled me on this one, I'll tell you that! But I love every inch of this place. Thank you."

John folded her into his arms and replied, "Since the Lord has given me the most beautiful and wonderful woman in the world, I've got to take good care of her."

It was almost twelve-thirty when Dottie Carroll answered the knock at her door and beheld her sister's beaming face and dancing eyes.

"Sorry I'm late, Dottie," Breanna said, "but wait till I tell you why!"

On several occasions Breanna had told her sister about the white house and her longing to have one like it. When Dottie heard the good news, she wept with joy.

After describing what the house looked like inside, Breanna showed Dottie a sketch of what she envisioned for a wedding dress, and together they walked toward the business district to look for material.

"Breanna," Dottie said. "I'm so glad the Lord brought John into your life. He's such a wonderful man."

"That he is. The Lord is so good."

Dottie was quiet for a moment, then said, "You've made two precious children very happy, Breanna. James is thrilled that he's to be your ringbearer, and Molly Kate is elated she's going to be your flower girl."

Breanna nodded and smiled.

"Have you asked Dr. Goodwin if he'll walk you down the aisle and give you away?"

"Yes, and you'd think I'd given him a million dollars. He was really touched."

"Well, he and Martha have been like parents to you ever since they took you in and let you live in their cottage."

"They sure have. Only…I wish Daddy and Mother were still here. I'd like them to know John. And, of course, I wish Daddy could be the one to walk me down the aisle and give me away."

Breanna felt her throat tighten, and tears filled Dottie's eyes.

They walked on silently, and when they reached Glenarm Street, turned and headed downtown.

"Has John asked Chief Duvall about being best man yet?" asked Dottie.

"Yes, and he was humbled by it. He told John there were lots of men around who would be honored to be his best man. He's such a dear Christian man."

Soon they entered the first store to begin looking for wedding dress material.

On March 28, Mark Gray looked out the open door of the old Comanche woman's shed and saw Cecil Yates riding up. Yates had a black custom-made Mexican saddle with silver trimmings tied behind his own.

Gray stepped outside into the warm Texas sunshine.

"Here's the saddle I promised you, Mark," said Yates. "I saw a fella ride into Guadalupe Springs last night and go into the saloon. He was half drunk when he staggered in, so I knew he'd be in worse shape when he came out. When nobody was around to see me, I took it off the fella's horse."

Gray's face showed his disappointment. "Sort of conspicuous, isn't it, Cecil? All this fancy silver trimmin' and all?"

"Sorry, but it's the best I could do. Stealin' saddles ain't the easiest thing in the world."

"Ah, it'll be all right. Main thing is that I have a saddle."

Yates hipped around, untied the saddle, and handed it down to his friend. "You takin' off right away?"

"Few minutes."

"Still goin' to Arizona to hole up at Jim Carter's ranch?"

"Sure am."

"What name did you say he's goin' by now?"

"Jock Hood."

"Oh, yeah. Your wound all healed up?"

"Seems to be. I've been goin' up in one of the canyons to practice my fast-draw the past few days."

"Aren't you afraid Sears might still have some of his hounds sniffin' around here? They might hear your gunfire."

"Oh, I haven't fired it...just workin' on my speed."

Yates nodded. "Well, ol' friend, I guess I'll be moseyin' along. You take care of yourself, y'hear?"

Gray reached up and shook Yates's hand. "You, too, Cecil. And thanks for everything."

He watched his friend ride away, then threw the saddle on the horse and cinched it tight.

"Mike, I'm telling you, this is nothing but a wild-goose chase," Gene Whitfield said. "Gray's probably somewhere way up north by now—Dakota Territory or Montana."

Mike Dorn gave his partner a sidelong glance. "I don't think so. When Cap'n Sears has a gut feeling, you don't want to ignore it. He sent us up here to nose around because something's telling him that Gray's in this area. He doesn't trust that Yates, either. He still thinks the guy lied when he told Hammett he hadn't seen Gray in four years. And so do I. I'm sure I've heard Gray say he's been up to see Yates within the past year."

They were coming up on a huge jumble of boulders and tall pillarlike rocks that were partially embedded in the side of the mountain. At their base was a small tumbledown shack.

A rider appeared, coming from the yard, and turned west at a trot.

"You get a good look at that fella?" asked Dorn.

"Not real good," said Whitfield, "but he wouldn't have to change much to fit Cap'n Sears's description of Cecil Yates. C'mon. Let's check out the shack."

Mark Gray heard Nana come out of her shack as he gave the cinch a final tug and dropped the stirrup. When he turned he saw a knapsack in her hand and a toothless smile on her face.

"This food for Mark Gray," she said.

"Thank you, Nana. And thank you for making me well. You've been very kind."

"Nana glad to help Cecil Yates's friend. You come back see Cecil Yates some day, you come see Nana."

"I sure will," he said, and turned back to tie the knapsack to the saddle.

Movement on the rolling cactus-strewn prairie to the northeast caught Gray's eye as he peered through the narrow opening between the shack and a towering rock pillar. He stiffened when he saw sunlight glint off metal as the two riders headed in the direction of the shack at a leisurely gait.

Nana blinked in amazement when Gray dropped the knapsack, swung into the saddle, and spurred the horse into an instant gallop, heading due west.

Dorn and Whitfield were about a quarter mile from the shack when Dorn said, "Let's split up, Gene. I'll go in from the east side, and you circle around and move in from the west. There's no way to sneak up on anybody on this open land. If Gray's in that shack and happens to look out, he might see one of us; but if we're coming from opposite directions, he might not see both of us."

"Makes sense. When we get in close—"

Ranger Whitfield's words were cut off by the sudden appearance of a rider from the back side of the shack. He was headed west, and riding hard.

"It's *him!"* said Dorn. "Let's go!"

Mark Gray lashed the mare with the tips of the reins. He glanced back and saw the Rangers coming after him at a full gallop.

The parched desert flats were stippled with greasewood and cholla cactus. Gray let the mare choose her own path, threading her way between them.

Five minutes of hard riding showed Gray that the bay mare was faster than the horses under the Texas Rangers. Gradually, he was pulling away from them. Another five minutes put enough distance between Gray and his pursuers that he began to relax a bit. He had to think—to plan. These men were like wild dogs that had seen their prey and were on the scent. They wouldn't give up till they'd hunted him down. The mare was fast, but she'd wear out soon if he kept pushing her this hard.

Up ahead, he spotted a winding dry wash. Fugitive and

horse topped the slight rise bordering the wash and plunged down its steep slope, showering sand in every direction. The tapered walls of the wash were thick with brush, but its sandy floor was bare and afforded more speed for the horse.

Up ahead, on one of the winding curves, was a thick entanglement of brush that jutted onto the floor. He rode past the heavy stand of brush, followed a slight curve, then halted and tied the mare to a mesquite tree where she couldn't be seen from the Rangers' approach.

He worked his way back up to the rim of the wash, staying low, and looked east across the desert. He could see the dust cloud raised by the galloping Rangers. Bending low, he dashed along the edge of the wash, plunged into the thick brush, and found the perfect spot. He pulled out his revolver, checked the loads, and snapped the cylinder shut with an experienced flick of the wrist.

"C'mon, Rangers," Gray said, smiling to himself. "You're already dead men. You just don't know it yet."

Soon the sound of thundering hooves met his ears. His mare's hoofprints were easy to follow on the bottom of the dry wash, and now the pursuers were drawing near.

When they came around the bend, Gray recognized both of them just before he cut loose with his gun. The first bullet knocked Dorn from the saddle, and the second one buckled Whitfield but left him on his horse.

Gray fired at Whitfield again, but not before Gene was able to get off a shot at the dark form in the brush.

To Gray it felt like a sledgehammer had hit him in the left shoulder. He fell backwards and righted himself as another bullet hummed past his ear, then fired again. This time, Whitfield peeled off his mount and hit the sand.

Gray's shoulder felt numb, but he knew the pain would come when the shock wore off. He carefully rose up to get a look at the Rangers. Whitfield was crumpled in a heap like a broken doll, and Dorn was sprawled facedown in the sand. Neither man was moving.

He would go back to Nana. She would help him. The dead Rangers—whenever they were found—were far enough from the Guadalupes that no one would know where the chase started.

He groped his way to the wash bottom and stumbled to his horse. It was all he could do to get himself in the saddle. His head felt light, and the wound was starting to come alive with pain.

Covering his trail as only a man who had been a Ranger could do, he made his way back toward the Guadalupes.

Nana was in her shack, kneading dough, when she heard hoofbeats. She flipped the latch on the door and eased it open. Her head bobbed when she saw the ex-Ranger bent over in his saddle, and a stream of blood running down his arm.

"Mark Gray!" she exclaimed, shuffling toward him.

With Nana's help, Gray got to the ground without falling. She gave him what strength she had as he leaned on her, and they made it to the shed. He fell back on the cot, sweating from the pain, and Nana quickly examined the wound.

"Bullet in shoulder. Nana take out."

An hour later, Nana left an unconscious Mark Gray in the shed and led the mare to her previous hiding place. Once more, the old Comanche woman would nurse the white man back to health.

✦

Jody Sleppy, having been promoted to sergeant, was leading a five-man band of Texas Rangers in search of Corporal Mike Dorn and Private Gene Whitfield, who had been missing four days.

After scouring the area around the Guadalupe Mountains, including the village of Guadalupe Springs, they'd come up with nothing. No one in the village had seen the two Rangers. They talked to ranchers in the vicinity, and even an old Comanche woman named Nana on the north side of the mountains, but neither the ranchers nor the old Indian woman had seen Dorn and Whitfield.

"We'll cover that area up there, men," said Sleppy, pointing northwest. "If we don't find somebody who's seen them within thirty miles or so, we'll head back to El Paso."

"Yeah, to a very upset captain," said one of the Rangers.

"Can't blame him," said Sleppy. "We've put a lot of time and effort into looking for Mark Gray. If something has happened to Dorn and Whitfield, Cap'n Sears is going to be a bearcat."

"Especially if what happened to them was caused by Gray," said another.

"Well, the captain believes Gray is still in west Texas," said Sleppy. "If something has happened to those two Rangers, even if it's unrelated to their pursuit of that no-good turncoat, the captain will blame Gray."

The Rangers rode across the desert floor, weaving among clumps of greasewood and cactus in a northerly direction.

It was midafternoon when they saw a small cloud of dust up ahead, and then spotted a rider coming fast from the north. They held their horses to a trot and watched the rider draw closer, riding as if he were being chased.

When the man was about thirty yards from them, he suddenly pulled rein, skidded his horse to a stop, and rode toward them. As he drew near, he called out, "I saw your badges flashing in the sun. Am I glad to see you!"

"What's up?" asked Sleppy, pulling rein. The other Rangers followed suit.

The man's horse snorted and blew as he said, "I found two dead Rangers in a dry wash back there about six or seven miles. Looked like somebody ambushed them. I was riding to El Paso to report it."

"In a dry wash, you say?" Sleppy said, his heart sinking at the thought of Dorn and Whitfield dead.

"Yes, Sergeant. My ranch is west of the wash a couple miles. I was riding to a neighboring ranch when I spotted two horses standing at the top of the draw. They were saddled and bridled, but they weren't ground-reined or tied to anything. I thought something must be wrong, so I took a look down into the wash and saw the bodies. I went down to see if either was alive. It was then I saw they were Rangers."

"Would you take us there, Mister—"

"Carpenter...Lloyd Carpenter, Sergeant."

Carpenter had tied the dead Rangers' horses to a mesquite bush before heading for El Paso. When the Rangers rode toward them, they pricked up their ears and whinnied.

"Keep a sharp eye as you go down, men," said Sergeant Sleppy. "If you see anything out of the ordinary, give a holler. Whoever shot Dorn and Whitfield might have left evidence of some kind."

Carpenter went down behind Sleppy as the others picked their way toward the bottom of the wash.

"Hey, Sarge!" called a private named Hec Withers.

Sleppy stopped and looked back up the slope where Withers stood in the brush.

"There's blood on these bushes. Looks like the ambusher took a bullet."

"Good," Sleppy said with a nod. "Maybe we'll find him lying around here somewhere."

When they reached bottom, Sleppy swallowed hard at the sight of his dead fellow Rangers. He noted the crumpled position of Whitfield, and that Dorn was sprawled facedown with his right hand stretched above his head.

Sleppy looked more closely and saw impressions in the sand near Dorn's hand. He blinked in surprise as he made out a word written there.

Lloyd Carpenter and the Rangers were coming up behind him, speaking in low tones.

"Take a look at this, men," said Sleppy, pointing to the sand next to the dead Ranger's hand. "Dorn wrote something. Do you see what I do?"

"It says, 'Gray,' Sarge," spoke up a Ranger.

Captain Sears was at the door of his office when Sergeant Jody Sleppy and his men rode up, leading two horses with dead Rangers draped over their backs. People on the street gawked at the sight.

Sears looked at his sergeant. "Where'd you find them, Jody?"

Sleppy explained about the rancher who had found the bodies, and the location of the ambush in the dry wash.

"It was Gray, sure as anything!" the Ranger captain said. "Nobody can tell me different!"

"None of us would do that, sir," said Sleppy. "We have evidence it was Gray. Dorn wrote Gray's name in the sand before he died."

Sears's face went livid with rage, and the veins in his temples swelled. He drew in a ragged breath and said, "That slimy snake! He tried to kill you, Jody, and now he's killed two Rangers!"

"One thing, Cap'n," said Jody. "There was blood in the bushes where Gray ambushed them. One of them got off a shot that hit its target."

"Well, good! I hope Gray bleeds to death, except I'd like to catch him and watch him hang!"

"We'd all like to see that, sir," said Sleppy.

Sears clenched his fists in frustration. "No wonder I haven't heard from any of the lawmen who received Gray's description. He's been here all the time."

Sleppy nodded. "Gray had his horse stashed in the wash around the next bend, Cap'n. We found the horse's tracks and Gray's footprints leading to and from the horse. There was blood on the sand, too. But it was impossible to tell which way he went when he rode out of the draw."

Sears rubbed his jaw. "I'm sending another band of men out tomorrow, and I'm sending wires to all the sheriffs and town marshals in west Texas and southern New Mexico to be on the lookout for him. I seriously doubt he'll go into Mexico."

"I agree, sir."

The captain turned to watch as the Rangers removed the bodies of Dorn and Whitfield from the horses. There was iron resolve in his voice when he said, "I'm going to get that filthy rat if it's the last thing I do."

10

APRIL CAME TO DENVER, bringing with it wetter snows that melted off much sooner than in the previous three months.

On the first Wednesday in April, Stefanie Langan went to her front door and pulled the curtain aside to watch her three children coming home from school. She was so proud of them. And all three were doing well in school.

"Lord," she said almost in a whisper, "You had your reasons for making my body so I could never bear children, and You know I've gotten over questioning Your wisdom in that. I'm so thankful for Jared, Susie, and Nathan. What wonderful children they are! And now they're my own!"

She brushed a tear from her cheek as the children turned into the yard and headed for the porch, and marveled at how quickly they had taken to her and Curt as parents.

She thought of how much the Hamilton children had suffered in their short lives, coming with their parents to New York from Wales, finding poverty instead of riches, and then watching both parents die of consumption. Stefanie thought of the "orphan train" that had carried the Hamilton children west from New York, and how by the hand of God, Breanna Baylor had boarded that train and cared for the children who were sick.

By God's grace, the Hamilton children became the Langan children through legal adoption, and Stefanie's mother, Mary Donelson, had "adopted" Jared, Susan, and Nathan as her grandchildren, and they in turn had adopted her as their grandmother.

Just as the children reached the porch steps, Stefanie opened the door and said, "Well, there are my three scholars! Everybody do well in school today?"

As they answered yes, Stefanie gave each child a hug and a kiss, then closed the door and waited until they put their light wraps in the hall closet before she picked up an envelope and held it behind her back.

It was Susie who studied Stefanie for a moment and said, "Mother, why are you smiling like the cat who ate the canary? And what are you holding behind your back?"

The boys' heads jerked around.

"I have something here for Jared. But all three of you are going to like it."

Jared's brow furrowed. "What is it, Mom?"

Stefanie showed him the envelope and held it upright so he could see his own name written in its center:

Master Jared Langan
c/o Sheriff Curt Langan
1123 Cherokee Street
Denver, Colorado

Then Jared's eyes flicked to the upper left-hand corner:

Bodie Walker
General Delivery
Georgetown, Colorado

His eyes bulged. "It's a letter from Bodie Brolin! Whoops! I mean Bodie Walker!"

"Bodie!" shouted Nathan, jumping up and down.

"Open it, Jared!" Susan said, her eyes dancing.

Jared ran his fingers under the sealed flap and took out the letter. He smiled as he unfolded the sheet of paper and read aloud.

April 2, 1871

Dear Jared,

I hope I'm not already too late, but I remember you telling me your birthday is in April. A great big thirteen, huh!

I just wanted to wish you Happy Birthday, and to tell you that I think of you a lot. Susie and Nathan, too. I turned fourteen in February. Pa was in Denver on a quick trip in March, and got your address from somebody he knows. I don't know when we'll be coming to Denver, but Pa says it won't be too long.

We'll come and see you. I'm very happy as Bodie Walker, with my wonderful Christian parents, and I love life on the ranch. We go to a good church in Georgetown, which is ten miles from the ranch.

Please tell Nathan and Susie hello for me, and your parents, too. And when you see Miss Breanna, tell her thanks again for leading me to Jesus on the Orphan Train. You may remember that she led my new pa, Cliff Walker, to Jesus in Santa Fe, New Mexico, about two years ago.

God bless you! Write to me at the address on the envelope if you have time.

Your friend,
Bodie

"I want to write him back," Jared said.

"I think you should," Stefanie replied. "It was awfully nice of him to write to you."

"Well, he only missed my birthday by three days—April eighth!"

"Yeah," Susan said, teasing him. "In three days, you'll be an old man! A teenager!"

Jared stepped close to his sister, looked down at her with a mock scowl, and said, "Well, you'll be eleven shortly. But that's still young and immature. *I* am a wise man of the world. Ask me anything...*anything*."

Susan placed her hands on her small hips. "All right, smarty. What do you get if you cross an elephant with a kangaroo?"

Jared thought on it. "An elephant with a pouch to keep his trunk in?"

"No, silly, you get huge holes all over Australia!"

Stefanie laughed, Nathan looked confused, and Susan marched triumphantly to the staircase and headed up to her room, giggling. "A wise man of the world!" they heard her say, as she topped the stairs.

The sun was almost touching the mountain peaks as John Brockman and Sheriff Curt Langan rode into Denver on Broadway, turned on Colfax Avenue, made their way west a few blocks, then made a right turn. The two men in handcuffs who rode behind them sat stiffly in their saddles, their countenances bleak.

Deputy Sheriff Steve Ridgway was on the porch of the Denver County Sheriff's Office, talking to a couple of merchants, when he saw his boss and Brockman with the two outlaws in tow.

Ridgway said something to the merchants and pointed with his chin. The men stepped away a few feet and joined the other spectators who had caught sight of the two outlaws being brought in.

Ridgway stepped off the boardwalk and paused at the hitch rail as his boss and Brockman drew rein. Smiling, he said, "Where'd you catch up to them, Sheriff?"

"Colorado Springs," Langan said, dismounting.

The deputy looked at the two outlaws and smiled. "Welcome to the Langan Hotel. We've got some very uncomfortable rooms waiting for you two gentlemen. I use that last word loosely, you understand." Then to Langan: "They give you any trouble?"

"Fisher has a broken jaw. He tried to get rough with John."

"Ooooh," said Ridgway, eyeing the man with the swollen jaw. "Getting rough with our friend John is a no-no, Mr. Fisher."

Langan chuckled. "He knows that now."

"In fact," said Ridgway, "shooting up a saloon and wounding the bartender is a no-no."

"They both know that now," the sheriff said. "Steve, I'll leave them with you to deposit in their cells. When you can get around to it, get one of the doctors to come and look at Fisher's jaw."

The outlaws dismounted their horses with help and sullenly

preceded Deputy Ridgway inside.

"Lock up after you've told those boys a nice bedtime story, Steve," Langan called after them. "I'm going home."

Ridgway grinned and escorted the prisoners inside.

Langan sighed and turned to John. "I appreciate you going along with me."

"My pleasure. Well, I'm going to Doc Goodwin's office and see if Breanna's still there. Maybe I can take her out for supper."

"Oh, yeah. You did tell me she's filling the empty spot since Doc's main nurse moved back east. Maybe he's hired a new one by now."

"Maybe. See you later."

Jared Langan was sweeping the front porch for his mother when he saw his dad riding down the street. He leaned the broom against the wall and leaped off the porch, shouting, "Dad! You're back!"

Curt dismounted and hugged Jared as the boy said, "I was getting worried you wouldn't be home in time for my birthday!"

"Well, son, you can stop worrying. I'm home, and your birthday isn't until Saturday."

"But what if you have to go after some more outlaws between now and then?"

Curt grinned, ruffled the boy's hair, and said, "Didn't I tell you? All the outlaws in Colorado are taking time off between now and Sunday. There won't be any to chase."

Jared laughed. "Did you catch Fisher and Melton?"

"Steve's got them behind bars right now."

"In the Langan Hotel, right?"

"Uh-huh. You about finished with your sweeping job?"

"Yes, sir."

"Well, you go in and tell your mother I'm home. I'll put the horse in the barn and be right in."

Moments later, the sheriff was greeted at the back door by Stefanie and the other two children. After he washed up, they sat down to eat.

During the meal, Curt told his family how he and John caught the outlaws, then the conversation turned to the big day on Saturday. Stefanie told him that her mother was coming to their house Saturday afternoon. She was going to cook up a special meal and bake a chocolate cake.

By Jared's request, Breanna and John had been invited to the birthday party Saturday evening, only John didn't know it yet. Stefanie was sure Breanna would tell him tonight.

Breanna was straightening up the reception desk when John opened the office door.

"Hello, darling!" She dropped a handful of papers and rushed to him. Since they were alone in the office, they shared a quick kiss.

"Did you catch those guys?" Breanna asked, returning to the desk.

"Yes. In Colorado Springs."

"Bring them back alive?"

"Yes, and they'll stand trial before Judge Harrington."

"Good. I missed you."

"Same here. You…ah…getting off soon?"

"Doctor's with our last patient of the day right now."

"I thought if you were hungry I'd take you to the Bluebird this evening."

"You might say I'm a bit hungry," she said, placing a stack of papers in a drawer. "We were so busy that neither one of us had a chance to grab lunch."

"Curt and I haven't eaten since we broke camp this morning. Doc Goodwin any closer to finding a gal for this job?"

"Might be. Two nurses have written in response to the bulletin he sent to the Kansas City Medical Association. They both look good on paper. I'm sure Doctor will choose one of them soon."

The clinic door rattled, and Dr. Goodwin held it open for an elderly woman as she shuffled into the office.

Breanna looked up and smiled. "Does Mrs. Dugan need another appointment, Doctor?" she asked.

"Yes. I should see her in a month."

"All right," said Breanna, opening the appointment book.

Gertie Dugan set her weary gaze on the tall man, and said, "Hello, Mr. Str— I mean, Mr. Brockman. Sorry. Breanna told me you'd let your real name be known, but I forgot there for just a moment."

"That's all right, ma'am," said John.

While Breanna and Gertie were working on a suitable time for the next appointment, Dr. Goodwin moved to John's side and said, "Getting closer to wedding time..."

"Yes, sir."

"Breanna took Martha and me out to the house. It's beautiful, John." A wistful look captured his face. "We're sure going to miss having Breanna in our cottage, though. She's the same as a daughter to us."

"I know that, sir," said John. "She loves both of you very much."

Goodwin's lower lip trembled. "I tell you, John, it means more than all the world to me to have the privilege of walking that sweet girl down the aisle to give her away."

John watched the older man's face, and his own expression softened as he said, "We're both honored to have you do it, sir."

"I was talking to Sol Duvall at church Sunday. He's walking on clouds because you asked him to be your best man. You really touched his heart, John."

"Well, we're the best of friends, and I'm happy that he'll be standing beside me when Breanna and I take our vows."

John and Breanna ate an early dinner at the Bluebird Café, enjoying each other's company as well as satisfying their hunger with the Bluebird's home-style cooking. The first item of discussion was their new house.

Breanna explained what things she had done to it since John had left to track down the outlaws, and he was pleased to hear she was putting her personal touches to the house.

She sipped her coffee, and then hurriedly placed the cup on the table. "Oh, darling, I almost forgot! Saturday is Jared's birthday. You and I are invited to supper and the party at seven o'clock in the evening, by personal request of Jared. Is there any reason you couldn't go?"

"None that I know of. And even if I had something else, I'd change it for Jared. He's one special boy. You have something in mind for a present?"

"I already bought it. Stefanie told me he needs clothes, so I bought him shirts and trousers."

"Mm-hmm. That's all well and good, but I've been thinking about doing something for him—not for his birthday, particularly, but since the occasion's coming up, I'll just make it a birthday present."

A smile crept over Breanna's lips. "Don't tell me...a gun?"

"How'd you know?"

"Because every time you and Curt take Jared target practicing, you mention that the boy has to use one of Curt's old rifles."

John nodded and said, "A boy like Jared ought to have a rifle of his own. The kid's good, honey. Excellent marksman."

"I know he's good with a revolver. Curt's trained him well, and he sure proved it when those two guys came to the cottage last summer when you were gone. If it hadn't been for Jared, they'd have killed me."

John's eyes looked bleak for a moment as he remembered that time. "I've thanked Jared many times for that. Like I said, he's one special boy."

Breanna smiled. "So what kind of rifle will you give him?"

"I'll look around a bit. I want it to be something extra nice."

Saturday evening came, and during the delicious meal prepared by "Grandma Mary"—with a little help from Stefanie and Susan—an excited Jared Langan couldn't keep his eyes off the presents piled on a small table in the corner of the dining room.

While they ate, the children reminisced about their ride on the orphan train. Jared mentioned Bodie Brolin and told Breanna about his letter.

"Oh, that was nice of Bodie to write you, Jared," she said.

"It sure was. He told me to thank you once again for leading him to Jesus on the train."

John looked at Breanna. "Didn't you tell me a Christian couple who live in the mountains adopted Bodie?"

"Yes—Cliff and Mary Walker."

"Well, if her name's Mary, she's got to be all right," spoke up Mary Donelson.

"Oh, she is, Grandma," said Susan, "but she's not as all right as you are!"

Everyone laughed, and Stefanie affectionately patted her mother's hand.

"You knew them from somewhere, didn't you, Breanna?" persisted John.

"I knew Cliff, darling. A little over two years ago I was in Santa Fe, helping a doctor there during a smallpox epidemic. Both whites and Indians were dying. Cliff was among the sick, and I had the joy of leading him to the Lord. He reminded me of it the day he and Mary adopted Bodie and told me that Mary has been a Christian since she was a young girl."

"The Walkers are going to bring Bodie to town sometime to see us," said Susan.

"That'll be wonderful," Breanna said, and smiled. "I hope I'm in town when they come. I'd love for them to meet John."

"Speaking of the name *Walker,*" John said to Breanna, "when I was in Butte City, I got to know the pastor of the church there quite well, and his wife. Their names are Bob and Phyllis Walker. I want to invite them to the wedding. I think they'd try to come."

"If Pastor Bayless knew they were coming," Breanna said, "he might let your friend have some part in the wedding ceremony."

"That's a good idea; I'll write to them soon."

Jared's eyes went to his presents once again.

Mary noticed her grandson's gaze and then looked at the faces around the table and said, "Looks like everybody's finished eating. Girls, let's clean up the table, put all the dishes in the kitchen, and then Jared can open his presents."

"Girls, nothing!" said the birthday boy. "I'll help you so I can get to those presents!"

"I'll help, too," Curt said.

"I guess I'm in, too," said John.

Within five minutes the dirty dishes were carted off to the kitchen. Curt and Stefanie piled the presents on the dining-room table and turned Jared loose.

He was elated with the new dress boots from his parents, as well as the new wide-brimmed hat that made him look more grown-up, and a brand-new Bible. Both Susan and Nathan gave him presents, as well as Grandma.

Soon Jared was down to two packages. One was a small box that was quite heavy for its size. The other was much larger, but very light in comparison.

He looked at John and Breanna. "Which one should I open first?"

"Well, the bigger box is from me," said Breanna. "Open it first. The other box is from Mr. John. Save it till last."

Jared gave Breanna a big smile when he lifted out the shirts and trousers, and thanked her warmly.

Curious as to what the small but heavy box might contain, he grinned at the tall man and said, "What could this be?"

"Open it and find out," said John.

Susan and Nathan drew near, eager to watch.

Jared slowly removed the wrapping paper and then tried to mask his disappointment by saying, "Oh, boy! Look, Dad! Forty-four caliber cartridges so I won't have to use yours when we go target shooting!"

"That's great, son," said Curt.

"Thank you, Mr. John," Jared said.

"You're very welcome, Jared," John replied. He pushed back his chair and rose to his feet, saying, "Oh, I forgot. There's something to go with those cartridges."

He stepped into the hall, opened the closet door, and picked up the nickel-plated Winchester .44 nine-shot repeater rifle. Breanna had tied a red ribbon to the barrel, and John now held the gun with the muzzle pointing toward the floor as he reentered the dining room.

Jared's eyes popped, and his mouth flew open as he sucked in a quick, short breath.

"Oh, Jared!" gasped Susan. "Look at that!"

"I am! I am!" he said, standing up.

John smiled from ear to ear as he placed the rifle in the boy's hand and said, "Suppose you can fit those cartridges in this?"

Jared, who was well trained in gun handling, kept the muzzle pointed toward the floor as he caressed the smooth nickel plate. "I sure can, Mr. John," he said with awe.

Jared moved around the table and handed the rifle to his father to hold, then went to the tall man and hugged him. Next he went to Breanna, hugged her and thanked her for the shirts and trousers, then made the rounds, hugging and thanking everyone for their gifts.

John looked on and touched Breanna's shoulder, and she grasped his hand and squeezed it.

When Jared took his rifle back from his father, he said, "I'll be able to outshoot you with this gun, Dad!"

Curt laughed. "Tell you what, son. It takes more than a fancy rifle to shoot straight. The guy who aims and squeezes the trigger has something to do with it, too! And I'll tell you, buddy, you've got a long way to go to outshoot the sheriff of Denver County!"

Jared chuckled. "Well, I'll practice a whole lot with this new rifle and then challenge the sheriff of Denver County to a shooting match!"

"If I may have your attention, everyone," said John, "we're not quite through here."

Again he stepped into the hall and opened the closet door. When he came back, he carried a brightly wrapped gift in each hand. "I couldn't leave out Susie and Nathan," he said.

Breanna smiled and shook her head. She hadn't known about this.

Nathan went through the wrapping in a hurry and gave a squeal as he found a toy rifle that looked a lot like Jared's. He rushed to John and hugged him as he said thanks.

All eyes were on Susan as she opened her gift.

"A *diary!*" she exclaimed. "Oh, Mr. John, I was going to ask for one on my birthday! Thank you!"

While John was getting his hug from Susan, he said, "I know that when girls start to become young ladies, they like to keep a diary."

Sister gave older brother a smug look. "See, smarty Jared. Mr. John doesn't think I'm so young and immature!"

Everyone had a good laugh, then Mary and Stefanie told the children to get seated, and they went to the kitchen.

Breanna found a moment to lean over and whisper, "That was thoughtful of you!"

"I love kids," he whispered back.

"That's good!" she whispered in return and was rewarded with a crooked smile.

Mary and Stefanie returned from the kitchen with Stefanie carrying a big chocolate cake bearing thirteen flaming candles. Everyone sang "Happy Birthday," and Jared blew out the candles in one try.

While the cake was being devoured, Stefanie set her gaze on Breanna across the table. "How's Dottie coming along with the wedding dress?" she asked.

"She's got it about half done already."

"She does such good work...I know it'll be beautiful," said Stefanie.

John ran his gaze between the two women. "I'm sure the dress will be beautiful, Stefanie, but not half as beautiful as the one who will wear it."

Breanna blushed and smiled softly.

"John, you're a romantic," Mary said. "I hope you stay that way."

John just looked into Breanna's eyes and said, "When God gives a man the most wonderful woman in the world, how can he be anything else, even when they're both old and gray?"

Breanna's heart swelled with emotion, and she gave John the sweetest smile he had ever seen.

11

IN MID-APRIL, MARK GRAY once again began practicing his quick-draw at his favorite hidden canyon in the Guadalupe Mountains. He was glad the Ranger slug he'd taken during the ambush had hit his left shoulder and not his right.

Within days he was back to his old speed. His strength had returned, and it was time to head for Arizona.

Nana was hanging her wash on the crude clothesline behind her shack when she saw Gray returning from his daily practice session in the nearby canyon.

"You are doing well with your gun, now?" asked the old woman.

"Perfect, Nana. Thanks to you, I'm feeling almost as good as new, so I'll be leavin' tomorrow mornin' before dawn."

The soft sound of hooves on sand came to his ears, and Mark whirled about, drawing his gun.

"Hey, it's just me!" said Cecil Yates from his saddle. "I thought you might be here, Mark."

Nana greeted Yates as he dismounted, then slowly walked to her shack and went inside.

Yates started talking as he limped toward Gray. "I was in El Paso day before yesterday. Got to talkin' to a couple old retired Rangers who keep close contact with Sears's men. They told me about you ambushin' Dorn and Whitfield, and that you left blood on the bushes. I figured if you were hurt very bad, you'd probably come back to Nana to get patched up. Got home late last night, so I rode over here this mornin' to find out, and to see if you were alive and still here."

Gray frowned. "Wait a minute. What makes Sears think it was me who ambushed those two? Could've been anybody."

Yates squinted against the morning sun. "Anybody named *Gray,* you mean. And how many fellas named *Gray* are the El Paso Rangers chasin'?"

Mark shook his head. "What are you talkin' about…'anybody named Gray'?"

"Well, Ranger Dorn wasn't dead when you left. He lived long enough to write your name in the sand before he died."

Mark looked toward the ground and frowned.

"Where'd the bullet get you?" asked Yates.

"Left shoulder," came the quiet reply. "I'm pretty well healed up now. Leavin' for Arizona tomorrow before dawn."

"Better be real careful, Mark. Sears is still playin' bloodhound. He's madder'n a teased rattler. Says you've not only killed two of his men, but you've put a black mark on the Texas Rangers for bein' a turncoat. All this on top of the fact that Jody Sleppy says you would've murdered him if you hadn't run out of bullets. He's sayin' you aimed your gun right between his eyes, when he was down, and pulled the trigger."

Gray's mouth thinned to a tight line, and his jaw muscles rippled.

"From what those old Rangers said, Mark, Sears is takin' it all real personal. He's makin' no bones about it. He'd like to see you dancin' at the end of a rope, and he means to put it on your neck, personally. He's not gonna rest till you're six feet under."

A red flush crept up Gray's neck and tinted his cheeks. "He ain't catchin' me," he said through gritted teeth. "I'm headin' for Arizona. Jim Carter will hide me where no Texas Ranger could ever find me, not even Sears."

He took a deep breath and ran a finger over his dark mustache. "But I'd sure like to find him! Just long enough to brace him for a quick-draw."

Yates shook his head. "That wouldn't be smart, even if you could meet him face to face, Mark. Sears has shown himself to be plenty fast with his gun."

"Bah! He ain't as fast as me. He's gettin' old. I'd shoot him down like a cur dog, while he was still huntin' for the butt of his gun."

"So how long you gonna hide in Jim Carter's shadow?"

"Right now I don't know. I'll just have to see how it goes."

"What're your plans when you do come out of hidin'?"

"Put together a good bank robbin' gang—make a pile of money. It sure didn't pay to stay on the right side of the law, but it'll pay real good on the other side."

Yates's mouth pulled down. "Mark, I hate to see you do this. It'll just mean more killin', and no doubt more killin' of lawmen."

"So what?"

"It was me who harbored you and brought you to Nana so's she could patch you up. And I was glad to do it. But it bothers me, knowin' you'll be usin' your gun to kill people. And you'll have to, if you go to robbin' banks. It's as if I'll have a part in every person you kill."

Gray threw back his head and laughed. "Cecil, you did what a real friend should do. I'll take the blame for anybody I have to shoot, includin' the lawmen. It ain't your fault what I do."

Without another word Cecil Yates turned and limped to his horse, mounted, and rode away.

"Hey!" Gray called after him. "Ain't you even gonna say good-bye?"

Yates gave no sign that he'd heard, and soon rode out of sight.

Two days later, Mark Gray rode into Deming, New Mexico. It was warm, and the town lay basking in the welcome springtime sun.

No one noticed him as he walked the bay mare slowly along the town's main thoroughfare. The people of Deming were used to strangers riding through. Their town was on a direct line between southern Texas and southern Arizona, and the street was always busy with people milling about.

Gray's dark eyes were drawn to the Deming Bank, situated on a corner in the center of town. His funds were low. He rode past the bank, giving it a furtive glance, then looked up and down the cross streets. He made a casual turn in the middle of the street and rode back to the intersection where the bank was positioned. There was a saloon two doors down from the bank, and four rough-looking men came through the batwings, laughing. One of them had a blaring voice, and could be heard by everyone within a block in either direction.

Gray dismounted at the hitch rail but left the reins looped on the saddle horn. The mare was not the kind to wander; she'd be there when he came out with the loot.

He watched people moving in and out of the bank intermittently. He slipped a bandanna out of his hip pocket and scanned the street for any sign of a lawman. Just as he started to put it on, a blaring voice said, "Hey…*you!*"

Gray paid him no mind, veering around the mare's rump to head for the boardwalk.

"You, cowboy!" yelled the man. "Did you just get off that bay?"

Gray paused and glanced over his shoulder at the hatchet-faced man. "You talkin' to me?" he asked.

"Yeah! You just got off that bay, didn't you?" The man rushed toward Gray with his three comrades following.

The man's tone had started a thread of anger in Gray's belly. "So what?" he said with a hint of a challenge in his voice

"'Cause that's my saddle! You're the skunk that stole it over in Guadalupe Springs!"

"I bought the saddle off a man in El Paso, mister—"

"Bart Dixon."

"Well, Mr. Dixon, I paid good honest money for that saddle. I had no way of knowin' it was stolen."

Dixon stared at Gray with angry eyes. "You're a liar! You stole the saddle, and you know it! Either I get it back this minute, or I'm goin' to the town marshal and have you arrested."

People had started to gather around, hoping to see a fight. He was about to tell Dixon he could have the saddle, when one of Dixon's pals said, "Hey, Bart, he looks like a gunnie. See how low he's wearin' that gun? Challenge him!"

Bart Dixon glanced over his shoulder and looked at his crony. "Think I should, Glenn?"

"Sure. Maybe he's a big name."

Dixon turned back to look at Gray and said, "What's your name, thief?"

"Look, pal," Gray said, forcing a smile, "I didn't steal your saddle, but I'll take the loss of the money I paid for it. Go ahead. Take it."

Dixon backed up a few steps and took the gunfighter's

stance, letting his hand dangle over his revolver. "Go for your gun, mister!" he said. "I'm countin' to three. If you haven't slapped leather, I'm goin' for mine. One...two...th—"

The gun was in Gray's hand and spitting fire before Dixon could finish the count. The slug hit Dixon square in the chest, its impact flopping him on his back. He lay still.

Glenn, Dixon's pal, swore and went for his gun.

Gray raised his smoking revolver, snapped back the hammer, and lined it on the man's face in one smooth move.

Glenn froze with his hand on his gun. He saw the little devils of temper dancing in Gray's dark eyes. He licked his lips and said shakily, "Y-you killed my friend, m-mister."

"Only because he made me. Don't make me kill you."

A man in the crowd cried out, "Somebody get the marshal!"

Another male voice responded, "He's outta town for a couple hours!"

Gray gave Glenn a cold look, backed toward the bay mare, and said to the crowd, "You folks saw what happened. I didn't steal the man's saddle, but I was gonna give it to him, anyway. He forced me to draw on him. I had to defend myself."

A silver-haired man spoke up. "We all saw it, fella. You tried to evade trouble. This drifter forced you to kill him. You were just better with your gun than he was."

"That's right," came a woman's voice from the crowd. "You had to defend yourself!"

"Since you folks all see that it was self-defense," said Gray, "I'll be movin' on."

Glenn, who was kneeling beside his dead friend, gave Gray a hateful look but said nothing.

Gray trotted his horse out of town, and as soon as he was out of sight from the people, he put the mare to a gallop. He hoped the town marshal would accept the word of the witnesses.

The next town was Lordsburg, New Mexico, but it was more than a day's ride.

When evening came, Gray rode into a small village. He spotted a corral where maybe a dozen horses were kept. Next to it was a rickety barn, which seemed to be the community stable.

He passed on through the village and rode past a large cluster of mesquite trees where he dismounted to eat some of the food Nana had provided and drink water from a canteen. When darkness fell, Gray walked back to the stable, crept inside the barn, and found a saddle.

Soon the saddle was on the mare's back, and he tied the Mexican saddle behind him and rode west till the moon came up, then found a spot beside a small brook where he would spend the night.

By the light of the moon, Gray found a deep spot in the brook, loaded the saddlebags with rocks, and dropped the Mexican saddle in the four-foot depth of water.

The next morning, he headed west again.

When darkness fell, Gray was some ten miles from Lordsburg. He slept beside a trickling stream that night and headed for town the next morning. Because of Bart Dixon, he had been deprived of robbing the Deming Bank. There would be no Bart Dixon to get in his way this time.

The wind whistled through Lordsburg, tossing sand against the weatherworn, unpainted buildings. Little dust devils spun across the sun-bleached street in front of Gray as he rode in.

The marshal's office was in the center of town. As Gray passed it, he could see two men talking just inside the door.

Gray was glad to see that the Lordsburg Bank was at the west end of town. When he came out of the bank with the loot and swung aboard the mare, he would only be a few seconds' ride from open country. The Arizona border was twenty miles away, and there was a maze of sandy hills near the border where he could easily elude a posse.

He hauled up in front of the bank and looped the reins over the saddle horn. He paused as he rounded the hitch rail, casually glancing in the direction of the marshal's office. No sign of either man he'd seen a few minutes earlier.

There were a few people on the street, a couple of wagons on the move, and a man riding into town from the west, dodging a dust devil.

Gray quickly tied the bandanna over his nose and mouth, pulled his gun, and rushed inside the bank. Moments later, he backed through the door, carrying a canvas moneybag in his free hand, and said, "First man sticks his head out this door will get it shot off!"

A quick glance up and down the street and then he was on the mare in a flash, and several hundred dollars richer. He galloped out of town with the wind in his face.

Gray expected a posse, and he pushed the horse hard, leaving the road a mile from town to angle northward. Soon he was over a low range of hills where he cut due west again, galloping across the desert.

It was a rugged and broken land, with deer and antelope trails running through the scattered rocks, greasewood, and dry bunch grass. Long, narrow lines of black lava ran down the hills and out onto the flat land as though reaching toward the alkali lake to the north.

Horse and rider topped a sandy hill sprinkled with clumps of Joshua brush and Spanish bayonet. As they plunged down the gentle slope, Gray spotted a ranch house and outbuildings off to the right. Suddenly the mare stumbled. She tried to right herself, but her right foreleg buckled. Gray sailed out of the saddle, and both man and beast rolled and came up on their feet, covered with sand.

Gray picked up his hat and dusted it off, then planted it back on his head and staggered toward the mare. She was swishing her tail and shaking her head. "Hey, girl," he said, looking her over, "are you hurt?"

The mare took a couple of steps, limping noticeably. Gray examined her and found that she'd lost her shoe, and part of the hoof had been torn off. Gray checked the moneybag, and found it intact. Glancing toward the ranch, he counted five saddle horses in the corral. He would lead the mare to the ranch and buy a horse from the rancher.

There was no sign of life around the ranch. The only movement was in the corral, where the horses swished their tails at pesky flies, and a couple of them drank from a water trough.

He halted at the back porch and called out, "Hello, anybody home?"

Silence.

He knocked on the door, but still there was no response. He led the mare to the barn and checked inside, calling out to announce his presence. Again, there was only silence. Then he found a spot where a wagon or buggy was usually kept.

Gray saddled and bridled a black and white piebald gelding. He looked all around him in the distance and saw no sign of human life, so he broke into the house and checked on the rancher's clothing. He and the man were very close to the same size.

Ten minutes later, he rode away. He was almost to the main road when he saw a dozen horsemen riding hard from the east, leaving a dust cloud behind them.

His first thought was to turn and ride behind the hills he'd just covered. But he knew that if he could see them, they could see him. He dropped the canvas moneybag in a shallow crevice next to a large boulder, and rode on toward the road.

The man in the lead veered his horse toward Gray, and the others followed. Gray smiled as they drew up in a cloud of dust. The lead man wore a badge.

"Howdy, gentlemen," said Gray in a friendly tone. "Posse?"

"Yes, sir," said the man with the badge. "I'm Marshal Dan Jones from Lordsburg."

"Frank Chase, Marshal," Gray said. He gestured over his shoulder. "I have a ranch beyond those hills."

"I assume you just came from there," said Jones.

"Yes."

"Did you happen to see a rider heading west on the road? He was on a bay with white stockings and would be pushing it hard."

"Come to think of it, I did," Gray said. "When I topped the hills back there on the road to my place, I saw a fella ridin' like he was in a real hurry. He was on a bay...and you're right. He was headin' due west."

"Thanks," said the marshal, wheeling his horse about. "Okay, men, let's go!"

Gray smiled to himself as the posse thundered away. When they had passed from sight, he trotted the piebald back to where he'd dropped the moneybag. He picked it up and rode north on the east side of the hills.

Captain Terrell Sears and Sergeant Jody Sleppy were walking back to the captain's office after delivering a captured outlaw to the El Paso County Jail. They watched Charlie Wilson, the Western Union operator, hurrying toward them, zigzagging through the people on the boardwalk.

"Captain Sears!" called the elderly man. "Telegram for you!"

Wilson was short of breath as he handed the yellow envelope to Sears and said, "I knew you'd…want to know about this…right away."

"Thanks, Charlie," Sears said as he opened the envelope.

"You want me to stay…so's if you want to reply, I can get it on the wire for you?"

Sears nodded.

"Who's it from, Cap'n?" asked Sleppy.

Sears pulled out the sheet of yellow paper, unfolded it, and said, "Marshal Bill Riggs, in Deming."

He read the message silently, then said, "There was a fast-draw shootout two days ago in Deming while the marshal was out of town. It wasn't until today that the description of the victor, as given by eyewitnesses, registered in Riggs's mind as the description of Mark Gray I'd sent him earlier. Gray left town in a hurry, heading west." Sears stroked his mustache. "Okay, Charlie. Send a wire back and tell Riggs I appreciate the information. Tell him I'll have Rangers on their way to Deming within the hour. They'll try to pick up Gray's trail."

On Saturday, April 29, the band of Rangers returned to El Paso, faces glum as they walked into the captain's office. Sears took one look at them and banged his fist on the desk.

"We went all the way to Lordsburg sir," said the lieutenant who had led the Rangers. "There's a good chance it was Gray who robbed the Lordsburg Bank a couple days after he was in Deming, but nobody can say for sure. Robber wore a mask. But we couldn't come up with a thing. He's disappeared again."

Sears ground his teeth and said, "Sooner or later he's going to be in the wrong place at the right time. His days are numbered."

Gray rode into Tucson the same day Sears's band of Rangers returned empty-handed to El Paso. He had plenty of money in his saddlebags. He boarded the piebald at a stable near Tucson's fanciest hotel, the Royal Crest, and rented himself a plush room, figuring to stay there three or four days to rest up. He placed the money-packed saddlebags in the closet and left the room with a wad of bills in his pocket.

When he found a clothing store, he bought himself a whole new outfit, including hat and boots. After eating in the hotel's restaurant, he ordered hot water brought to his room and took a long, refreshing bath.

The next morning, Gray slept in till nine o'clock. Lazily, he shaved, combed his hair, and put on his new clothes and boots. He ate a late breakfast at the restaurant, then decided to take a stroll around town. Tucson had grown immensely since he'd last been there.

As he moved leisurely along the boardwalk, feeling the touch of expensive clothing next to his skin, he told himself what a fool he'd been to exist on the low pay of a Texas Ranger. He was going to live differently from now on.

He flinched when he saw a man wearing a badge come out of a store and walk toward him. A cold chill slithered down his spine as the lawman drew near and the badge identified him as Pima County's sheriff. The man's line of sight was fixed on Gray's unfamiliar face, and Gray knew he was about to be stopped. Butterflies flitted about in his stomach.

The sheriff slowed as they came near each other.

Gray forced a smile. "Sheriff," he said, nodding.

"Howdy. Stranger in town, aren't you? My name's Mitchell Bromley."

"Frank Chase, Sheriff. Yes, I'm a stranger here. I've been down in Mexico for a few days. Own a ranch down there. South of Nogales about seventy miles. Near a town called Magdalena. I'm on my way to Flagstaff to visit my brother and his family."

The sheriff scrutinized him for a few agonizing seconds, then let a smile curve his lips. "Well, I hope you have a nice stay in Arizona, Mr. Chase."

Cold sweat trickled down Gray's back. "Thank you, Sheriff."

Relief washed over him as Bromley started to move past. But the relief was short-lived when a man stepped out of a store beside them and said, "Hey! If it isn't Lieutenant Mark Gray!"

12

FOR A SUSPENDED MOMENT, Mark Gray could neither move nor speak. His blood ran cold as he recognized the high-pitched voice of C. B. Hardy, who had owned the gun shop in El Paso until two years ago.

As he turned to look at Hardy, he saw Sheriff Bromley going for his gun. Panic-stricken, Gray surprised the sheriff by sending a savage blow to his jaw. A woman on the boardwalk screamed as Bromley went down and Gray kicked the lawman's gun into the street.

Silver-haired C. B. Hardy stood with mouth agape as Gray ran a fleeting glance along the street. He needed a horse, quick. Several were tied at the hitch rails nearby, but it would take precious seconds to untie the reins.

His gaze fell on a rider who was just dismounting. Gray bolted for the street, but his concentration was so fixed on his ticket out of town that he didn't see the fast approaching wagon.

He was no more than three steps into the street when he ran right into one of the horses pulling the speeding wagon. The impact slammed him into a wagon that was parked parallel with the hitch rail. He felt a blow to his head and slumped to the street, unconscious.

The man driving the wagon hauled his team to a stop, hipped around on the wagon seat and pointed to the woman beside him, who was great with child and doubled over in pain. He called back to the men who were helping the sheriff to his feet. "Hope that guy's all right! I'm taking my wife to the doctor! She's about to give birth!"

One of the men waved him on and headed for Mark Gray.

Moments later, Sheriff Bromley stood over the disarmed fugitive, who looked up at him with glassy eyes. C. B. Hardy blinked in confusion as he heard Bromley say to Mark Gray, "Frank Chase, eh? I had a funny feeling about you." Bromley pointed to Hardy. "This man here called you Lieutenant Mark Gray. Would that be *ex*-Lieutenant Mark Gray of the Texas Rangers?"

Gray didn't reply.

"Sheriff, what's this all about?" asked Hardy. "I've known Lieutenant Gray for a long time. He was always a good Ranger. He told you his name was Frank Chase?"

"Yes, he did. He may have been a good Ranger at one time, but he's not a Ranger at all anymore. I had a wire from Captain Sears in El Paso back in December. You know him, I suppose?"

"Yes, sir."

"Well, Sears said Gray murdered a teenage boy and shot a fellow Ranger. He then stole a horse and disappeared. I'm sure the same wire went to lawmen all over the West. Then a few weeks ago, I received another wire, telling me that Gray was still on the loose and had ambushed two Rangers who were chasing him, killing them both. That's what it's all about, sir."

While Hardy digested the information, the sheriff looked hard at Gray, pulled a pair of handcuffs off his belt, and said, "On your feet."

Gray staggered to his feet, still a bit dizzy from the crack on the head. The gathering crowd watched with interest as the sheriff ushered him down the street.

Deputy Sheriff Hugh Scott was cleaning a rifle in the office when Gray stepped through the door in front of Bromley, his hands cuffed behind his back.

"Well, who have we here, Sheriff?" Scott said.

"You remember we had a couple of wires in the last few months from a Captain Sears over in El Paso, 'bout a Ranger gone bad?"

"Oh, yeah. He shot some boy in the back and killed him, and later murdered two Texas Rangers. Name was Mark Gray. This him?"

"Sure is. Take him back and lock him up."

"With pleasure," said the deputy, rising to his feet. "Let's go, killer."

As Scott shoved Gray toward the door to the cell block, Bromley said, "I'll wire Captain Sears right away. He'll no doubt send a couple of Rangers to take him back to El Paso to hang."

Gray looked over his shoulder at Bromley with dark, angry eyes and held his gaze until Scott nudged him through the door.

Charlie Wilson darted out the door of the Western Union office and hurried down the street as fast as his aging legs would carry him. He was panting when he stepped into the Texas Ranger office, eyed the two Rangers who stood talking, and said, "I've got a very important message...for Cap'n Sears! Where is he?"

"Over at the general store," replied Jody Sleppy. "Wouldn't be about Mark Gray, would it?"

"Now, you boys know I can't divulge anything that's in this here envelope to anybody but the person it's addressed to. But I can tell you this much, you're gonna like what's in here! See you later. Gotta get this to Cap'n Sears."

"We'll go with you," said Sleppy. "If we're going to like what's in there, we want to like it as soon as possible."

They were hardly out the door when they saw the tall Ranger captain coming their way, weaving his way around the people on the boardwalk. Sears noticed Charlie with his two Rangers and then saw the yellow envelope in his hand. "Looking for me?" he said, as he drew up.

"Yes, *sir,* Cap'n! Got a wire here from the Pima County sheriff over in Tucson. You're gonna like it!"

Less than a minute later, people on the street heard a loud *"Ya-a-a-hoo!"* come from the Texas Ranger office.

After another minute, Charlie Wilson came out the door, and voices on the street called to him, asking what was so exciting in the Ranger office. Charlie hurried down the boardwalk, saying, "Ask Cap'n Sears!"

Soon Charlie was sitting at his desk, tapping out a message in Morse code:

> Sheriff Mitchell Bromley
> Pima County Sheriff
> Tucson, Arizona Territory
>
> Sending Sergeant Jody Sleppy and Corporal
> Ben Oliver by stagecoach tomorrow morning
> STOP Watch Gray close STOP Thank you
> STOP
> Terrell Sears, Captain, Texas Rangers
> El Paso, Texas

⁂

On Monday, May 1, John Brockman entered the federal building in Denver, greeted two deputy U.S. marshals in the hall, and turned into the office of Chief U.S. Marshal Solomon Duvall.

"Good morning, Mr. Stranger—I mean, Mr. Brockman," said the young deputy at the desk. "The chief said to send you in as soon as you arrived."

Brockman smiled as he passed the desk. "You doing all right, Jerry?" he asked.

"Yes, sir. Thank you."

Brockman tapped on the door and turned the knob. Easing the door open, he saw Duvall at his desk. "Jerry said I should come in."

"Then do what he says," said the silver-haired lawman with a smile.

Brockman closed the door behind him, and Duvall gestured toward a chair before his desk. "Have a seat, John."

Brockman removed his black, flat-crowned hat, laid it on the chair next to him, and said, "What can I do for you, my friend?"

A serious look etched itself on Duvall's features, and John noticed that the deep lines in his face were growing deeper, especially at the corners of his eyes.

"I received a letter from Chester McCarty in Washington, D.C., John. He thinks there's a problem at the Phoenix U.S. Marshal's office. Have you met Tom Wall, who heads up that office?"

"Yes. Know him well. I believe you could call us friends."

"And you know the Phoenix office is in my jurisdiction..."

"Yes. What kind of problem are we talking about, Sol?"

Duvall leaned forward, placing his elbows on the desk. "As

you know, every U.S. marshal's office in the country has to send a quarterly report to McCarty."

John nodded. "Yes...the arrest, conviction, sentencing, and/or execution report."

"That's right. Each report has to show who the marshal or his deputies arrested, and for what crime. It has to show the results of the court trial, and if sentenced, whether it was prison or the gallows. It has to show how many years they were sentenced to prison, and which prison. And if it was a sentence of death, when and where the hanging took place."

"I follow you," said John.

"Well, McCarty thinks there's something fishy going on with Wall's office. The reports for the past year seem to have some discrepancies."

"What kind of discrepancies?"

Duvall hesitated as he thought of the friendship between John and Tom Wall. "It's...it's looking like Wall is falsifying arrests, John. McCarty thinks Wall—and quite possibly his staff—are making up arrests, as well as court convictions, and all the rest. It could easily be done, if the judge was in on it. How would anyone in Washington know if a man went to a certain prison, or was hanged on a certain day? Besides, they don't have the time or manpower to ride herd on all the federal marshals, or anyone else, way out here."

John's brow furrowed. "But why in the world would they want to invent arrests that never happened?"

"Washington knows the average number of arrests for every state and territory west of the Missouri for the past ten years. That average is increasing every year, of course, because the population out here is increasing. But some lawmen go on the 'take' and let outlaws they've caught go free...for a price."

"Oh, so that's it," said John. "They falsify the reports by making up arrests that never happened."

"Right. Otherwise, the decrease in crimes in that area would look strange compared to the rest of the country, which is showing an increase."

"So McCarty suspects this kind of thing is going on with Tom Wall?"

"Exactly. And it would involve the circuit judge, too, since he would have a pretty good idea what the average in his territory is."

John shifted in his chair, and Duvall waited for him to speak. Finally John said, "So what raised McCarty's suspicions?"

"About a month ago, the regular circuit judge, Clarence Whitcomb, took sick quite suddenly. There was a case of a particularly brutal murder in Maricopa County, so the territorial governor sent another judge to hold the trial. While he was at Tom Wall's office, he asked one of the deputies about a case that was supposed to have been handled by the other circuit judge a few weeks back. The deputy had no knowledge of an outlaw bearing the name the judge mentioned. When Wall returned to the office, the judge asked him about it, and Wall told him there must have been some mix-up in the records. No such outlaw had been arrested by his office.

"Shortly thereafter, McCarty received a wire from the substitute judge, asking about Wall's report. McCarty sent a wire back, confirming the arrest and trial of the outlaw in question. It had been reported by Wall's office. When Wall received a wire from McCarty about it, he answered back that somehow an error had been made in the report. He didn't know how it got in there. McCarty has a feeling something's awry. He wants an investigation before he accuses Wall or Judge Whitcomb."

John thought on it. "Mm-hmm. But not by someone Wall knows is doing it."

"Right. It's going to take some clever work right there in Wall's office by a man who's one of his deputies. But it must also be a man Wall knows and trusts."

John grinned. "And that would be yours truly?"

"Now, how did you guess that?"

"Just call it intuition."

Duvall laughed, then said, "You're the perfect man for the job."

John didn't look convinced. "You said the clever investigation would have to be done by one of Wall's deputies."

"That's right. An inside man."

"So how would you get me on his staff of deputies?"

"Easy. The Phoenix office just had a deputy killed a week ago in a gun battle with stagecoach robbers. Washington told Wall by wire three days ago that they would send a replacement soon. All you have to do is show up there with official papers in your hand and tell Wall you've decided to wear a deputy marshal's badge. He knows you and trusts you, John. And we need to stop Wall and Whitcomb—if they're guilty—before this goes on any longer. Like I said, there may be some deputies in on it, too. Now, how about it?"

John rubbed his angular jaw. "I'd say yes, Sol, but that could take time, and I'm getting married June 4. That's barely more than a month away. I'll need to be here at least a few days before it takes place. I doubt I could make the trip to Phoenix, conduct the investigation, make arrests, if necessary, and get back here in time. You'll have to come up with someone else."

Duvall sighed. "John, this is very important. There may be outlaws out there in Arizona getting away with murder."

"I know, Sol, but my wedding is important, too. It's so important that I won't jeopardize it. It's set for June 4, as my best man knows, and I can't take a chance on not being here."

"Look," argued the chief, "as proficient as you are, you'll wrap up this case in a matter of days. The U.S. marshal's office in Phoenix will be cleared up or cleaned up, and you'll be back here well ahead of June 4. John, you can't let me down. This thing has to be handled."

"There are plenty of other men in your organization who can do the job."

"Not like you. Please, John. I'm asking you to go do the job as only you can do it."

Brockman shifted in his chair again and sighed. He looked his friend square in the eye and said, "All right, Sol, but—"

"Good."

"I have a stipulation."

"What's that?"

"If I haven't taken care of the situation by May twentieth, I pull out, regardless. I want to be back in Denver no later than the twenty-third."

"The way you work, you'll have it wrapped up in less than a week."

"Accolades are fine and appreciated, Sol," John said evenly, "but please understand. If I don't have it wrapped up by the twentieth of May, I'm heading home, no matter what. Now, if you'd rather not have this stipulation, my feelings won't be hurt if you find yourself another man."

"No, no! I'd rather have you with the stipulation than someone else with no stipulation."

"Okay. You've got me."

"All right," said Duvall with a wide smile. "I appreciate it more than I can tell you, John." As he spoke, he opened a desk drawer and pulled out a deputy U.S. marshal's badge. "You'll have to wear this."

John chuckled. "Tell you what, Sol, how about I stay here and wear your badge, and you go to Phoenix and wear that one?"

Duvall touched the badge on his chest. "Tell you what, John. You'd look real good sitting behind this desk and wearing this badge."

"Oh, no!" said Brockman, throwing palms up. "I was just kidding!"

Duvall's features remained serious. "Maybe someday you will wear this badge, John. With all your experience, you'd make a good chief U.S. marshal."

"No, thanks! I'd rather ride a horse than a desk. And besides that, you're going to wear that badge another fifty years."

Duvall ran splayed fingers through his thick mop of silver hair. "I doubt that."

Brockman stood up. "I'll go book a seat on the next stagecoach to Phoenix."

Duvall rounded the desk and put an arm around John's shoulder. "You're the best friend I have, John. Thank you for coming to my rescue. I really need your help on this one."

John playfully cuffed the older man's chin. "You're the best friend I have, too, Sol. That's why you were chosen to be best man at my wedding."

The Colorado sun was setting behind the majestic Rockies, slanting golden streamers of light across the Mile High City, as John Brockman rode up the circle drive in the Carroll yard and swung from the saddle. He noted Breanna's buggy—borrowed from Dr. Goodwin—parked next to the Langan buggy. He could hear the happy laughter of the children coming from inside the house.

The front door stood open, and as the tall man stepped up on the porch, the aroma of hot food met his nostrils and made his mouth water. He lifted the heavy knocker and let it drop, which brought an instant response from inside. Molly Kate came running down the hall, calling over her shoulder, "I'll get it, Mama! It has to be Uncle John!"

When she reached the foyer, she saw the outline of the man through the screen door. "Hi, Uncle John!" she said excitedly, her blond curls bouncing on her shoulders. "Come in."

John stepped through the door and gathered Molly Kate into his arms. "How about a big hug?" he asked.

The sweet child hugged him and kissed his cheek.

"Oh, a kiss, too?" he said.

Molly Kate giggled. "I thought since Aunt Breanna won't let very many ladies kiss you, I'd keep you supplied, Uncle John."

Brockman laughed and set her down as the rest of the children came down the hall, calling their greetings to him. John greeted them individually, making each child feel special.

As they headed toward the hall, Matt appeared on the winding staircase, and Breanna showed herself at the other end of the hall, holding a dish towel in her hands. "Hello, darling," she called. "Some welcoming committee you have there!"

"I'll say!"

"We've got Curt out here in the kitchen, carving the turkey. If you can get away from your admirers, come on back."

Matt went on to the kitchen while John looked down at Nathan Langan's abundant supply of freckles and mussed his hair. "Nathan," he said, "where'd you get those freckles?"

The boy shrugged. "I don't know."

"Well, *I* know," said John. "At the freckle store!"

Susan Langan laughed. "Oh, Mr. John. There aren't any stores where you buy freckles!"

"Well, where'd he get them, then?"

"I don't have as many as Nathan, Uncle John," spoke up Molly Kate, "but Mama told me that I got mine when I was real little. She said when I was asleep one night, an angel came into my room and painted the freckles on my nose."

Jared Langan elbowed his little brother. "As many freckles as you have, Nathan, it must have taken a hundred angels to paint them on in just one night!"

James grinned at his sister and said, "Well, Molly Kate, the angel who painted your freckles on must've run out of paint, 'cause he used most of it on Nathan!"

An impish look gleamed in Nathan's eye as he retorted, "Well, at least he thought Molly Kate and I were important enough to paint!"

"Hold on!" said the tall man. "I didn't mean to start trouble, here. Why don't you kids go back to whatever you were doing before I showed up?"

The children returned to the sitting room and resumed their game, and John entered the kitchen and was greeted by Dottie and Stefanie.

Curt Langan dropped a slab of white turkey meat on a large plate, then he looked up from the table where he was wielding a long-bladed carving knife, and said, "Hungry, John?"

"If I wasn't before I came in here, I would be now. Sure smells good."

"We're just about ready to sit down and eat," said Dottie.

Just then, Breanna came from the dining room, touched John's arm, and said, "Everything's on the tables but the turkey."

Stefanie chuckled. "Well, if the turkey carver wasn't so slow…"

Curt paused, grinned at his wife, and said, "You mustn't hurry an artist at work, Mrs. Langan. Great art takes time."

She laughed and said, "Well, when I see some great art, I'll check it out."

Stefanie's laugh was infectious. Soon everyone in the kitchen was laughing, except Curt. "You're all just jealous 'cause you can't carve a turkey and make it a thing of beauty."

"Who wants to *look* at it?" said John. "I just want to *eat* it!"

Curt trimmed off the last piece. "Okay. It's ready. But I want everyone to notice the exquisite symmetrical design of each slice, and to appreciate the care and forethought that went into it." There was more laughter as Curt carried the large platter of sliced turkey to the table.

On first call, the children rushed to the dining room. "The smaller table is for you children," Dottie said. "After we've prayed, you can make your way around the table and load your plates."

As Susan silently counted chairs at both tables, a puzzled look came over her face. "Miss Dottie…"

"Yes, Susie?"

"There are two extra chairs and settings at the adults' table, and an extra chair and setting at our table."

The adults exchanged glances and smiled.

"You are quite observant, Susan," Matt said. "And you're correct. The reason there are three extra chairs and places is because we have a little surprise for you, Jared, and Nathan. Three more guests will be joining us for dinner."

The Langan children looked at each other.

"Okay, folks!" the doctor said, calling over his shoulder. "We're ready!"

Footsteps sounded on the winding staircase, then in the hall. The first person to appear at the dining-room door wore a wide smile and walked with a slight limp.

"Bodie!" Jared exclaimed, dashing to his friend's side. Susan and Nathan followed.

Cliff and Mary Walker stepped around their adopted son and his friends as they excitedly greeted each other, and Mary embraced Breanna and Cliff greeted her warmly. When Bodie spotted Breanna, he hurried toward her with arms open wide. After they had enjoyed their moment of reunion, Breanna introduced Bodie to John.

Bodie extended his hand. As John met his grip, the boy said, "I'm so glad to finally meet you, Mr. John. Miss Breanna talked about you so much when we were traveling west on the orphan train. I'm glad to know that you and Miss Breanna are getting married. And…you're just as tall as she said you were!"

John grinned at the boy, and then Breanna introduced everyone to the Walkers, starting with John.

After the meal and the enjoyable evening, John drove Breanna home in the Goodwin buggy, with Ebony tied behind.

As they moved through Denver's lantern-lit streets, John said, "Honey, I sent a letter to Pastor Bob Walker and his wife in Butte City today, inviting them to come to the wedding."

"I hope they come," she said, squeezing his arm. "Is he paid very well? Maybe they can't afford to make the trip."

"I'm sure the church is as generous to him as possible, but it's small. So I put a check in with the letter. I told them to use the money for the trip if they could come, and if they couldn't come, to use it for whatever they need."

"Oh, John, you're such a generous man. That's one of the multitude of reasons I love you so."

"God's been good to me, Breanna. It's only right that I share it."

"I was thinking just this morning about all the money you gave to the building fund for the hospital. There wouldn't be such a fine hospital in this town if you hadn't given so generously. And then there's the church building—"

"Let's not brag on John Brockman, sweetheart. He's just a sinner saved by grace."

When they were near the Goodwin house, John said, "Breanna...if Pastor Walker's letter comes when I'm gone, and he says they can come, will you let Pastor Bayless know? Tell him I'd sure like to see Pastor Walker have some part in the wedding ceremony."

John could feel her eyes on him. "When you're gone, John? I wasn't aware you had a trip scheduled. Where are you going? It won't be far away, and it will be brief, won't it...since the wedding is only four weeks away?"

"Oh, I'll be back in plenty of time for the wedding, honey. Don't you worry about that."

"So you're traveling somewhere in Colorado?"

"Well, not exactly," he said, clearing his throat slightly. "I'll be leaving tomorrow morning on the stage to Phoenix."

Breanna straightened on the seat. "Phoenix, *Arizona?*"

"Well...yes. As far as I know, it's the only Phoenix in this country." John drew rein and brought the buggy to a halt.

"Is this an assignment for Chief Duvall?"

"Yes. But let me explain the stipulation I put on it, sweetheart."

Breanna folded her arms across her chest. "Please do."

She listened as John explained, and he made sure she understood that he would allow nothing to keep him from being back in Denver by May 23.

"Darling," she said softly, "I was only acting uneasy at the news. You know I would never question any decision you ever made."

"I appreciate that, sweetheart," he said, turning to kiss the tip of her nose.

"Of course," she said, muffling a laugh, "if you don't show up for the wedding, you won't like what I'll do to you."

13

MARK GRAY LAY ON HIS COT inside the Pima County jail in Tucson, trying to concoct a plan for escape. There were six cells in the jail; only two others were occupied. Across the cell block from Gray, two men, who had been brought in the night before on drunk and disorderly charges, were yelling at each other through the bars of their adjacent cells.

Gray's head ached. The loud voices were making it even worse, and they were disturbing his concentration. He put up with it for several minutes, then leaped to his feet and shouted, "Hey! You two shut up! I'm sick of listenin' to you!"

"You shut up, buster!" bellowed one of the men. "Or I'll—"

"You'll what?" challenged Gray.

The door to the sheriff's office opened, and Deputy Sheriff Hugh Scott appeared. "What's all the noise about back here?" he asked. "A deaf man could hear you!"

"These two have been screamin' at each other for an hour," said Gray. "I'm sick of listenin' to it. Make 'em shut up."

"I've only been gone half an hour, Gray," said Scott, "so I know it hasn't been that long." He turned to the other men. "But I don't want any more from you two, do you hear?"

"We weren't hurtin' him any," said one of the men.

"If we want to argue, that's our business," said the other.

"It's my business when you're carryin' on and I can't even hear myself think!" said Gray.

"All three of you shut up," Scott warned, "or you'll be missing some meals. We don't feed rebellious prisoners."

The door to the office opened again, and Sheriff Bromley came in, making a beeline for Mark Gray's cell. He glanced at the deputy. "Problem, Hugh?"

"There was, but we got it ironed out."

Bromley nodded, then stepped close to Gray's cell and grinned slyly. "Good news, Gray. Captain Sears has two Rangers on their way here. They'll arrive by stagecoach in three days."

"Sheriff, you can't let those Rangers take me! All the Rangers in El Paso have it in for me. They hate me. They'll kill me before we ever get to El Paso! I know they will! Please! Don't let 'em take me!"

Bromley laughed. "Come on, Gray. Who do you think you're kidding? You don't fear those Rangers. You fear the noose they'll put on your neck."

"Sheriff, I'm tellin' you, they'll kill me between here and El Paso! You gotta listen to me!"

"Come off it, Gray," said Bromley, giving him a disgusted look. "Even if there were no other passengers on that stage, there would still be a driver and a shotgunner. It would be pretty hard for the Rangers to kill you with the crew on board."

"You don't know how those Rangers hate me, Sheriff. If there aren't any other passengers, they could still shoot me in the ribs and tell the driver and shotgunner I tried to escape. And if there are other passengers, they'll find a way to kill me, anyhow. You want that on your conscience?"

Bromley turned to his deputy. "Come on, Hugh. We've got important things to do."

"What is it, Bromley?" Gray said. "Haven't you got a conscience?"

"Conscience I have," said the sheriff over his shoulder, as he and his deputy moved toward the door. "What I don't have is patience with birds like you who wear a badge and tarnish it."

The door closed before Gray could reply. He turned away from the bars and ran shaky fingers through his coal-black hair. He rubbed his aching head, wishing he'd seen the wagon before he'd darted into the street. Seeds of panic were beginning to take root inside him. He had to find a way to escape.

He turned back to the barred door and looked across the space between the cells. "Hey, fellas, I'm sorry I lit into you like that. It's just that I took a real crack on the head before they brought me in here, and I've got a headache that would stagger an elephant." Both men looked at him impassively. "How long you guys gonna be locked up?"

"Three days, if we agree to pay the fine for breakin' a five-hundred-dollar chandelier and a eighty-dollar mirror at the Cactus Needle Saloon," said one.

"You fellas got the money?"

"Yeah," said the other prisoner. "Stashed where nobody'll find it."

"So how long will you be in here if you don't come up with the money?" Gray asked.

The men looked at each other, then back at Gray. "Probably ninety days," said one.

"So I guess you'll tell Bromley you'll pay if he lets you out in three days. By the way, my name's Gray. Mark Gray."

"Ed Stagler," said one of the men. "I take it you used to be a Texas Ranger."

"Yeah. Used to be."

"Millard Frye," said the other. "What did you do to tarnish your badge?"

"Long story. Tell you about it later. Is that what you two were arguin' about? Payin' or stayin'?"

When they nodded yes, Gray said, "Guess what you have to decide is whether ninety days in jail is worth savin' all that money."

"I already made the decision to pay it and get outta here," said Stagler. "Millard thinks we ought to sit it out."

"I don't any more," said Frye. "I've decided you're right, pal. Let's pay it and walk. We *have* to do the next three days, but that's gonna be enough of this place."

"Well, okay," Ed said, and grinned. "Let's tell Bromley we'll cooperate. All he has to do is go with us to where we have the money stashed. We'll pay the fine and ride outta this no-good burg."

Gray leaned against the bars. "How would you boys like to get out of here real quick, and keep your money, too?"

Stagler and Frye rose from their cots, giving Gray their undivided attention.

"I was noticin' that when the sheriff or the deputy talk to us, they like to stand real close to the bars..."

Captain Terrell Sears was humming an unrecognizable tune as he cleaned up his desk. It was time to close up the office and go home to his wife for a promised fried chicken dinner. He flipped the page of his desk calendar in preparation for the next day and settled his gaze on the page. Thursday, May 4, 1871. He thought of Sergeant Jody Sleppy and Corporal Ben Oliver. They should have arrived in Tucson today.

He grinned to himself and pulled at his mustache.

"Tomorrow, they'll head back with that scumbucket cuffed between them!" he said out loud. His mouth curved in a smile of triumph. "Can't wait to see your ugly puss when they walk you in here, Gray. I hope the ghosts of that Mexican boy and those two Rangers dog your tracks all the way to the gallows."

Charlie Wilson and his wife, Evelyn Ruth, lived in the apartment above the Western Union office. The stairs to the second floor were on the inside of the building at the back, and Charlie had been smelling the aroma of Mexican food for ten minutes. His stomach growled as he used a feather duster to make the office presentable before going upstairs for the night.

"Charlie!" came Evelyn Ruth's voice from the top of the stairs. "Supper's almost ready!"

"Okay, sweetie pie," Charlie called back. "I'm just about—"

The telegraph key began to click. He dropped the duster on a chair, sat down at the desk, and picked up a pencil.

"Charlie-e-e! You coming?"

"Just a minute," he called over his shoulder. "Got a message comin' in!"

"Okay! But come up as soon as you get it. Supper's getting cold!"

As Charlie's practiced ear translated the coded message, and he began writing, his countenance fell. "Oh, no," he said, sighing the words.

When the last click came, Wilson laid the pencil down, folded the yellow slip of paper, and placed it in a yellow envelope. "It's times like these when I don't like my job," he mumbled to himself.

He paused at the bottom of the stairs and called up, "Sweetie pie…"

"Yes?"

"You'd better go ahead and start eatin' without me. I've got to take this telegram to Captain Sears. He'll probably want to send a reply, so I'll have to come back and get it on the wire."

Evelyn Ruth appeared at the top of the stairs. She was a small, pretty woman with lovely silver hair. "Honey, when are you going to get to eat?"

"Soon's I take care of this matter. But you go ahead."

"Well, all right. I'll keep your food warm."

As Charlie hastened down the street, he told himself it must be about time to retire. He couldn't run like he used to.

As he entered the block where the Texas Ranger office was situated, he saw two Rangers ride up in front of the office and dismount. He recognized Lieutenant Chad Beckwith and Sergeant Orville Paulsen. He was glad to see Captain Sears step through the door and greet them. Sears was wearing his hat, which told Charlie he had almost missed him.

The captain and two Rangers spotted Charlie as he drew near. His stomach gave a nervous quiver.

"Hello, Charlie," said Sears. "That telegram in your hand for me?"

"Yes, sir," said Wilson, puffing to a halt.

"From my Rangers in Tucson, maybe?"

Charlie handed him the envelope. "Yes, sir. Rangers Slcppy and Oliver. I…I'll wait to see if you want to reply."

Sears waved the envelope at Beckwith and Paulsen. "Ben and Jody!" he said laughing. "In Tucson to pick up Mark Gray!"

"Yes, sir, we know," Beckwith said, and smiled.

Sears unfolded the telegram and angled it toward the fading light. When his eyes had taken in the message, his head moved as if he'd been slapped, and he gave out a strangled cry.

Charlie Wilson's face pinched.

"What is it, Captain?" asked Paulsen.

Sears took a deep breath and let it out slowly through his nostrils, then drew in another. With effort he kept his voice low as he said, "Sleppy and Oliver arrived in Tucson on time, at three-fifteen this afternoon. Gray and two other prisoners escaped from the Pima County Jail yesterday. They managed to overpower Deputy Sheriff Hugh Scott, and took off, leaving him unconscious, possibly with a fractured skull. No details."

He took another deep breath and said, "Sheriff Mitchell Bromley and a posse are searching for Gray and the other two escapees." His hands began to tremble. "I can't believe it. I just can't believe it! They had him behind bars, ready for Ben and Jody to bring back here. And now, the slithering snake is on the loose again."

"Captain, excuse me," said Charlie. "Did you want to send a message back to the Rangers?"

"Yeah. Right away. Tell them to wait there till Bromley and his posse return. If they've caught Gray, Sleppy and Oliver are to bring him back to El Paso in chains. Of course, they're to wire me immediately so I'll know Gray has been caught again. If Bromley comes back without him, Sleppy and Oliver are to wire me that message, and I'll tell them what to do next."

Mark Gray traveled the back country and rode hard toward Phoenix. He and the men who escaped with him had parted company when they stole three horses off the street in Tucson. Stagler and Frye had gone east; Gray had headed north.

Summer had almost arrived in the desert, and Gray squinted through the shimmering heat haze across the desert's rolling, sun-bleached surface. It seemed to stretch endlessly in every direction. There were pockmarked arroyos and wind-washed rocks, along with stunted piñon, palo verde, and cat claw clinging to the desert's surface, taking what water it could afford to give. Gray knew that sometimes the deeper arroyos held water in their basins. His canteen had been empty for hours, and soon he would need food.

As he rode over cactus-strewn hills and into sandy valleys, he told himself he would have to rob another bank. There was one in Eloy, and one in Casa Grande. But he'd have to be very careful. No doubt, Bromley had a posse on his trail and probably had wired lawmen all over Arizona to be on the lookout for him.

The sun was going down. He would have to find water for the horse, if at all possible, and then for himself. He could do without food until he robbed the Eloy bank.

In the orange light of sunset, his horse skirted a thick patch of creosote bushes that stippled the area. When the sun was gone, and its light faded into deep purple, the Silver Bell Mountains rose mistily from what seemed to be the western edge of the world.

As complete darkness fell, Gray knew he would have to stop without finding water. It was too risky to traverse the rugged and uneven land at night.

"Well, horsey," he said, pulling rein, "it's time to call it a day. You and I will get us some rest."

The light of the gathering stars showed him a level spot beneath a huge boulder by a dry brook. He had started to dismount when a flicker of light caught his eye near the foothills of the Silver Bells.

He blinked and squinted to bring it into view. Sure enough, a campfire!

The winking fire looked to be maybe two hundred yards away. He nudged the horse forward and guided it toward the fire. When he drew near, he could see a couple of men hunkering down, holding skillets. Outside the ring of light, a pair of figures darker than the gloom could be seen moving about, tending to the horses.

When he was almost close enough for them to hear the soft hoofbeats of his horse, he drew rein and called out, "Hello, the camp! Permission to ride in!"

The two men at the fire leaped to their feet, drawing their guns, and the two in the shadows swiftly appeared in the firelight, flanking them. They peered into the night and said something among themselves that Gray couldn't hear, then one of them called, "Prove you ain't Apache!"

Gray's ears picked up the sound of a stream running nearby. He licked his lips, and his horse nickered at the smell of water.

"My name's Frank Chase," he called out. "I'm on my way to Flagstaff to visit a friend. If you'll allow me to come within the circle of light, you'll see I'm not Apache!"

"Your hands better be empty, mister!" warned the one who stepped ahead of the others. "Or you're a dead man."

"Comin' in," Gray said. "All I'm holding are the reins."

He nudged the horse forward and felt the hard scrutiny of the men as he came into view.

"Well, he ain't Apache, Chuck," said one.

"Never saw one with a mustache," said another.

The aroma of hot coffee and food cooking teased Gray's taste buds.

"Sorta dangerous for one man to travel alone on this desert, Mr. Chase," said the man who stood closest to him. "What with Apaches runnin' wild and outlaws as thick as ants at a picnic."

"I know," said Gray. "This visit is more than casual. Somethin' I have to do."

"Well, I hope your friend in Flagstaff appreciates the risk you're takin' to pay him a visit."

"He does, I assure you."

"What exactly did you come to our camp for?"

"I ran into some trouble back in Tucson and lost all my money and what food I was carryin'. My canteen's dry, and so is my horse. I was wonderin' if you could spare me a morsel of food. I wasn't aware of the stream, so if you don't mind, I'll let my horse get a drink, and take one myself."

"Come on down, Mr. Chase," said the man in front of the others. "There's enough grass along the bank of the creek for your horse. Ours are takin' their share right now. We were about to eat supper. Got beans, hardtack, and some buffalo jerky. You're welcome to a belly full of it."

"Thanks," said Gray, swinging his leg over the saddle and touching earth. "I appreciate this more than I can tell you."

"Take your animal on over to the creek, Mr. Chase. We'll have you a cup of coffee poured and a plateful of beans ready in a minute."

The fugitive ground-reined his stolen horse at the creek so that it could drink, and munch on the grass. He knelt on the bank upstream from the horses, removed his hat, and stuck his face in the cool stream, taking his fill. He then splashed water all over his head, put his hat back on, and returned to the campfire.

The man who had spoken to him earlier stood near the fire, while two others were loading beans onto tin plates from steaming skillets, and the fourth man was pouring coffee into tin cups.

The first man, who seemed to be the leader, stuck out his hand and said, "My name's Chuck Griswold. This fella pourin' coffee is Harry Draper. This guy right here is E. J. Lessig, and the big ugly one is Gus Pulford."

Gray clasped Griswold's hand in a tight grip.

"Watch it, Chuck!" said Pulford. "Or I'll poison your beans!"

Griswold laughed. "You've been doin' that ever since we've been ridin' together!"

Mark Gray laughed with the rest of them.

Soon they were sitting around the fire, eating.

"So you ran into trouble in Tucson, eh?"

"Yeah," nodded Gray.

"Sounds like you may have been robbed."

Mark gave a lopsided grin. "You could call it that."

"What business you in?" asked Lessig.

"Well…I'm sort of between careers right now. Worked cattle ranches all over west Texas. My friend in Flagstaff is gonna help me get started in the cattle business in that area."

"Oh. A herd of your own, eh?"

"Yeah." Gray filled his mouth with beans and smiled at Lessig. He ran his gaze over the faces of his benefactors. "What business you fellas in?"

The rugged-looking foursome exchanged glances.

"We're sorta what you'd call travelin' men," spoke up Griswold. "We move about, doin' odd jobs."

A look passed between Harry Draper and Gus Pulford, and they both grinned.

Griswold bit off a chunk of buffalo jerky, and while he chewed, he said, "You ain't done much desert travel, I take it."

"Oh, I've done plenty of it," said Gray. "Why?"

"Well, no man who's desert wise will let his canteen go dry. You're not that far from Tucson. Are you tellin' me you rode through there and didn't fill your canteen?"

Gray met his gaze but kept silent.

When he didn't reply, Griswold said, "Pardon me if I'm wrong, Mr. Chase, but I think maybe that trouble in Tucson you spoke of put you on a new horse real quick-like. Tell me if I'm wrong."

Gray laughed. "Okay, I'll come clean. I was caught and jailed in Tucson for robbin' a bank in Lordsburg. The New Mexico authorities were sendin' marshals to take me back for trial. I managed to escape, and I'm headin' for Flagstaff to hide out from the marshals."

Big Gus Pulford laughed. "See, Harry? I told you he was on the dodge. He just had that look about him."

Gray glanced at the big man. "I do, huh?"

"Yep."

"Guess we might as well tell him, boys," said Chuck.

Gray's dark eyes swerved to the leader.

"We're in the bankin' business, ourselves. Makin' withdrawals at gunpoint, I mean."

"Doesn't surprise me," Gray said. "You fellas just have 'that look' about you."

"Tell you what, Frank," said Chuck. "We just made a good haul at the bank in Casa Grande. But we've been talkin' about movin' on south to Tucson and cleanin' out the big one there—the Altar Valley Bank. Only thing that was holdin' us back from makin' definite plans was that we needed another man. Be a lot safer with five than with four."

"Makes sense," said Gray, his mind working.

"How about joinin' us, Frank?" asked Griswold. "We'll hit the Altar Valley Bank and ride for California. Those New Mexico marshals won't look for you, runnin' with a gang."

"Let me think on it while I put down some more beans," Gray said. "Be a big change in my own plans. However, a fifth of whatever we get at the Tucson bank would be pretty nice."

The outlaws exchanged glances as Gray dished up more beans from the skillet.

"Well, now…uh…I need to explain somethin', Frank," said Griswold. "Whenever we add a new man to the gang, he works at a lower percentage of the take for three months. He sticks with us that long, he gets his full percentage."

"Oh," said Gray, nodding. He set the plate of beans down and poured his coffee cup full. He rose to his feet and held the steaming cup in his left hand. "I can understand that."

Griswold looked up at him and smiled. "So you'll join us?"

Suddenly Gray flung the hot coffee in Griswold's face and whipped out his gun. Griswold howled as he lifted his hands to his eyes, and the other three stiffened in shock. Gus Pulford started to go for his gun.

"Don't do it, Gus!" snapped Gray, lining the cocked revolver on his face. "All right, now. Since you fellas just made a good haul at Casa Grande, that'll be good enough for me. I assume the money's in your saddlebags…"

The outlaws glared at him while their leader whined and held his burning face.

"Okay. One at a time, I want you to pull your guns out real slow-like, empty them, and toss them in the fire."

"What?" bellowed E. J. "Now look, Chase, you can't leave us out here without our guns! You—"

"Shut up and do as I say! You've got rifles. I saw them on your horses. You go first, Lessig. One quick move and it'll be your last."

One by one the outlaws punched the cartridges from the cylinders of their revolvers and dropped the guns into the fire.

"Now your boots," commanded Gray.

Moments later, the outlaws stood in their socks, watching their boots and guns getting ruined in the fire.

Gray took Harry Draper with him at gunpoint and made him remove the money from each saddlebag and stuff it in the saddlebags on the horse he'd stolen in Tucson. He then made Draper untie the gang's horses. When he fired two shots in the air, the horses bolted and soon disappeared in the darkness.

As Gray mounted up, he smiled at the outlaws and said, "You gentlemen ought to be glad I didn't just shoot you down. Be thankful you're still alive."

The outlaws were still cursing him as he rode away.

14

CHARLIE WILSON STOOD BEFORE Captain Sears's desk, thinking even more seriously about retiring. He hated delivering telegrams like this one.

As the captain read the message, a pulse began to hammer at his temple, and then he crumpled the yellow sheet of paper.

Three of Captain Sears's Rangers watched him, then Sergeant Orville Paulsen said, "The sheriff didn't catch him, sir?"

"The mangy skunk got away. They lost his trail somewhere north of Tucson. Uncanny, that's what he is. How does he do it? How does he manage to elude the law every time?"

"Maybe it's because he *was* the law for so many years, Captain," said Corporal Tim Castle.

Sears shook his head and threw the crumpled paper in the wastebasket. "I'm afraid you're right. The Ranger organization trains its men well. When one of them goes bad, he really goes bad."

"Do you want to send a message back to Sleppy and Oliver, Captain?" asked Charlie.

"Yes. Tell them to come on home."

When Charlie had gone back to his office, Paulsen said, "Sir, don't let this Gray situation get you down."

Sears eased back in his chair. "Easier said than done. This has got to end. Gray can't keep this up. Sooner or later he's got to make a big mistake."

"Oh, he will, sir," said Castle. "It's inevitable. Mark has adopted violence as his way of life, and he'll die a violent death, as sure as Monday follows Sunday."

Sears eyed him speculatively. "I'd like to believe that's so, but how can you be so sure, Tim?"

"The Word of God."

"Pardon me? I don't understand what you're saying."

"Me either," said Orville Paulsen.

"Proverbs 13:2," said Castle. "It says 'the soul of the transgressors shall eat violence.' It's an Old Testament parallel to what the Lord Jesus Christ said: 'All they that take the sword shall perish with the sword.'"

Sears brushed at his mustache. "A lot of wisdom in that Bible, isn't there, Tim?"

"That's for sure, sir. You rest on it. Mark Gray's going to end up in a bad way one of these days."

"I hope I'm there to see it," said Sears with gravel in his voice.

All day, hot silence had smothered the rolling acres of the Bar-H Ranch, but as cool twilight settled over Arizona, the cattle on the hills began to bawl.

The Bar-H, coveted by ranchers far and wide, lay five miles northeast of Phoenix. A rippling creek ran through ex-Texas Ranger Jim Carter's ranch. Carter, known in these parts as Jock Hood, had laid hold on these choice three thousand acres upon first coming to Arizona in early 1863.

More than half of the ranch was knee-deep in rich green

grass at this time of the year, and the tall green pines that dotted the land added to its beauty. To come upon the Bar-H from any direction was like riding from dry desolation into a lush, beautiful park. In addition to the creek, which was spawned by deep springs at the north edge of the ranch, were other springs among the jagged rock formations that appeared frequently across Bar-H land.

Hood stepped out on the front porch of his sprawling ranch house and let the breeze blow through his thinning carrot-red hair. His gaze took in some of his ranch hands at the corral, who had just returned from a long day riding among the herd. Others were moving about outside the bunkhouse, situated in a cove of yellow pines.

Movement caught his eye toward the west, where the main trail to the house came from the Phoenix–Flagstaff road. He could see five riders coming toward the house. Purple shadows flowed along the ridge slopes, dropping into all the pockets, barricades, and arroyos of the broken country that made up the Bar-H. The shadows were too deep for him to identify the riders, but Hood was sure three of them were his own men.

The breeze grew cooler as Hood waited for the riders to draw up. Even with the semi-darkness, he recognized the two men who had been escorted in by his "sentries."

"Well, look who's back," said Hood. "Perry Jocelyn and Shelby Revis. Jail break, or did you serve full time for your latest escapade?"

"Jail break, Mr. Hood," said Jocelyn, who was nearly thirty, but looked scarcely more than nineteen.

"Six months ago we were sentenced to ten years at Deer Lodge up in Montana, sir," said Revis, who was about the same age as his partner, but looked older. "Broke out the last of April. Been movin' real careful-like, so it's taken us a while to get here. We need you to hide us for a good stretch."

"Well, then, let's go inside and talk about it."

Hood's three riders trotted away, and the fugitives dismounted. He led them down a long hall to his den, which was a virtual museum of bear rugs, deer, buffalo, and elk heads on the walls, and a gun rack that could almost furnish a small army.

Hood gestured toward two chairs made of bison horns and cushioned with pillows made from buffalo hide. He took a seat behind the desk as the two outlaws sat down.

"So, did you boys rob some banks or stagecoaches along the way?" queried Hood.

"You mean, do we have the money to pay for your help?" asked Jocelyn.

"Yeah. That's what I mean."

"We wouldn't have come here askin' for shelter if we didn't have the money, Mr. Hood," said Revis. "How much is it since the last time? More?"

"A little. Hundred and fifty dollars a month, apiece. Last time you were here, I think it was something over a hundred."

"Hundred and ten, sir," said Jocelyn. "But that's okay. We figure to stay at least seven or eight months."

"Well, you can pay me for six, if you want. We'll see how it looks to you then."

"Sure," Jocelyn said, reaching into his pocket.

When each man had counted out and laid the correct amount of money on the desk, Hood scraped the green bills toward himself, and said, "You can stay here tonight. I'll make arrangements tomorrow for you to stay with a rancher friend of mine up north a ways. His name's Nate Langford. Nate's expecting me to send him the next three or four fugitives who come along. Same arrangements. You do the work he asks, and he'll see that you're safe, fed, and clothed."

"And we can come and go at our own risk, if we please, like with that rancher Ernest Banks?" asked Revis.

"Yes. Nate understands that you might need to get away for a breather and to pick up some cash. But if you pull a robbery and lead any lawmen to the Flying L, he'll deny he knows you, and so will the other men. And if somehow you escape the law, you won't escape Langford. He'll put a price on your head no bounty hunter could refuse."

"We understand, sir," said Jocelyn. "We'll make sure nothin' like that ever happens."

"Fine. I guarantee you'll be safe as long as you stay on the Flying L. Nate will take good care of you."

Hood had one of the Bar-H men summoned to lead Revis and Jocelyn to the bunkhouse.

Hardly had they left the den when Hood's four sons came into the house and headed down the hall. They were talking as they walked, and Hood picked out the voice of United States Marshal Tom Wall. Harold, Mason, Virgil, and Billy Hood entered the den, accompanied by Wall.

"Pa," said Harold, who was the oldest, at thirty-three, "Tom just rode onto the ranch. He wants to talk to all of us at once."

"Have a seat, Tom," said Jock, gesturing toward a single chair in front of the desk.

The Hood brothers gathered around.

"I'll get right to the point," said Wall. "Since I've been taking money from you to look the other way when your outlaw friends commit crimes all over Arizona Territory, I've falsified a lot of arrest reports to the U.S. marshal's office in Washington. So far, I've been able to keep my eleven deputies from finding out what I'm doing. A couple times I've come close to getting caught. I really had to lie a heap to convince one of my deputies that what he thought he saw, wasn't so. I've probably sent you nearly thirty outlaws to harbor since the first of the year. I'm taking big chances to help you make money off these guys, and to put it bluntly, I think I should get more pay."

Jock Hood's features were impassive as he ran his gaze over the faces of his sons. "What do you think, boys? Any raise in pay for Tom will have to come from the central fund."

Billy, who was the youngest, at twenty-one, said, "As I see it, Tom is worth whatever he asks. After all, he's smart enough to fool his deputies, and he's risking his career as a lawman. Not only that, but if he gets caught letting our outlaw pals get away with their crimes, he could go to prison for the rest of his life."

"I agree," Mason said.

Jock set his gaze on Virgil.

"Me, too, Pa," Virgil said.

Jock's line of sight swerved to his eldest. "Harold...?"

"Without Tom, we wouldn't be bringing in most of the money. I say, let's give him a raise."

Tom Wall smiled.

"Okay, Tom," said Jock, "how does a 30 percent raise sound?"

"Oh, that would really help. It's hard to make it on a U.S. marshal's pay these days. I don't know how those deputies of mine do it."

"Things are tough all over," grunted Hood, smoothing his thinning hair. "Guess they'll have to get tougher for outlaws who want help, too. We'll just have to raise the fee so we can pay you better."

Wall stood up. "I won't take up any more of your time, Jock. Thanks a lot."

"Thanks a lot, yourself," Hood said, as he rose to his feet.

"I'll walk Tom to the door, Pa," said Billy.

The older brothers remained with their father as Billy and the U.S. marshal walked outside. A ranch hand was lighting the lanterns that were set on posts next to the steps. He spoke to Wall, then headed toward the bunkhouse.

Wall laid a hand on young Billy's shoulder. "Thanks for speaking up for me in there."

"Thank *you* for teaching me the fast-draw."

Wall moved down the steps. "Talk about risk, kid. If your pa ever finds out I taught you the fast-draw, he'll have my hide."

"He isn't going to know," said Billy, following him.

As Wall moved to his horse, he said, "Billy, without a doubt, you have the natural ability to one day be a big name gunfighter. I've trained you because you asked me to. Just watching you, I'd say you're faster and more deadly than eight out of ten gunhawks in this part of the West."

Billy studied the marshal's face in the light of the lanterns. "But you still think I should forget it, don't you?"

"Why waste your life, son? Find yourself a better goal."

"But it's what I've wanted to be ever since I was sixteen years old."

"Why not just be a lawman who's exceptionally fast on the draw?"

Billy snorted and laughed. "You think Pa would explode if he found out I was planning on being a gunfighter. He'd *really* come apart if I told him I was going to be a lawman! Besides, I want men to quiver and quail in my presence, because they know I'm death in a pair of high-heeled boots. That wouldn't happen if I was wearing a badge, no matter how fast I was."

Wall rubbed his chin. "So that's all you're living for?"

"Yep."

"No matter what your pa thinks of it when he finds out?"

"Yep."

"He'll probably disown you."

"I don't care. I know what I want, and I know I can achieve it. Pa's scorn won't bother me. I just want to be a big-name gunfighter."

"Billy, you and I have faced off with our guns empty, and you've been outdrawing me every time for the past two months. But you've never drawn against a cold-eyed man who would just as soon kill you as swat a fly."

"So what? I can take any man who'll face me."

"Not *any* man, kid. Like I said, if my estimation of you is correct, you're faster than eight out of ten gunhawks in this part of the West. But there are always the other two. One of these days, you're going to find your first man to challenge. You'd better make sure he isn't one of the big names. You'll get yourself killed right off."

Billy shook his head. "I know me better than you do, Tom. I'm telling you, I'm ready to take on a big name and leave him lying in the dust. That would make Billy Hood a big name in a heartbeat, wouldn't it?"

"You mean a big name on a tombstone?"

The kid laughed. "C'mon, Tom, don't be an old grandma. I'm telling you, I'm ready for a big-name gunfighter. I'm gonna challenge the first one that shows up in Phoenix."

John Brockman stepped out of the stagecoach in Phoenix on Monday, May 8. A buggy from the Desert Rose Hotel was waiting for him. After signing up for his room and depositing his luggage there, he walked down Main Street to the office of the United States marshal.

Two deputies were just dismounting at the hitch rail as

Brockman approached. Both men saw his badge at the same time and smiled.

"Howdy, gentlemen," said the tall man in black. "I'm John Brockman. Replacement for Deputy Trent Hale."

They shook Brockman's hand and introduced themselves as Ansel Krebs and Vince Porter.

"We really miss Trent," said Krebs. "He was a good lawman."

"I'm sure of that," said Brockman. "You fellas know if Marshal Wall is in?"

"We just rode into town ourselves, Mr. Brockman," said Porter. "We're supposed to report to him, so we hope he's here."

Krebs hurried ahead and opened the door, allowing Brockman and Porter to enter first, then followed.

U.S. Marshal Tom Wall and another deputy were bending over an open map on a desk top. When Wall glanced up and saw the towering man in black, now flanked by Krebs and Porter, he gasped.

"John Stranger!" he said, extending his hand. As they gripped in a steady handshake, all three deputies looked on wide-eyed. They knew the name, *John Stranger.*

"So your real name is Brockman, sir?" asked Krebs.

John nodded.

"What?" said Wall. "You told these men your real name? How come you never told *me?*"

"I'll explain that later," John replied, reaching into his shirt pocket for a folded sheet of paper.

"I'm Cliff Barnes, sir," said the other deputy.

"Oh, I'm sorry," said Wall. "Didn't mean to ignore you, Cliff."

As John shook hands with Barnes, the deputy said, "I saw

you over in Apache Junction a year or so ago, Mr. Str—I mean, Mr. Brockman."

"I was there, all right," said John.

"So, John, to what do we owe this visit?" asked Wall.

"This will explain it officially," Brockman said, handing Wall the paper he'd just removed from his shirt pocket.

Wall's eyes showed his surprise as he looked up after reading the paper. "I can't believe this, John. With your travels and all, it seems a deputy U.S. marshal's job would be rather mild and uninteresting."

"Fella needs a change now and then, Marshal. It'll be temporary, but Chief Duvall sat me down, told me about Deputy Trent Hale being killed, and said you were already shorthanded out here, so he asked if I would come and take the job till someone else could be found to fill it."

"I am shorthanded, all right. Without Hale, I have eleven deputies, and until Krebs and Porter just rode in, I had exactly one deputy here—Cliff. He's best acquainted with all the paperwork that goes on around here, so I don't let him chase bad guys as much as he used to. I might just have you help me handle trouble right here in town most of the time, John. Or even to watch over things when I ride after lawbreakers, myself."

"That would be fine. Just point mc in the right direction at the right time. I'm sure there'll be plenty to keep me busy."

"You can count on it," Wall said, and grinned. "And when we're between outlaws, I'll give you some of this paperwork to do."

"I'm here to serve, boss," John said.

"I guess I'll need to find you a place to stay…"

"Not necessary. I'm already in the Desert Rose Hotel."

"Oh, all right. It's that temporary, then, is it?"

"Like I said, till someone else can be found to fill the job."

Wall smiled. "Glad to have you for whatever time you can be here, John. How soon do you want to start?"

"How's tomorrow morning? That'll give me a chance to get settled in a bit."

"Fine. I'll have Cliff take you over to the stables and let you pick out a horse that suits you. In the morning, you can go with Cliff to make an arrest over by the Vulture Mountains. Know where they are?"

"Northwest of here about fifty miles."

"Right. I was just showing Cliff where the outlaw hides when he's in the area. I found out yesterday that some neighbors saw him. Seems his brother is giving him a place of refuge from the federal authorities. That's us."

Brockman grinned. "Yes, sir. That's us."

As Breanna Baylor cleaned up the examining room, her mind was on John, the wedding, and her new house. She was glad the approach of summer brought more daylight, because there was so much to do today. She would eat supper at the Carrolls, then she and Dottie were going out to the house. Stefanie would meet them there, and the three of them would work together, fixing it up like Breanna wanted.

Doctor Goodwin was in the outer office, talking to a female patient he had just treated in the examining room. Breanna heard the woman leave, and a moment later, there was the sound of a male voice.

"Breanna!" came the doctor's voice through the partially open door. "Telegram for John. You want to accept it for him?"

She hurried into the office. The Western Union runner was a boy from the church.

He smiled at her and said, "Hello, Miss Breanna. This telegram came for John, so I brought it to you, knowing he's out of town."

Breanna thanked the boy, signed the necessary slip, and opened the yellow envelope. "Oh, it's from John's friend, Pastor Bob Walker, in Butte City. John invited him and his wife to the wedding. This confirms that they're coming."

"That's nice," said Goodwin. "John told Martha and me about Pastor Walker. They must've become pretty good friends when John was up there on that snow ghost thing."

"Mm-hmm. John said if I heard from the Walkers, and they were coming, he wanted me to ask Pastor Bayless if Pastor Walker could have a part in the wedding ceremony."

Goodwin smiled. "Well, if John wants it that way, I guarantee you, Pastor Bayless will go along with it."

The sun was still a couple of hours from touching the ragged peaks of the Rockies when Dottie and Breanna drove up to find Stefanie standing in the yard, admiring Breanna's handiwork. Spring flowers bloomed in multi-colored profusion along the front of the house and down both sides.

"It's beautiful, Breanna," said Stefanie, as the two women alighted from Dottie's buggy.

"Thank you," said Breanna, smiling at her friend. "Let me show you the backyard too."

The cottonwoods and willows in the backyard stood over two large flower gardens, and the apple trees were in full bloom.

"Oh, it's marvelous!" said Stefanie. "Breanna, you have a special touch."

"I just love flowers and green things," said Breanna, pleased that her friend liked the yard.

Breanna led her sister and Stefanie inside and explained how she wanted to change things in the parlor. She had bought two small still-life pictures, along with some bric-a-brac she wanted to place on small shelves, the mantle, and some of the lamp tables. She also had an assortment of dried flowers to go in vases on a couple of the lamp tables.

While they worked, Stefanie said, "Doesn't it worry you that John might not make it back from Arizona in time for the wedding?"

"Well, I do think about it a lot," Breanna replied, "but I pray about it a lot, too. I just have to trust the Lord to let John handle this job in Phoenix and return home in time."

"John told you he would come home by the twenty-third, no matter what, didn't he?" asked Dottie.

"That's what he said. Oh, I know how things can happen, and I won't say I don't have thoughts that something could come up that would keep him there, even though he's set his mind to leave by the twentieth."

"Well, the Lord's going to take care of it, Breanna," said Dottie. "This wedding is very important to Him. He let you and John meet and fall in love. And even though you were kept apart for quite some time, He let you find each other again. He's not going to let anything get in the way of you and John tying the knot on June 4."

That night, as Breanna lay in her bed at the Goodwin cottage, she thought of the conversation with her sister and Stefanie. Nagging doubts began pricking at her mind, keeping her from sleep.

Other thoughts intruded. She had prayed for those outlaws,

Max Richter and Hank Chatham, asking the Lord to use her witness to bring them to Himself before they hanged. Even though Richter had ordered her out of his room, she knew she had sown the gospel seed, and she'd prayed it would take root before it was too late.

She had also gone to the Denver County Jail and witnessed to Chatham. But like Richter, he had angrily told her to leave him alone. In spite of her prayers, both men had been hanged without heeding her witness. And now, she was having doubts about John getting home in time for the wedding.

She prayed again, asking the Lord to bring John home in time and to give her the faith to believe He would answer. Even when she was getting drowsy, it seemed that the Holy Spirit was saying to her heart, *Breanna, think of all the people the Lord Jesus preached to. Even under His powerful preaching, most of them never called on Him for salvation.*

That thought seemed to calm her spirit, and soon she was asleep and dreaming again of her wedding day…

Breanna smiled at little Molly Kate as she strewed rose petals from a hoop basket. Breanna had not yet let her eyes go to the groom. She would wait until she was a little closer. She set her gaze on the groomsmen who stood in a fan shape, waiting for the bridesmaids and the matron of honor. Inside their line stood Chief U.S. Marshal Solomon Duvall, John's best man. And next to him—

John wasn't there!

Suddenly Breanna was sitting up in bed, gasping for breath. As moonlight flooded through her bedroom window, she breathed a prayer. "Oh, dear Lord, please don't let anything happen to prevent John's return in time for the wedding."

15

JOCK HOOD AND HIS YOUNGEST SON, Billy, were walking from the barn to the big ranch house as the sun set in a fiery display of red, orange, and yellow clouds.

A galloping rider caught their attention, coming from the direction of the Phoenix-Flagstaff Road.

"Looks like Marshal Wall, Pa," said Billy.

Hood squinted at the approaching horse and rider. "I'd say so, son," he said.

Hood could tell it was Wall when the man came within fifty feet, already swinging out of the saddle. He touched ground while the horse was still in motion, saying, "Jock, we gotta talk!"

"Okay, okay. Come on inside."

With Billy standing beside his father, and the two older men seated in overstuffed leather chairs, Jock said, "Okay, Tom. You look upset. What is it?"

"I'm sure you've heard of that tall, dark guy who calls himself the Stranger?"

"Sure. Who this side of the wide Missouri hasn't? The outlaws and gunslicks fear him, and the lawmen admire and love him. He's got a way of tracking outlaws and catching them like no man I know. Why do you mention him?"

"He's in Phoenix right now. Came in on the stage from Denver today."

"Well, I know Stranger tracks outlaws for Marshal Duvall. In fact, they're close personal friends, from what I've heard. But why's Stranger here?"

"Duvall sent him. Authorized by the big U.S. marshal's office in Washington."

"To do what?"

"Be one of my deputies."

While the marshal gave every detail of the tall man's arrival, young Billy's mind was working. He knew about John Stranger. The man was famous for his "greased lightning" draw, although he had never been known as a gunfighter. It was Stranger who took out the fastest gun in the West—Tate Landry—a couple of years before, over in Lander, Wyoming. If Billy were to beat the man who had outdrawn and killed Landry...

Billy's attention drifted back to the conversation as his father said, "Of course I agree, Tom. With this Stranger—I mean, Brockman—on your staff of deputies, we'd be foolish to carry on business as usual. I'm glad he told you his stay will only be temporary. When he's gone, we'll go back to things as they were."

"If we can," Wall mumbled.

"Hmm?"

"I'm worried, Jock. What if Washington wanted Brockman here because they suspect what's going on? I don't have a good feeling about this."

Hood chuckled. "Come on, now, my friend. Don't let Brockman's presence spook you. It's probably just as he told you. Duvall wanted to send you the best he had available until he can send you a permanent deputy. Don't get an ulcer over it. Just go on and do your job. We'll make plenty more big bucks when Brockman's gone."

For the next several days, Billy Hood made up reasons to be gone from the Bar-H for three and four hours at a time. Each time, he went to the place near the Superstition Mountains east of Phoenix where Tom Wall had secretly schooled him in the fast-draw.

There, he practiced drawing and firing until he surprised himself at how fast and accurate he was. With each practice session, he became more confident that he could outdraw the famous John Stranger.

On May 14, Mark Gray rode about a half-mile west of the Phoenix-Flagstaff Road behind rolling hills and through dense thickets, following a crude map drawn by an old-timer he'd met south of Phoenix. The old man knew where Jock Hood's Bar-H Ranch was, marking it on the map with a shaky "X." It was near a jumble of large rocks and boulders, east of the road.

Gray kept the road in sight periodically, and soon came to the spot the old-timer had described. He led his horse into a ravine near the road to wait until after dark to cross the road onto Jock Hood's spread.

When a pale half-moon peeked over the eastern horizon, Gray led the horse out of the ravine and across the road to the rocks and boulders. He left the horse ground-reined at the base of a huge boulder and climbed up to see if the ranch house was within sight. He smiled when he saw twinkling lights from windows in two buildings that looked to be maybe fifty yards apart. One would be the ranch house, and the other the bunkhouse. He estimated them to be about two miles from where he stood.

He was just turning to descend the boulder when he heard his horse whinny, followed immediately by a sharp voice.

"Hey, *you!* What're you doin' up there?"

At the bottom of the boulder were two dark figures. Gray could make out the rifles in their hands, and they were both pointed at him.

"I...I'm a friend of Jim Carter—I mean Jock Hood's," said Gray. "I've never been here at the ranch before. I was just wantin' to see if the ranch house was visible from the road."

"Take that gun out of your holster, mister," said the heavier of the two men. "Real slow-like. Toss it down here to me."

Gray quickly complied. When the gun was in the man's hand, he said, "All right, come down."

As Gray jumped off the last rock, he said, "I assume you men are with the Bar-H?"

"That's right," said the thinner man. "And we don't cotton to people snoopin' around like you're doin'."

"Look, my name's Mark Gray. You've got the guns, I'm unarmed. Just take me to Jim—Jock—and you'll see that I'm tellin' you the truth. I came here to see him because I need his help. Okay?"

"Let's go," said the heavier one.

Jock Hood and his sons were in the den, discussing a steer that two of the ranch hands had found dead late in the afternoon.

"No question about it," said Harold, "that steer was killed by a cougar. Problem is, he'll probably not move on for a while. He's tasted the blood of Hood cattle, and he knows there are plenty more."

"Then we'll just have to go cougar hunting," said Hood.

"We'll get on it first thing in the morning," Harold assured him.

"Good. I want his hide stretched out on the floor right over there on that bare spot."

"You'll have it, Pa," said Virgil.

The housekeeper, a woman in her early sixties, appeared at the door of the den and looked toward Hood.

"Yes, Hazel?" he said.

"Couple of your sentries caught a man skulking on the property, Mr. Hood. They'd like to bring him in."

"Sure. Send them in."

Hazel turned and moved down the hall.

"Wonder if it's a lawman," said Mason.

"If it is," said Billy, "what're we gonna do with him?"

"Don't cross a bridge till you come to it, son," said Hood. "Let's see if it's a lawman, first."

The sentries appeared at the door. The heavyset one said, "Mr. Hood, we caught this guy snoopin' at the ranch."

As he spoke, he brought Mark Gray into view.

Hood jumped to his feet. "Mark!"

Gray moved toward him, extending his hand. "Jim, it's good to see you!"

While the two were shaking hands, Hood looked at the sentries. "It's all right, boys. He's an old friend."

"Like I told you," said Gray, giving them a wide smile.

"You on a horse, Mark?" asked Hood.

"Yes."

"Take care of his horse, fellas."

"Oh," said Mark, "could I have my gun?"

The big one pulled a revolver from under his belt and handed it to Gray, then said, "Your horse will be in the corral."

"Fine. Thanks."

When the sentries were gone, the Hood brothers gathered around Gray, welcoming him to the Bar-H. When each had shaken his hand, Mark laid a hand on Billy's shoulder and said, "You've really grown up since I saw you last, boy!"

Billy grinned.

"So what brings you here, Mark?" asked Jock, noticing there was no badge on Gray's chest.

"I know you're in the fugitive-hiding business. Found it out through another ex-Ranger."

"Mm-hmm. Are you telling me you're a fugitive? No longer a Ranger?"

"Yeah."

"Are you running from the law?"

"Yeah."

"What did you do?"

"Long story. Shall we sit down?"

When every man had found a seat, Gray told them of his wife's murder by Mexican banditos, the fact that he'd killed the Mexican boy and shot Ranger Jody Sleppy, and everything that had happened after that. "So," he concluded, "I need a place to hide out."

"Well, I know Terrell Sears," said Jock. "Most lawmen would give up when they don't catch their man in a reasonable amount of time. Not Sears. He'll dog your tracks as long as there are tracks to dog."

"How well I know," said Gray. "I was thinkin' maybe we could make it appear that I died."

"Be pretty hard to do that," said Hood. "It'd have to be foolproof, and Sears isn't easy to fool. Let's just hide you real good and let things cool down. Maybe if Sears thinks you've skipped the country, that'll be enough to get him off your back."

"You're the boss," said Gray.

Hood nodded. "I've got several remote ranches where I send men on the dodge...for a price, you understand."

"Oh," said Gray, reaching in his pocket. "What's the fee?"

"Not for an old friend," said Hood. "I was just explaining my operation. I've got several remote ranches where I send fugitives who come to me for help. I'll send you to the L-Bar-S. Rancher friend named Lowell Stanton. He's about forty-five miles north of here in the shadow of the New River Mountains. Stanton will give you refuge in exchange for work. It'll be like you're a hired hand, you just don't get paid any money. He'll feed you and give you shelter, but you'll have to figure out how to come up with your own cash."

"I see. So he'll let me leave the ranch to rob a stagecoach or a bank, eh?"

"Yeah. You just have to be real careful. If you lead the law to the L-Bar-S, he'll deny he knows you, and so will his men. And if the law doesn't punish you, Stanton will. And believe me, you'd rather have the law's punishment. Understand?"

Gray nodded. "I understand. Appreciate your help, Jim. Ah...I mean, Jock."

Hood grinned. "Takes a little getting used to. Anyway, I'll write a letter for you to take to Stanton, and I'll give you a map so's you can find his place. Just present yourself at the gate, tell his men I sent you, and show them the letter. Stanton will welcome you. The letter will explain that you're an old friend. He owes me a favor, so he'll keep you for no charge. Any questions?"

"Only one. How long do you think I should hole up?"

"At least six months. A year would be better. Make Sears think you vanished off the face of the earth."

Mark nodded. "Anything would be better than hangin'."

"That's for sure. You can stay here in the house tonight. We'll feed you breakfast in the morning, then you can be on your way. You'll be safer if you stay in the back country. Don't use the road."

"That's the way I got here."

Hood laughed. "You're a smart man, Mark. You'd make a good outlaw."

"I'm findin' that out," said Gray, chuckling.

"So you're a friend of Jock Hood's, it says here," said the big beefy Lowell Stanton. "How long you known him?"

"Since about five years before he left the Texas Rangers. We did some ridin' after outlaws together."

Stanton laughed. "And now you've both become the kind of guys you used to chase."

"Life has its little changes," said Gray.

They were standing on the front porch of the ranch house. Stanton used his chin to point toward the barn and corral where several men were working, and said, "About half of those guys over there are outlaws, Gray. You'll fit right in."

Gray nodded.

"Did Jock explain that you'll give us a good day's work the same as if you were being paid?"

"Yep."

"And did he tell you the rules about going and coming from the ranch?"

"Yep."

"You understand that it's your neck if you pull a robbery of some kind and you leave a trail the law can follow to this ranch?"

"Jock made that very clear."

"Good. Another rule: No fighting amongst the men on this ranch. Fella that starts a fight will wish he'd never been born. Understood?"

"Yes, sir."

"Okay. Let's put your horse in the corral and take you to the bunkhouse. You can go to work immediately."

"Fine with me," said Gray, feeling a sense of victory already. Terrell Sears and his hounds would never find him here.

Gray was put to work with the men at the barn, who introduced themselves one by one. They knew he was being harbored, and the other outlaws made sure he knew who they were.

The next day, Gray was setting fence posts with another man on the dodge, whose name was Boone McKeever. While they worked, McKeever asked why Gray was running from the law. Gray told his story briefly and spoke his dislike for Captain Sears, saying he would like to catch him alone and make him go for his gun.

McKeever was a tall, lanky man with an evil eye. "I know how it is to want to put a guy six feet under," he said, showing his teeth. "I got one of those, myself. But I sure wouldn't want to brace him in a fast-draw."

"Oh? Some hotshot gunhawk do you wrong?"

"Nobody thinks of him as a gunhawk. He's better known as an outlaw catcher. But he's lightnin' with his gun. You've probably heard of him. They call him the Stranger."

Gray's eyes widened. "You met up with *the* Stranger? *John* Stranger?"

"Yeah," said McKeever, his eyes like flint. "I'd heard about this guy and how fast he was with a gun. Course I didn't know who he was at first."

"What do you mean, 'at first'?"

"Oh. Sorry. I'm gettin' ahead of my story. You see, I robbed the bank in Rock Springs, Wyomin', little over a year ago, and I was comin' out with the moneybag in my hand when the town marshal saw me and started chasin' after me on foot, hollerin' for me to stop. I got a clean shot at him and put a bullet in his heart. I was already a block from the bank *and* from my horse. People were gatherin' around the marshal, and some of the men were pointin' at me. I jumped on the closest horse on the street and took off. I didn't know it then, but at the same time, this John Stranger rode into town at the opposite end of town. He'd been there before, so the people knew who he was. They told him what happened, and that I was gettin' away.

"That lowdown Stranger come after me. Like I said, I didn't know it was the famous John Stranger comin' after me. I figured he must be some kind of lawman, though I'd never seen one dressed all in black before. Anyway, I emptied my gun, tryin' to shoot him outta the saddle. I'm a good shot, Gray, but I couldn't seem to hit him. And ridin' like I was, there was no way to reload. Stranger's got a big black horse that's faster'n anything I've ever seen that didn't have wings. He caught up to me real quick, leaped from his saddle, and took me to the ground. I tried to fight him, but the next thing I knew, I was wakin' up in a jail cell.

"It was then I learned who he was. He came to see me before leavin' town. I was supposed to be hanged in two days for killin' the marshal. He started preachin' Bible stuff to me."

"I've heard he's a preacher," said Gray, sneering.

"Well, I told him I didn't want nothin' to do with that stuff.

He left, sayin' he was sorry for me. Without Jesus I'd go to hell when I died."

"Don't you hate somebody preachin' to you like that?"

"Yeah."

"So, obviously you didn't hang…"

"Nope. Stranger left town, and all they had around there to handle me since the marshal was dead was an old retired sheriff. Well, before they could hang me, I got the best of the old man and made my escape. I knew they'd have a posse after me, or even worse, they might find Stranger and put him on my trail. Friend of mine told me about Jock, so I beelined for Arizona. I found Hood, and he put me with Mr. Stanton. Been here ever since."

"So you hate this John Stranger, since he's the one who ran you down and took you in to be hanged?"

"Yeah. If it had been left up to him, I'd be dead."

"I've heard a lot about this guy," said Gray. "Some say the reason he's so fast with that gun and so tough with his fists is because he isn't human. He seems too clever, too tough, and too good with a gun to be mortal. Not to mention the fact that he's downright indestructible."

McKeever nodded. "I've heard that too since my run-in with him. But if I ever get him in my gun sights when he ain't lookin', I'll find out if he's human. I'll shoot him full of lead and see if he dies!"

While John Brockman was carrying out his duties as a deputy United States marshal, he carefully watched for any sign of outlaws being purposely overlooked when they should have been arrested, or being allowed to escape after being arrested. He even watched for any indication that outlaws were being coddled, in any way, by Wall and his men.

In the days since he'd been in Phoenix, Brockman had been involved in capturing and arresting his share of outlaws who warranted federal attention, and every man who had been arrested had either gone to trial or had it pending. One by one, they would get their just due.

He wondered if Wall was onto him and was keeping things legitimate for now. All he could do was watch the calendar and keep doing his job. If Wall and his men were dirty, as Duvall and the Washington office suspected, in time they would make a mistake. John just hoped it would be before May 20. He'd like to leave, knowing he'd done his job.

At the Bar-H, Jock Hood was giving work instructions to a group of his men near the barn, when he saw Tom Wall ride up.

"When you've finished hauling the hay and putting it in the loft, fellas," he said, "you can go check on that stretch of fence we were talking about."

As the men walked away, Hood turned to Wall. "Come on down, Tom. What can I do for you?"

"You asked me to let you know how things were going with Brockman around."

"Oh, sure. And…?"

"Well, he's beefed up the population of the jail."

"I see. We sure don't need him around here too long. Any word from Duvall about a new man to replace him?"

"Not yet. Course he's only been here a few days. But as nervous as I am with him around, it seems like a month."

"Don't get nervous," said Hood. "That's when you'll make a

mistake. Just stay calm. Soon he'll be gone, and we can get back to normal."

Wall took a deep breath. "I sure hope you're right."

"Anything else?"

"Nope. Just wanted to report, as you requested."

"Fine. Thanks. Now, get back to your job, and stay calm. Got it?"

"I'll do my best."

16

THREE RIDERS SKIRTED THE SOUTHERN EDGE of the Palo Verde hills, with the stiff, hot wind plucking at their hat brims. It was Thursday, May 18, and John Brockman rode northeast toward Phoenix, leading the other two horses. On each horse sat a hard-faced man with his hands cuffed behind his back.

The sun had reached its apex and was on a downward slant, and the wind was coming from the north, blowing hard. A tawny, shifting cloud of sand drifted toward Mexico from beyond the Palo Verdes, but to the north and west it was clear. So clear, that Brockman could see the Mazatzal Mountains beyond Phoenix well enough to distinguish deeply shaded vertical apertures and huge outcroppings of rock.

As they approached the town, John thought of the cool breezes coming off the snow-capped peaks of the Rockies west of Denver, and Breanna came to his mind's eye. "I'll make it, sweetheart," he whispered low enough that his prisoners couldn't hear him. "Just need a little time when Wall's out of town."

They headed up the town's main thoroughfare, which was a wide, dusty street lined with false-fronted clapboard buildings, some new, some old. Even some of the new ones were showing wear from the heat and wind.

John guided his horse to the hitch rail in front of the Maricopa County sheriff's office and was surprised to see Sheriff Howard Fremont emerge with his deputy, Art Winslow, beside him.

"Well, howdy, Sheriff," said Brockman, swinging from his saddle. "I didn't expect to see you yet. Art said you'd be gone another few days."

Fremont stepped off the boardwalk, shook John's hand, and said, "I got my business in California taken care of quicker than I anticipated, John. First thing Art told me when I hit town two hours ago was that you were here, wearing a deputy U.S. marshal's badge. Surprised me a little. 'Specially to learn that you're working for Tom Wall."

"Just filling in till they can come up with a replacement," Brockman said. "Got a couple federal prisoners to lock up in your jail."

"Fine. We take all kinds."

Art Winslow moved toward the outlaws and said, "Let's get them off these horses, and I'll lock them up."

A moment later, as the deputy was ushering the men inside, Fremont said, "Art also told me you've let your real name be known."

"Yes, sir. I guess it's about time. My reasons for keeping it a secret are now in the past."

"Brockman, is it?"

"Yep."

"What caused you to reveal your name?"

John towered over the other man and grinned down at him. "I'm getting married June 4."

"Married! To that little gal you told me about… ah… Deanna, wasn't it?"

"Breanna."

"Oh, yeah. Breanna. You still making Denver your roosting place?"

"I am. That's where Breanna is."

"Oh, of course."

"It was Breanna who brought it up about my name a few weeks ago. Said she could hardly be called Mrs. Stranger, and our children couldn't be called little Strangers. So the name's out."

"How about where you're from? Is that out, too?"

The tall man grinned again. "Nope."

Fremont shrugged. "Oh, well, one out of two ain't bad."

"It's sure good to see you again, Sheriff," said John. "Maybe we can get together while I'm here."

"That won't be long if you're planning to be in Denver before June 4."

"You're right. We'll just have to squeeze it in."

"You name the time."

"Okay. I'll get back to you on it. Right now, I've got to report to the head marshal that I caught the guys he sent me after."

Fremont chuckled. "Don't you always?"

"Well, a few have given me the slip."

"Very few, I'm sure."

"Will you see that these horses are boarded, Sheriff?"

"Sure."

"Thanks. See you soon."

Brockman swung into the saddle for the two-block ride to the U.S. marshal's office. As he nudged the horse forward, Fremont called, "John…!"

John pulled rein and looked over his shoulder. "Yes?"

"Congratulations on your wedding. I think it's time some little gal put a bridle on you."

John gave him a slanted grin and rode up the street.

It was just after twelve o'clock noon when Billy Hood emerged from the big ranch house, picking his teeth with his fingernails. He stepped off the back porch and headed toward the barn.

A blocky figure appeared at the door behind him. "Billy…"

"Yeah?"

"How about picking me up a couple boxes of .45 cartridges while you're in town?"

"Sure, Virg. You can pay me later."

Virgil was listening to a voice from inside the house, and Billy waited until he turned back. "Pa said while you're picking up that medicine from Doc Axton, you should tell him the rash on Pa's leg is still bothering him. Maybe Doc could send some more of that salve."

"I'll tell Doc," said Billy, and moved on to the barn.

Billy trotted his horse into town, tugging at his hat brim to keep the wind from stealing it away. The gun shop would be his first stop. Doc Axton's office was at the other end of town, just past the U.S. marshal's office.

After a few minutes in the gun shop, Billy returned to the street, placed the cartridge boxes in his saddlebags, and swung into the saddle. He was near the main intersection of town when he noted Sheriff Howard Fremont talking to a tall man, dressed in black, in front of his office. Billy's attention was drawn to the low-slung, bone-handled Colt .45 that hung on the man's hip. He wore a badge, but Billy was too far away to make out what kind it was.

The man in black turned and mounted a sorrel gelding. He

rode a few feet, then halted and turned back to look at Fremont, who had called after him. The man grinned at Fremont, then rode away.

Billy observed the man's broad shoulders, and admired the way his back tapered to a slender waist. There was something about him...

Fremont was taking the reins of two horses that stood near the hitch rail when he saw young Hood riding toward him. "Hey, Billy!" he called. "How're things at the Bar-H?"

Billy veered toward him and drew rein. "Things at the Bar-H are just fine, Sheriff. Welcome home."

"Thanks, kid. It's nice to be back."

"Say, Sheriff, that fella you were just talking to...is he the new deputy U.S. marshal? The one they call the Stranger?"

"That's him, Billy. I've known him for some time. One fine man. He's going by his real name now."

"I heard that. Brockman. John Brockman."

"Yep. I hope you can meet him before he leaves town. Job here is only temporary."

"Yeah. I heard that, too. Maybe I'll just stop in at the U.S marshal's office and meet him. See you later."

Billy rode his horse into the second block past the town's main intersection. As he passed the U.S. marshal's office, the door was wide open and he could see Brockman standing at the desk, talking to Deputy Cliff Barnes.

He rode on to the doctor's office and came out a few minutes later with a small paper bag, which he placed in his saddlebags next to the cartridge boxes. He looked back toward the U.S. marshal's office and saw that the door was still open, though he couldn't see inside from that angle.

This is William Ronald Hood's big day, he thought to himself. When he walked away with John "The Stranger"

Brockman lying dead in the dust, he would be among the most admired and feared gunfighters in the West!

Maybe when his father learned who Billy had taken out, he'd be proud of him instead of disown him. And if not, well, he'd just move on and strut his way from town to town and watch men quiver and quail when they learned who he was.

He patted his horse's neck and said, "Be back in a few minutes, boy."

Billy's adrenaline was flowing full charge as he adjusted his gunbelt lower on his hips, pulled a leather thong from his hip pocket, and tied the lower tip of the holster to his thigh, then headed down the dusty street.

When he was in front of the U.S. marshal's office, he stopped six feet from the boardwalk and faced the open door. John Brockman was still standing at the desk with his back toward the street.

Billy made sure the Colt .45 in his holster was sliding easy. He got the attention of people on the street as he shouted at the top of his voice, "Hey! You in the U.S. marshal's office! John Stranger! I'm calling your hand! No matter what they say about your fast-draw, I say you're slower than molasses in January! Come out here and let me prove it!"

Just before Billy Hood had left Sheriff Fremont, Deputy Cliff Barnes looked up from the desk in the outer office as the shadow of a tall man appeared in the open door, momentarily blocking the glare of the sun.

"Well, Deputy Brockman," he said, laying his pencil down, "I'm glad to see you back. Get 'em?"

John moved inside and said, "Yes, I just deposited them in Sheriff Fremont's jail."

"Brought 'em back alive, eh? With those two, I'm surprised you didn't have to shoot it out."

"Would've," John said, "but I got the drop on them."

Barnes eased back in the chair. "You really go to great pains to keep from killing a man, don't you?"

"Whenever I possibly can," replied John, looking around. "Marshal Wall here?"

"No. He and two of the deputies you haven't met took off about three hours ago in pursuit of some outlaws who just robbed the stage from Yuma. Had federal money on it, so it fell on our office to go after them."

Brockman stepped closer to the desk. "Cliff, does anyone other than Marshal Wall handle the arrest records and the reports that go to Washington?"

"Why, no. Marshal Wall feels that's his personal responsibility. But if you have questions regarding the arrests we've had over a period of time, maybe I can answer off the top of my head."

"Well, I'd really like to—"

"Hey! You in the U.S. marshal's office! John Stranger!" came a loud voice from the street.

"What's this?" John said, turning to see who was calling his name.

His gaze focused on a tall, slender, dark-haired young man with his gunbelt slung low and his thumbs hooked in his pants belt.

"I'm calling your hand!" came the loud challenge.

"That's Billy Hood," said Barnes in a half-whisper, rising from the desk.

"Hey!" came the voice from the street. "No matter what they say about your fast-draw, Stranger, I say you're slower than molasses in January! Come out here and let me prove it!"

"So who's Billy Hood, Cliff?" John asked, keeping his gaze on the young man.

"Son of the biggest rancher in these parts—Jock Hood."

"John Stranger!" Billy shouted again. "I see you in there! My name's Billy Hood! Come on out here and square off with me! I say you're overrated! I'm gonna show all these nice people on the street that I'm faster'n you!"

"What're you gonna do, John?" asked Barnes, moving up beside him.

"Go out there and send him home to his mother."

"Can't do that. She's dead."

"Then I'll send him home to his father. Kid's still wet behind the ears."

"What if he draws on you?"

"I'll cross that bridge when I come to it."

As he spoke, Brockman stepped through the door into the hot sunlight. People lined both sides of the street, looking on, some with eager anticipation, others with trepidation. All traffic came to a standstill.

A wolfish grin spread over Billy's mouth when he saw Brockman come through the door. He backed up till he was in the center of the street, motioned with one hand, and said, "C'mon, Stranger! Let's show all these people who's fastest!"

Brockman stepped off the boardwalk, leaving Cliff Barnes in the office doorway, and assessed the young man with steady gray eyes. "You don't want to do this, Billy," he said. "Go on home."

Billy laughed. "I'll go home after I leave you for buzzard bait, mister high-and-mighty John Stranger!"

Someone had alerted Sheriff Fremont, who rushed toward the gathering crowd and bounded off the boardwalk into the street, darting up beside the youthful challenger. "Billy!" he said. "What are you doing? You don't know who you're dealing with, here! That's the man who out-drew and killed Tate Landry!"

"I know," Billy said, keeping his wolf-like eyes on Brockman. "That's why I'm doing what I'm doing."

"You fool! This man has been challenged by experienced gunfighters who thought they'd make a big name for themselves. And they did...on their tombstones! Now, get this foolish idea out of your head and go on home. Besides, you're challenging a deputy United States marshal."

"I didn't know there was a law against that, as long as he's not trying to arrest me and I'm meeting him head-on."

Fremont sighed. "I'm just trying to get you to use your good sense and forget this foolishness. I've never seen you like this before."

"That's because nobody like this Stranger guy has come to our town since I learned how to quick-draw."

"Think of your father and brothers. Why make them stand over your grave and weep because you played the fool?"

"They're not gonna stand over my grave," said young Hood, still keeping his eye on Brockman. "Now, step aside and let us get this on, Sheriff."

"Billy, listen to me. I'm sure John can list a lot more names he's had to face than I know about. But I know that after he was forced to kill Landry, he was challenged by Rick Tatum and Manny Bixler. You know their names, don't you?"

"Yeah."

"Well, they're six feet under because they challenged Stranger. Don't be the next to die at his hand."

Billy's mouth twisted in a devilish grin. "I won't, Sheriff. This is John Stranger's day to die."

Brockman took a couple more steps toward Billy. "Listen,

kid. You're alive and breathing. Let's keep it that way. Believe me, you can't beat me. I've had years of experience. You're still wet behind the ears. Don't force this on me. Just swallow what pride you've built up here in front of these people, and walk away to see another sunset."

Billy pivoted and lined himself to face John parallel with the street. When John turned to meet him, Billy backed up till there was a space of some forty feet between them. He spread his feet apart, taking the gunfighter's stance, and let his hand hover over the butt of his Colt .45.

"Okay, Stranger" he said. "Go for your gun."

Sheriff Fremont shook his head. "Any last words for your father and brothers, Billy?"

"Sure. Tell them I'll be home for supper."

"Look, kid," said Brockman, "I'm begging you to just turn and walk away. Don't make me draw on you."

Billy waggled his head in a cocky manner. "So that's it. You're afraid of me, aren't you? You're a sniveling coward, Stranger."

"He's no coward, Billy," came a voice from the crowd. "No man who faces the likes of Tate Landry, Rick Tatum, and Manny Bixler is a coward. He's just tryin' to keep from killin' you!"

Billy ignored the voice and dug his boots a little deeper in the dust. "Go for your gun, Stranger!" Even as he spoke, Billy's gun hand snaked downward.

Before he could wrap his fingers around the curved handle of his Colt .45, Brockman's gun was out, cocked, and aimed at him.

The kid's face blanched, expecting the hammer to drop and a bullet to rip into his chest. For a moment, he froze with his hand touching his gun.

"You're still alive, kid," said Brockman. "Keep it that way. There's a thin line between life and death. You're very close to that line. Don't cross it."

Billy clawed for his gun, screaming, *"I'll kill you!"*

Before he cleared leather, John Brockman's Peacemaker roared. The bullet struck young Hood where his gun arm joined the shoulder. The impact of the slug knocked him flat.

Sheriff Fremont got to Billy first and knelt beside him. "Somebody get Doc Axton!" he yelled.

"I'm right here, Sheriff," said the doctor, hurrying toward him from the crowd.

Brockman hunkered down to find the kid clutching his bleeding shoulder and clenching his teeth in pain as the town's physician drew up and knelt on Billy's other side. The doctor moved Billy's hand from the wound and began ripping away his shirt.

"He could've killed you just as easily, Billy," said Fremont. "You ought to be thankful he didn't, and you ought to realize how foolish you were to challenge him."

Young Hood glared at Brockman. "I'll work on my fast-draw some more, Stranger," he hissed through clenched teeth. "I'll track you wherever you are and make you draw against me. I'll kill you yet!"

"You'll have to do it with your left hand, Billy," said Axton.

"Huh?" Billy swerved his gaze to the doctor. "What are you talking about, Doc?

"Mr. Brockman's bullet tore up your shoulder joint and shattered the clavicle. You'll have trouble with that shoulder for the rest of your life. I doubt you'll ever use a shovel or a pitch-fork again, and for sure you'll never be able to draw a gun with any speed or accuracy. He did you a favor, Billy. You'll never die trying to outdraw some gunhawk who wouldn't have mercy on you, as he did."

Billy's eyes closed and he gritted his teeth, breathing hard.

"Let's carry him to my office," said Axton. "I've got to get the slug out of his shoulder, clean out the bone fragments, and patch him up."

Billy Hood gave John Brockman a venomous look as four men picked him up and carried him away.

"The kid still doesn't realize what you did for him, John," Cliff Barnes said, as he and John returned to the U.S. marshal's office.

"Maybe he will someday," John said quietly.

Cliff paused at the desk. "Now where were we before all of that started?"

"We were discussing the monthly arrest reports."

"Oh, yes. Is there some question I can answer for you?"

"Well, just before we were interrupted, I was about to say that I'd like to see copies of the reports Marshal Wall has sent to Washington in the past nine months."

John watched Cliff Barnes's eyes closely as he made this request, but he could see no sign of alarm or agitation.

"That shouldn't be a problem," the deputy replied. "They're kept over here in this filing cabinet." Cliff led John to the files. "These drawers are kept locked, but I know where the marshal keeps the keys. Be right back."

The deputy went into a small cabinet and returned with a key in his hand. "Why do you want to see these?" he asked, as he unlocked the drawer that held the designated reports.

John looked the deputy square in the eye. "I was sent here by Chief Solomon Duvall because the Washington office has reason to believe Marshal Wall has made false arrest reports."

Cliff's eyes widened and his mouth dropped open. "Why would he do that?"

"I really don't have all the particulars as to why they suspect him, but I was sent here to find out if he's guilty."

"Oh, I hope not," said the deputy, trying hard to swallow, but finding his mouth suddenly dry.

"Mind if I take the reports and sit down at the desk?" asked John. "Be easier to go through them."

"Go right ahead. I'll finish what I was doing."

John thumbed through the drawer and pulled out the reports that covered the past nine months and went through them slowly, taking a little more than an hour. When he had scanned the latest report, he stood up and said, "Be back in a few minutes."

"Where are you going?"

"To my hotel room. I have copies of the reports Wall sent to Washington. Now that I've familiarized myself with these reports, I want to compare the two sets."

No more than fifteen minutes had passed before John returned, carrying a slender briefcase. Cliff watched him as he sat down and began to compare the reports one by one. After a few minutes, John chose three out of six sets, and said, "Take a look, Cliff."

A few seconds later, Cliff's face turned pale, and he seemed to shrink within himself. "John, I—I can't believe what I'm seeing here. He's been making up outlaws who don't exist, saying we've arrested them, and then he's falsified court trials, prison sentences, and executions. John, these reports are out-and-out lies!"

"You know what he's been doing, then, don't you?"

"Sure. He's looked the other way when men should have

been arrested and weren't. To make things look normal to Washington, he's made up arrests that never happened. He's probably getting paid by the outlaws he's helping. I can't think of any other reason to do it."

"Do you think any of the other deputies are in it with him, Cliff?"

"No. They're not in the office that much. If anybody could've been a partner with Wall, it would be me. And I assure you, this comes as a total surprise."

John smiled. "I believe you, Cliff."

The stunned deputy eased back on his chair. "So what's next?"

"I want to check his bank account. See what kind of money he keeps in it."

"Can you do that?"

John tapped his briefcase, and said, "With the authorization papers I have in here from the U.S. Marshal's office in Washington, the bank will tell me anything I want to know. Which bank does Wall deal with?"

"Maricopa Bank."

When John Brockman and Cliff Barnes came out of the Maricopa Bank, Cliff said, "Everything's normal here. What now?"

"We'll check the other banks in town. He might have been putting his crooked money in one or more of those."

When they came out of the fourth bank, Cliff said, "Okay, so he's made deposits that far exceed his salary in each and every one of these last three banks. Is that enough to make an arrest, along with the falsified reports?"

John nodded as he said, "More than enough."

17

WESTERN UNION
May 18, 1871
Chief U.S. Marshal Solomon Duvall
Office of United States Marshal
Federal Building
Denver Colorado Territory

Have the goods on Wall STOP He is out of town STOP Will arrest upon his return unless past May 20 STOP You must appoint new head of this office STOP

John Brockman Deputy U.S. Marshal out of Denver Office

"Yes!" Solomon Duvall said, shaking the yellow telegram in a victory sign. "I knew you'd do it, John!"

WESTERN UNION
May 18, 1871
Deputy U.S. Marshal John Brockman
Office of United States Marshal
Phoenix Arizona Territory

Excellent work STOP Deputy Clifford Barnes hereby appointed interim U.S. marshal STOP Arrest and jail Wall if still in Phoenix upon his arrival STOP Otherwise Barnes do same STOP Duvall will leave for Phoenix tomorrow STOP Will carry out prosecution of Wall and establish new permanent head of Phoenix office STOP

Solomon Duvall Chief U.S. Marshal
Western District

John Brockman stood by the desk, looking down at Cliff Barnes. "Cliff, if Wall shows up before Saturday, we'll nail him together. If not, as you see in the telegram, it'll be on your shoulders. Of course, the deputies who are with him aren't going to understand. If you've got others in town by then, show them the proof of what we've found and let them help you make the arrest."

"I just hope he gets back here before you leave," said Cliff.

"Be all right with me. But right now, I've got to send Duvall another wire."

WESTERN UNION
May 18 1871
Chief U S Marshal Solomon Duvall
Office of United States Marshal
Federal Building
Denver Colorado Territory

Regarding your wire about coming to Phoenix STOP Reminding the chief that he is to be best man at wedding June 4 STOP Not enough time to come here and return by June 4 STOP

John Brockman Deputy U.S. Marshal out of Denver Office

Duvall read the telegram and said to the telegrapher, "Send one back. Tell John I'm still leaving for Phoenix tomorrow morning. I can clean up the mess, appoint a permanent marshal as head of the office, and be back in Denver by June first or second."

"I'll get right on it, Chief," said the telegrapher.

John Brockman pushed his flat-crowned black hat to the back of his head as he read Duvall's last telegram. "Well, I hope he's right, Cliff."

"What if he isn't? What'll you do if your best man isn't there?"

John folded the telegram and shook his head. "Don't even think it, Cliff. He's *got* to be there."

Dr. Lloyd Axton was careful to guide the buggy over as few bumps as possible as he drove Billy Hood to the Bar-H Ranch. Billy's horse was tied behind. The boy sat hunched over, not speaking, as he held the arm that was in a sling. He hadn't spoken since they left town.

"Billy," Doc said, "remember now, I want to check your arm and change the bandage on Monday. Don't try riding in on your horse. Have your father or one of your brothers bring you in."

Billy didn't answer. But when the buggy hit an unavoidable bump, he let out a howl.

"Sorry, kid," Doc said, grunting from the jolt. "I'll give you some more powders to help ease the pain as soon as we get you in bed."

Still Billy said nothing. Hatred for John Brockman was festering within him.

When they drew near the tall rock formation amid the jumbled boulders, they saw two Bar-H cowboys with rifles in hand move from the shade at the base into the sunlight. Doc recognized them as Bus Kendrick and Amos Trapp.

"Howdy, Bus…Amos," he said.

"What happened to Billy, Doc?" asked Amos.

"Got himself shot."

"How'd that happen?"

"Gunslinger named John Stranger shot me," said Billy in a strained voice.

Bus looked at Billy in disbelief. "Stranger? You mean the one that took out Tate Landry?"

"Yeah, that's him."

"Fellas, Billy can tell you the story later," said Doc. "Right now, he's in a lot of pain. I need to get him to his pa and brothers, and into bed."

"Doc, Mr. Hood and his sons took off about an hour ago for Jack Wasson's ranch up by Prescott. Wasson sent a rider down to invite Mr. Hood and his boys to some kind of big gathering. Mr. Hood said to tell Billy to come on up if he wanted to. Otherwise he'd see him late Sunday afternoon."

"Guess I won't be going, Amos," Billy said through clenched teeth.

"Guess not, kid. You go on and let Doc get you bedded down."

As the buggy moved across the rolling land toward the ranch house, Trapp scratched his head. "Bus, how in the world did Billy get himself shot by that Stranger guy?"

Bus shook his head, then said, "My question is *why* would Stranger shoot a wet-nosed kid like Billy?"

Midmorning on Friday, May 19, John Brockman and Cliff Barnes were in the U.S. marshal's office when Tom Wall and two deputies rode up and dismounted.

"Here we go, John," said Barnes, pointing out the window as he got up from the desk. "I'm sure glad they got back before you had to leave."

"Better this way, I'm sure," said John, rising from the chair in front of the desk. "You be ready for whatever happens when I tell him he's under arrest."

"I'd rather be fishing a clear mountain stream," said Barnes.

"What's these other fellas' names?"

"The taller one is Brad Hines. Short one is Monte McAndrews."

John nodded. "Okay, Cliff…normal face."

Marshal Wall, who entered the office ahead of his deputies, ran his gaze from Cliff to John. "They got away," he said.

"It happens, Marshal," said Cliff.

"How goes it? Anything exciting happen around here?"

"Pretty quiet," John said. Then, turning to the deputies, "Well, let's see now, which one of you is Deputy Brad Hines?"

"Oh, sorry," said Wall. "This is Hines." John shook the deputy's hand. "And this is Deputy Monte McAndrews."

While Brockman and McAndrews shook hands, Tom Wall looked toward the desk, where the arrest reports lay in plain sight. "Ah…Cliff?"

"Yes, sir?"

"What are those reports doing on the desk?"

"If you'll look close," John said, "you'll see another set of reports right beside them. They are copies of the ones you've been sending the Washington office for the past nine months."

Wall's whole body stiffened.

"They don't match," said Brockman. "But then, you already know that."

"Marshal, what's he talking about?" asked McAndrews.

"Mr. Wall can tell you if he wants to, gentlemen," said Brockman.

When Tom's hand moved toward his gun, John looked him in the eye and said, "Don't do that, Tom. Just take it out slowly and hand it to me. You're under arrest."

Hines and McAndrews stood with their mouths gaping open.

"Cliff, what is this?" demanded McAndrews. "What's he talking about? How can he arrest the marshal?"

"By authority of Chief U.S. Marshal Solomon Duvall," replied Barnes. "Mr. Wall, here, has been falsifying arrest reports to Washington. The proof lies before you."

Both men looked at Wall, whose face had lost all color. His voice was tight as he said, "I...I had to do it, John. These gangs will shoot a lawman in the back if he doesn't do what they tell him. It was to save my life, I—"

"Save your life," Brockman said, "or fill your pockets?"

"Now, look, I never took any money. No, sir, I—"

"Stop lying, Tom! Your bank accounts tell a different story."

Wall sighed as he eased his gun out of its holster. He handed it butt-first to Brockman.

Cliff Barnes glanced at Hines and McAndrews, who were still in shock. "You two look like I did yesterday," he said.

Finally Hines found his voice. "Another tarnished badge," he said in disgust.

"Always makes the good lawmen look bad, too," said McAndrews.

Wall looked everywhere but at his deputies.

"Chief Duvall's on his way down here," said Brockman. "He'll take care of appointing a new marshal. And he'll begin the prosecution process for Mr. Wall. Let's take him down to the jail, Cliff."

The Denver-bound stage stood ready to go on Saturday morning, May 20. Driver and shotgunner were just loading the last of the luggage. An elderly couple would be riding with John Brockman as far as Durango, Colorado.

Cliff Barnes stood near the door inside the stage office and watched John buy a copy of the *Phoenix Sun* from the agent. The front-page headlines read: *U.S. MARSHAL THOMAS J. WALL INDICTED FOR CONSPIRACY WITH OUTLAWS!*

"Well, I guess you can read all about it on the trip, John," said Cliff.

"I already know more than I want to," he replied, chuckling. He ran his gaze down the page. Near the bottom were small bold lines that read: *Apaches on Warpath! Bloodshed at Fort McFarland!* "Guess I'll read about the Apaches instead," he said.

"Okay, folks," said the driver, standing at the open door of the stagecoach. "We're ready to go!"

Cliff extended his hand. "Thanks for everything, John," he said. "You made my job a lot easier."

"Glad I could." John paused, then said, "I have a feeling you'll be the man to wear the marshal's badge here. Chief

Duvall seems to have a lot of confidence in you."

"If he offers it to me, I'll take it. I hope you have a wonderful wedding and a happy life with that beautiful lady!"

"Thanks. Maybe I'll see you again sometime."

"I wouldn't doubt it. Who knows? Maybe you'll be appointed chief U.S. marshal of the western district when Solomon Duvall retires. Then I'll have to answer to *you.*"

John laughed. "No way! I'd rather ride a horse than a desk."

Phoenix had barely passed from view when John adjusted his long legs to give more room to the older couple sitting across from him. They were holding hands. John liked that. He figured they had to be well into their seventies, maybe even their eighties.

He thought of Breanna and the wedding, and told himself that if God let him and Breanna live as long as this couple, they would keep the romance in their marriage, too.

He smiled at the couple, and said, "Well, folks, I guess we ought to get acquainted. My name is John Brockman."

The silver-haired man smiled back. "A lawman, I see. My eyes ain't so good that I can make out the lettering, but I can tell that's a badge on your shirt."

"Oh. Yes. Of course." John had forgotten to remove the deputy U.S. marshal's badge.

"Anyway," said the old gentleman, "my name is Hosea Cordell, and this is my wife, Ella Mae."

John touched his hat brim. "Ma'am...sir. Glad to make your acquaintance."

"It's nice to meet you, too, young man," said Ella Mae. Her hair was a shiny silver, and her eyes were bright. John thought how lovely she was. Though the years had lined her face, they had not stolen her beauty.

"I like the name *Hosea,"* said John. "A man by that name in the Bible was quite a prophet."

"That he was," said Cordell. "I'm honored my parents gave me his name. Course *John* was a pretty good Bible name, too. I like 'em both—John the Baptist and John the Apostle."

The tall man smiled. "Hard to pick a favorite between those two. Both of them certainly exalted the Lord Jesus Christ."

"Honey," Hosea said to Ella Mae, "I have a feeling we just might be sitting in the presence of another child of God."

The stage was rocking and swaying, leaving a cloud of dust on the road behind them.

"You sure are," said John. "I've been born again by the Spirit of God and washed in the blood of the Lamb!"

There was an immediate kinship between John and the Cordells. They exchanged testimonies about the joy of walking with Christ.

As the stage rolled on, John picked up the newspaper he'd purchased at the stageline office and began reading.

"Terrible about that U.S. marshal," said Ella Mae.

"Yes," said John. "Always hurts the name of the law when a lawman goes bad."

"You knew him?" asked Hosea.

"Yes, sir. Real shame."

John scanned the Tom Wall story on the front page, then let his eyes drop to the article about the Apache Indians and Fort McFarland, which was about fifty miles southeast of Phoenix. When he turned to page three for the rest of the article, Ella Mae's eyes picked up on the bold print about the Apache story.

"Mr. Brockman...?"

John lowered the paper. "Yes, ma'am?"

"What's that about the Apaches being on the warpath? Does that say something about Fort McFarland?"

"I'm reading the story right now, ma'am," he said. "Yes, there was an attack on Fort McFarland. Many soldiers were killed and wounded, as were many of the Apache warriors. I'll tell you the whole story when I finish, or you're welcome to read it for yourself."

"We'll just let you tell it to us," said Hosea.

John continued to read, and it wasn't long before the Cordells fell asleep.

After three hours of travel from Phoenix, the stage rolled in to a small settlement near Towers Mountain. The Cordells were still asleep, but they stirred awake as the coach came to a dusty stop in front of the stage office. The passengers stretched their legs while a fresh six-up team was hitched to the stage, and soon they were on their way again, winding through the mountainous forests toward Flagstaff.

As the old couple settled on the seat once again, Hosea said, "You finish reading about the 'Paches, Mr. Brockman?"

"Yes, sir. About two hours before we made the stop, but you two were sleeping so soundly, I didn't want to wake you."

"'Preciate that. But now that we're awake, what's the story? I don't like to hear about 'Paches puttin' on war paint."

"Me, either," said Ella Mae.

"You folks ever hear of an Apache sub-chief named Gardano?"

Both nodded solemnly.

"Bad one," said Hosea. "Real bad. He works under the most vicious war chief in Arizona—Dogindo."

"Well, a few days ago, Gardano and five of his warriors attacked a rancher and his family over on the east side of the Superstition Mountains. They killed every member of the family and were setting the house and barn on fire when a patrol unit out of Fort McFarland happened along. They surrounded the

Apaches, disarmed them, and took them to the fort as prisoners."

"Oh, boy," said Hosea. "That would stir Dogindo's wrath, I'll guarantee you."

Brockman nodded. "It did. Article says that Dogindo and three dozen warriors showed up at the fort the next day, demanding the release of Gardano and the other five warriors. Colonel Clyde Westerman, the fort's commandant, flat refused, saying Gardano and his men must be punished for what they had done. Dogindo became very angry and warned Westerman that he would attack the fort unless his six men were released. Still, Westerman refused. So the next day, Dogindo went against the fort with about a hundred and fifty warriors. The army repelled them, but not until ten soldiers were killed, some sixteen or seventeen wounded, and at least a dozen Apaches were killed."

Ella Mae shook her head and made a clicking sound against her teeth. "When will all this bloodshed stop?" she asked.

"Not until the Indians are subdued and kept on reservations, dear," said Hosea. "Or not until us white folks can't take it any more and go back where we came from."

"That about sums it up," said John.

"So what's going on now?" asked the old man.

"All-out warfare in the Fort McFarland area. Dogindo has attacked the fort two more times. The last attack was the day before yesterday. Westerman's troops have held fast so far, and they still have Gardano and his men. If we weren't heading north—away from the troubled area—this stage wouldn't be running without an army escort."

The passengers and crew of the Denver-bound stagecoach spent the night at a way station some twenty miles west of Flagstaff. The next morning they were up and on the road by five-thirty.

It was midafternoon when the driver shouted, "Here comes the other Denver stage, folks!"

John stuck his head out the window and caught sight of Solomon Duvall's face in the rear window as they met and passed. He waved just as Duvall saw him and waved back.

Ella Mae fanned dust from in front of her face and asked, "You know the driver of that stage, Mr. Brockman?"

"No, ma'am. I was waving to a passenger. Friend of mine. I happened to know he was going to be on the stage from Denver."

"I see," she said, patting her husband's hand. "Hear that, Hosea? Mr. Brockman saw a friend of his on that stage we just met."

Hosea's eyelids were drooping sleepily, but he let a smile curve his lips. "That's nice, dear," he said, his head bobbing.

Ella Mae looked at John and shrugged.

Late in the afternoon of May 23, the stage pulled up in front of the Wells Fargo station in Denver. Two young men, who had ridden the stage since Durango, stepped out to meet friends. As they alighted, John looked through the window and saw his bride-to-be standing beside Dr. Goodwin's wagon. He quickly stepped out of the stagecoach and headed toward her.

Breanna gave him a bright smile as she dashed up to him and said, "Oh, darling, I'm so glad you're back!"

He kissed her tenderly. "Me, too."

"I saw Chief Duvall on the morning he left, John," said Breanna. "He told me you'd wrapped it all up—as far as you could go, at least."

"That's right. My only concern now is whether he'll be back in time for the wedding."

"I mentioned that to him," said Breanna, "but he told me not to worry."

Breanna's eyes were dancing as they headed for the buggy. She gripped his arm and said, "I'm so excited! Would you...would you like to see the house?"

"I sure would!"

As Breanna took John through their new house, he was amazed at what a beautiful job she had done. They finished the tour, standing in the front yard by the porch, and watched the sun turn the jagged peaks of the Rockies aflame.

John folded Breanna into his arms, kissed the tip of her nose, and said, "You've done a terrific job with the house and yard. They're beautiful."

"Nothing but the best for the most handsome and wonderful man in the world," she replied.

John cupped her chin, and said, "As long as I can keep you thinking that, I'll be happy."

He helped her into the buggy, then climbed in and picked up the reins, clucking to the horse to head back toward town.

"So what about your wedding dress?" John asked, as she sat close to him, holding onto his arm.

"Dottie finished it two days ago. It's beautiful. She did such a wonderful job!"

John gave her a crooked grin and said, "I want to see it."

"John! What are you talking about? You're not going to see that dress until I wear it a week from Sunday!"

He laughed, put an arm around her, and hugged her to him.

18

HAZEL CRUMPTON OPENED the bedroom door and looked in on young Billy. It was late Sunday afternoon, and he had been sleeping for some three hours after taking the powders Dr. Axton had given him.

Hazel closed the door, and as she walked toward the kitchen, she heard horses' hooves and male voices. Hazel felt a pang of dread. She wished someone else was there to give Jock Hood the bad news about Billy.

Her heart quickened as the four men mounted the steps and crossed the porch. She waited till they came through the door, then stepped up and said, "Welcome home, Mr. Hood ...boys."

"Sure hope you've got something real good on the stove, Hazel," Mason said.

"And plenty of it," Virgil said.

Hazel forced a smile, trying to cover her nervousness, and said, "You're having Hazel's beef stew. And I've made plenty."

"Good!" said Jock. "Billy on the place?"

"Why, ah...yes," she replied, avoiding eye contact.

Jock took off his hat, squinted at her, and said, "Something wrong, Hazel?"

"Well, yes, sir. You see...well, it's Billy, Mr. Hood. He—"

"What's wrong? What about Billy?"

"He...he's been shot, sir."

"Shot!"

"Yes, sir."

The brothers looked stunned.

"Where is he?" demanded Jock, throwing his hat on a chair.

"In his bed."

"How bad is it? Where's the wound?"

"In his shoulder, sir. His life's not in danger."

"At least we can be thankful for that," said Virgil. "Is he awake?"

"He's sleeping right now," she replied.

Jock scowled. "Who shot him? How'd it happen? Has Doc Axton seen him?"

"The shooting took place in town, sir. Dr. Axton was there. He took Billy to his office and removed the bullet. He had him all bandaged up and his arm in a sling when he brought him home. He left powders to give Billy for his pain. That's what's got him sleeping right now."

"Which shoulder?"

"The right one."

Jock looked at his other sons. "His good arm."

"I can't give you much in the way of details, Mr. Hood," Hazel said. "But the man who shot Billy is somebody they call the Stranger."

"What?"

"That's what the doctor said, sir. Do you know the man?"

"I know *of* him. He's a gunfighter of sorts. Faster'n a rattler's tongue. Why would that lowdown skunk shoot my boy?"

"I really don't know, Mr. Hood," said Hazel. "But..."

Jock's gaze locked on her face. "But *what?"*

"There's something I haven't told you yet."

"Well, what is it?"

"Doc says Billy's arm and shoulder will never be the same again. He'll probably never be able to use a pitchfork or a shovel."

Hood's face darkened. "You mean he'll be a cripple? He won't be able to use his arm?"

"I'm afraid that's it, sir. Dr. Axton can give you the details. He said something about the arm being shattered at the shoulder joint."

Hood's eyes sparkled and his lips thinned. *"Stranger,"* he said, as if the name tasted bitter on his tongue. "Dirty scum. Billy's just a kid. Why would a man who's been through countless gunfights want to harm an innocent boy?"

"Well, let's just go into town and ask him, Pa," said Harold. "There are four of us. There's only one of him."

"Ask him? We're gonna *kill* the skunk!"

Mason looked at the housekeeper. "Hazel, you said Doc Axton was there and took Billy to his office. Did Doc say if he saw the shooting?"

"No, he didn't."

"Why you asking that, Mason?" Harold asked.

"Well, I thought before we go after this Stranger…er…we ought to find out more about the shooting."

"We can talk to Doc," said Hood. "But no matter what he tells us, Stranger shot and crippled your kid brother, and that makes him a dead man."

"You want to go now, Pa?" Virgil asked.

"Sure. But I'd like to see Billy first."

Billy was still asleep when Jock and his other sons tiptoed into the bedroom. They stood over him for a few minutes, then Jock motioned toward the door.

When they stepped into the hall, his features were livid. "Let's go," he said in a half-whisper. "We're gonna find that scum and ambush him tonight!"

Doctor Axton answered the knock at his door and held up a lantern to see who was on his porch.

"Oh, hello, Jock...boys," he said pleasantly. "I guess you've been home."

"Yeah," said Jock, "and we'd like to know if you saw the shooting."

"Yes, I did."

"Good. Then please tell me why Stranger shot my boy."

"It was Billy's fault, Jock."

The Hoods looked as if the doctor had slapped their faces.

"What are you saying?" demanded Jock.

"I'm saying that Billy's the one who challenged Stranger—whose real name is John Brockman, by the way—to draw on him. Saw it with my own eyes, and so did about two hundred other people."

"Why would the kid do that, Doc? He knows Brockman, as you say, is considered to be the fastest gun in the West."

"That's the point. Your boy figured he could out-draw the man."

Jock looked at his three sons. "Any of you boys ever get the idea Billy wanted to be a gunfighter?"

All three agreed they'd seen no sign of that.

"Well, I won't dispute what you're telling me, Doc," said Hood, "but an experienced gunfighter like Brockman could've kept a green kid like Billy from drawing on him."

"He tried, Jock," said Axton. "But Billy went for his gun and forced it. Brockman didn't have a choice."

Hood's face flushed. "Doc, from what Hazel said, Billy's right arm will never be the same. That lowdown scum crippled my boy for life!"

"That's true," Axton said with a nod. "But keep this in mind...Brockman could have killed the kid. He hits what he shoots at."

"Yeah? Then why didn't he just wing him? Why did he have to destroy his right arm?"

"So Billy wouldn't challenge another gunfighter somewhere down the road and get himself killed."

"Well, I'm just gonna have me a talk with Mr. Brockman about that," Jock said.

"You'll have to shout pretty loud," said Axton.

"What do you mean?"

"Brockman left on the stage to Denver yesterday morning."

"You mean he isn't coming back to Phoenix?"

"Not any time soon that I know of."

Jock thought for a moment, then said, "Well, thanks for taking care of the boy, Doc. Send me your bill."

"You can pick it up when you bring Billy in tomorrow so I can look at the wound and change the bandage. Or whoever brings him can pick up the bill. I told Billy not to ride in by horse."

"We'll have him here tomorrow," said Jock.

Hood and his sons swung into their saddles and rode through town. "We're gonna kill Brockman," Hood said. "There's no way we can catch that stage now. But some time, some day, we're gonna find a way to kill that lowdown scum."

On Thursday morning, June 1, Deputy U.S. Marshal Alex Stone—who was in charge of the Denver office in Chief

Duvall's place—had just sat down at his desk when there was a tap on his door.

"Come in."

The door opened to reveal the tall figure of John Brockman. "Sorry to bother you, Alex," said John, "but have you heard from him?"

"No. But didn't he tell you in his wire he'd be back June first or second?"

"Yes."

"Well, he'll probably be on the stage today from Phoenix, or certainly on tomorrow's."

"I'd really like to know. It's getting awfully close to Sunday. Think I'll go on over to Western Union and send a wire to Cliff Barnes in Phoenix. See if the chief is on today's stage."

It was midmorning when John Brockman rode Ebony into the Goodwin yard and greeted Martha Goodwin, who was working in her flower garden.

"I can imagine you're getting awfully excited, aren't you, John?" said Martha, pausing in her work.

"Sure am," he said, not showing the concern he was carrying in his heart.

As he dismounted in front of Breanna's cottage, she came outside, having seen him ride up. "What did you find out, darling?" she asked.

"Doesn't look good, honey."

"What do you mean?" She studied his gunmetal gray eyes.

"Well, when I asked Alex if he'd heard anything, he said he hadn't, but he figured Sol would be on today's stage, or certainly on tomorrow's."

"Yes...?"

"I went to Western Union to send a wire to the Phoenix office. The telegrapher told me the line has been down for several days. As I told you, the Apaches are on the warpath down there, and it appears they've cut the telegraph lines. There's been no contact with the Phoenix Western Union office for six days."

"No wonder we haven't heard."

"Well, there's more. I went to Wells Fargo to see if I could find out if Sol's stage had made it to Phoenix. I told you I'd seen him on the stage as we passed."

"Yes."

"So I asked the agent if he knew if the chief got off the stage in Phoenix. The driver of that particular stage happened to be there, and he said the chief got off the stage with the other passengers."

"Well, that's good," said Breanna. "Then you know he got there all right."

"But I was just coming out of the Wells Fargo office when the telegrapher called after me and said he'd just made contact with their Phoenix office. So I had him tap out a message, asking the Phoenix man to go to the U.S. marshal's office and see if the chief was there. Cliff Barnes said he never showed up."

"Sol never showed up?"

"That's right. Barnes has been trying to get a wire through to us to see what happened, and why the chief never got there."

"Oh, John. Something's happened to him!"

"Had to. Right there in Phoenix...between the Wells Fargo station and the U.S. marshal's office."

"Does Alex know?"

"I stopped by and told him. He said he'd wire the Washington office and advise them that Chief Duvall is missing. And—"

"There's Alex, now," said Breanna, looking beyond John.

Deputy Stone came trotting up on his horse. "Hello, Miss Breanna," he said as he drew rein. Then to John, "I just got a wire back from Washington. They said President Grant will be notified as soon as he returns to Washington from Illinois. He's en route by rail right now."

"I'm sure the president will do something right quick," said John. "Let me know of any further developments, okay?"

"Sure will, John," Stone said, turning the horse about. He paused and said, "I know Chief Duvall is a very close friend of yours. I'm sorry for the burden this puts on you."

"I appreciate that," said John. "Keep me posted."

Stone nodded and rode away.

John took Breanna by the hand. "Honey, let's go in the house and pray."

Together, John and Breanna prayed for Solomon Duvall, asking God to protect him, wherever he was, and to let him be found soon. After they had prayed, Breanna said, "What about the wedding?"

"We'll go ahead as planned."

"But who will you ask to be your best man?"

"Well, there are a few men in town who are close enough friends to ask. There's Curt Langan…and Steve Ridgway, for example. But I'm going to ask your brother-in-law."

"Oh, Matt will be thrilled!"

"Do you suppose it'd be all right if I go to the hospital right now and talk to him?"

"Of course. He might be in surgery, or he might be tied up in a dozen other ways, but it's worth a shot."

"Okay. See you in a little while."

An hour later, Breanna stepped out onto the porch to meet John as he rode up. "Well?" she said.

John smiled as he dismounted. "It was like you said, sweetheart. Matt's thrilled to be my best man."

"Wonderful!" she said, moving into his arms. "Oh, John, we both love Sol, and we've entrusted him to the Lord's hands. We can't let his absence put a damper on our wedding."

"Of course not," John said. "It's going to be a wonderful day! Just think of it, the most beautiful and wonderful woman in all the world will be my wife!"

On Saturday, June 3, Mark Gray was feeling confined, and decided he needed to get off the *L-Bar-S* Ranch.

Lowell Stanton nodded when Mark made the request. "Sure, Mark. I understand. But you be plenty careful. Don't go near a town. Just ride across the desert or into one of the forests."

"Well, Mr. Stanton, I was sort of thinkin' of ridin' into that little town called Bumble Bee."

"Best not to."

"Tell you what, boss," said Boone McKeever, who stood with Gray. "I'll ride along with Mark. Make sure he stays away from town."

"Good," said the rancher. "Don't stay gone too long."

As the two outlaws rode across the sun-bleached hills, McKeever veered his mount toward the nearby forest.

"Uh…Boone," said Gray.

"Yep?"

"I'd really like to see that Bumble Bee."

"We told Mr. Stanton we'd stay away from there."

"Aw, c'mon. It won't hurt anything. We won't dismount. We'll just ride through, quiet-like, then go on to the forest. How about it?"

Boone chuckled. "Oh, all right. But that's all we'll do. Just ride through."

"Good enough."

Thirty minutes later, they rode slowly into Bumble Bee.

"A town!" said Mark. "It's so good to see a town!"

As they drew near the center of the small town, Boone said softly from the side of his mouth, "Don't look sudden-like, Mark, but the town marshal is standin' in front of his office. I just noticed his badge."

"S'pose we ought to turn around? I never figured on this."

"Too late. He's spotted us. We turn around now, he'll suspect somethin'. Just keep your pace. Smile at him if he looks directly at you."

"Okay."

There was little traffic on the wide street. The town was small enough that strangers were easily spotted. Mark's heart skipped a beat as the marshal stepped off the board sidewalk into the street, angling toward them.

"Howdy, gents," he said, expecting them to stop.

Mark saw the marshal's name on the sign above the office door: Dan Thornton. He smiled amiably, and said, "Mornin', Marshal Thornton."

Boone did the same.

"How'd you know my name?" Thornton said.

Mark chuckled, pointing to the sign above the door.

"Oh yeah!" the marshal said, and laughed. "Sometimes I forget about the sign. You gentlemen just passing through?"

McKeever said they were from a ranch south of Phoenix and were on their way for a short visit with a friend in Flagstaff.

"Nice town, Marshal," said Gray. "Seems quiet enough."

"Yes, and that's the way I like it," Thornton said, adjusting his hat brim. "*Real* quiet."

"Don't blame you. For your sake, I hope it stays that way."

"Well, we'd better be goin', pal," McKeever said. "Bye, Marshal.

"So long," said Thornton, as two elderly men strolled up to him. He watched the strangers ride away while the old men tried to get his attention.

An hour later, Thornton was sitting at his desk, his thoughts returning to the two riders. There's something about that dark one, he said to himself. Something...wait a minute! I know who he was!

"You sent for me, Cap'n?" asked Sergeant Jody Sleppy on entering the Texas Ranger office in El Paso.

"Yeah, Jody," replied Terrell Sears, smiling broadly. "Take a look at this!"

Jody read the telegram from Marshal Dan Thornton in Bumble Bee, Arizona. "Well, whattaya know? Gray didn't vanish off the face of the earth after all. Too bad Thornton didn't realize who he was at the time."

"Too bad, nothing!" said Sears. "I want to take Gray down personally. Get your gear together, Jody. We're going to Phoenix!"

On that same day, at three o'clock in the afternoon, Pastor and Mrs. Bob Walker from Butte City, Montana, arrived in Denver by train. John and Breanna were there to meet them. Walker was pleased to know that Pastor Bayless had granted John's request, and Walker would pray over the bride and groom when they knelt at the altar.

The wedding practice was held at First Baptist Church that

evening, and the Baylesses and the Walkers struck up a warm friendship. Everyone in the wedding party did well through the practice, including James and Molly Kate.

Doctor Goodwin and Martha provided a special dinner for the wedding party in the church's fellowship hall. There was much joy at the dinner, but the unknown whereabouts of Solomon Duvall became part of the conversation around the table.

The Carroll family sat across the table from the bride and groom. Breanna looked at her niece and said, "Molly Kate, you did a beautiful job in the practice. I know you'll do fine tomorrow."

"Thank you, Aunt Breanna," said the bright-eyed little girl.

"And you did a perfect job, too, James," said Breanna.

"I'll do my very best tomorrow, too, Aunt Breanna," James said.

"Just think, James," Molly Kate said to her brother, "tomorrow Uncle John will be our *real* uncle!"

John smiled at the two children and gave them a wink.

"And you'll be my brother-in-law, John," said Dottie, her eyes sparkling.

"Guess you're stuck with me, Dottie."

"What does that make us, John?" asked Matt. "Brothers-in-law-in-law?"

"Something like that," John replied, chuckling.

Breanna set her eyes on her brother-in-law. "Matt, I want to thank you for filling in so graciously as John's best man."

Matt smiled broadly. "Hey, sis, I know the long relationship John's had with the chief. I'm very happy and honored to be best man in his stead. Of course, I wish Chief Duvall could be here, and I pray he'll be found alive and well."

Before the meal was over, Pastor Bayless rose to his feet and said, "Folks, the Walkers and I were just discussing Chief Duvall. And as we're all concerned about him, I want Pastor Walker to lead us in prayer, asking the Lord for Sol's safe return."

All heads were bowed and eyes closed as the Montana preacher offered heartfelt words to the Lord on behalf of Chief U.S. Marshal Solomon Duvall.

God's cricket orchestra was giving its nightly concert as John helped Breanna from the buggy in front of her cottage. The moon sprayed its silver light on them as he walked her to the door. "Well, Miss Baylor, tomorrow night at this time you will have been Mrs. Brockman for over six hours."

Tears glistened in Breanna's eyes as she looked at him and said, "And I'll be the happiest woman in all the world."

John pulled her close and held her for a long moment. Then he put the tips of his fingers under her chin and tilted her face upward, kissing her tenderly.

"Good night, Miss Baylor. I'll see you at the altar tomorrow."

19

ON SUNDAY AFTERNOON, June 4, wagons, buggies, and riders on horseback came from every direction to the white frame church building on the south edge of Denver. Rolling green meadows, sprinkled with wild flowers of various colors and dotted with towering cottonwoods, made a picturesque scene against the deep-blue sky. Crystal white clouds rode the lofty breezes, casting their moving shadows over the land.

The church was already filling up with guests when the organist began to play the pump organ at 2:45.

In a side room, just off the vestibule, Mary Donelson was putting the final touches on Breanna's hair, while Dottie Carroll made sure the gown, veil, and train were just right.

There was a tap on the door of the adjoining room.

"Yes?" Dottie said, moving to the door

"It's Kathy," came the voice of the pastor's wife.

Dottie opened the door just enough to allow Kathy Bayless to slip into the room.

"Oh, Breanna!" she said. "You look beautiful!"

Breanna already had high color, but her cheeks tinted just a bit more as she said, "Thank you. I hope John thinks so."

"Are you kidding?" said Dottie. "You'd be beautiful in John's eyes if you were dressed in a gunnysack! When he sees you in this, he's going to wonder if you didn't just fall down from heaven!"

"Just wanted to let you know, Breanna," said Kathy, "that we've got everybody ready to go. Dr. Goodwin is in the next room. Your bridesmaids are there, too, and we've got two excited children."

"I hope they aren't *too* excited," said Dottie.

"They'll do fine," Kathy assured her.

Breanna thought about her recurring dream, especially the last one. She looked past Mary, who was fussing with her veil, and said, "Kathy, have you seen John?"

"Oh, yes. And does he ever look handsome! Everybody's here who's supposed to be. The groomsmen are here. Dr. Carroll is here. Stefanie's on the platform, ready to sing, and even my husband is here."

Breanna laughed nervously. "Well, I'm sure glad the preacher made it!"

The women laughed and Kathy went back to the adjoining room.

Breanna's thoughts went to Solomon Duvall. O Lord, she said in her heart, take care of that dear man. Please bring him back to us safely.

In Pastor Bayless's study, which was located at the rear of the building, a nervous John Brockman paced back and forth, thoughts of Solomon Duvall crowding into his mind. He shook them off, knowing he must keep his mind on the great moment at hand.

Pastor Walker smiled at him and said, "Settle down, John. Everything's going to work out as practiced."

John stopped abruptly. "It's not what we practiced that's got me nervous, preacher. I've never been a husband before. There's no way I could practice that."

Curt Langan and Steve Ridgway looked on, standing with Matt Carroll in their dark suits. "I don't know if I ever want to get married," said Ridgway. "Not if it does this to a fella."

Langan chuckled. "John'll be all right. The groom always lives through the ceremony."

"Never had one die yet," Bayless said.

John rubbed the back of his neck. "I've faced many a cold-eyed gunfighter. I've fought many a battle with savage Indians. And I've been in many a fistfight with rough, tough men. But I've never been so nervous in all my life."

Bayless grinned. "I still say you'll live through it."

"And if you pass out before it's over, John," said Matt, "the doctor's here to revive you!"

The men burst out laughing, but their laughter was cut short when the organ stopped playing.

The pastor looked toward the closed door that led to the platform. "It's three o'clock," he said. "Time for Stefanie to sing."

Just before three o'clock, Dottie took Breanna by the hand and led her to a full-length mirror on the back of the door. "There you are, honey. Take a good look at yourself."

Mary and Dottie watched the strikingly beautiful bride look at herself in the mirror. Dottie was so proud of her sister, she felt she would burst.

Breanna's gown was made of soft white satin with a round neck and delicate gathers at her slender waist. The back buttoned from waist to neck with fabric loops and tiny pearl buttons. The bodice was adorned with intricate lace and pearls in a flower design that trailed up into the shoulders of the dress. A wide band of gathered lace graced the edge of the elbow-length sleeves.

A strand of mellow pearls glowed at Breanna's graceful neck, and she gazed at their reflection in the mirror, reaching up to caress them. She remembered when her maternal grandmother had given them to her. They had been passed down through many generations.

Her blonde hair was gathered into shiny curls that cascaded onto her shoulders, and ringlets caressed her rosy cheeks. The gossamer veil, covering her face, flowed from a crown of soft white flowers that Dottie had placed on her head. The veil fell over the back of her dress and covered the lacy train in a sheer film of loveliness.

Dottie turned and picked up the white Bible from a small table. "Here's your Bible, Breanna."

Atop the Bible was a bouquet of delicate white roses and wispy baby's breath tied with pink ribbons.

"Thank you," said Breanna. "I love you."

Dottie carefully embraced her sister and looked at her tenderly. "I love you, too," she said.

Suddenly the organ music stopped.

Dottie patted Breanna's shoulder. "Time for yours truly to get in position. See you out there."

Stefanie Langan moved to a spot near the organ as the organist began the introduction to the love song she would sing. Following that, she would sing a special hymn chosen by John and Breanna.

The church was packed. Not only were there people from

the church, but also from the populace of Denver and the surrounding area.

The altar was beautifully decorated with white, lavender, and deep purple lilacs, placed amidst glowing candles in tall silver candelabras on each side of the kneeling bench. The air was filled with the fragrance of flowers.

When Stefanie had finished singing, she quietly stepped off the platform and joined her children.

As the organ went into the first low notes of the wedding march, the door of the pastor's study opened, and the men emerged. Pastors Bayless and Walker made their way to the platform, where Walker stood slightly behind and to the side of Bayless.

Groomsmen Langan and Ridgway stood in position to meet the bridesmaids, young ladies of the church. Just ahead of them, the tall, handsome groom, and the best man, took their places. They angled themselves to see up the aisle where the bride would soon appear on the arm of Dr. Lyle Goodwin.

The organ continued to play as the bridal procession began, directed in the vestibule by Kathy Bayless.

The crowd looked over their shoulders as the two bridesmaids emerged from the vestibule and started slowly down the aisle side-by-side. Behind them came Dottie Carroll, the matron of honor.

Then James Carroll moved into the aisle behind his mother, carrying a small white satin pillow to which the rings were attached with ribbons. People smiled at the way the boy stood erect, shoulders squared, keeping his eyes straight ahead.

Kathy leaned close to Molly Kate's ear and said, "All right, sweetheart, you're next. Be sure to drop the rose petals just as your mother and I showed you last night."

Molly Kate, clad in a frilly dress of light blue and white, with her long blonde hair done like her Aunt Breanna's, moved slowly down the aisle, carefully sprinkling the delicate petals and evoking smiles from the audience.

When the bridesmaids reached the end of the aisle, the groomsmen offered their arms. Together the four mounted the wide steps to the platform, then separated to take their places. Next came the matron of honor, who smiled sweetly at her husband, the best man, as he gave her his arm to mount the steps.

James and Molly Kate had been instructed to mount the steps together. On the night before, both had performed the climb perfectly, but Molly Kate's dress had been slightly shorter than the one she was wearing today. As she stepped up, her foot caught on the hem and threw her off balance. She stumbled and spilled the remaining petals from her little basket. Her cheeks flushed bright red as she moved to her mother and looked up at her. Dottie gave her an everything-is-all-right smile.

John Brockman stood alone on the floor in front of the platform as he waited for Breanna to appear.

Kathy Bayless looked through the open door and then turned back to indicate to Breanna and Dr. Goodwin that it was their turn. Breanna looked up at the silver-haired physician and said softly, "Thank you so much for doing this."

"I wouldn't have it any other way," he said.

Kathy nodded for them to enter the vestibule and moved her lips in a silent, *God bless you, Breanna.*

The organist raised the volume of the organ to "Here Comes the Bride."

Martha Goodwin rose to her feet and turned toward the rear of the church. The capacity crowd followed her cue, and everyone craned their necks to get their first view of the bride.

When Breanna appeared on Dr. Goodwin's arm, John felt an exhilaration he had never known before. As he watched her regal procession, the only thought in his mind was, She's the queen of my heart.

For a brief instant, John thought of the honeymoon they had planned. They would leave the next morning for a cabin high in the Rocky Mountains. How wonderful it would be to have Breanna all to himself, with no one needing her medical attention, and no one needing him to help them out of trouble.

All eyes were fixed on the bride in her shimmering white gown, and Breanna keenly sensed every eye on her. She felt her heart thumping in her breast as her gaze was riveted on the tall man with the twin jagged scars on his right cheek.

Her line of sight flicked to Martha Goodwin, who was like a mother to her. Martha was smiling and dabbing at her tear-filled eyes with a hanky.

Breanna's smile was radiant as she and her escort drew near John. The organist let the music fade as the bride and her escort came to a stop.

From his place on the platform, Pastor Bayless asked, "Who gives this woman to be married to this man?"

Dr. Goodwin cleared his throat softly and replied, "In place of her deceased parents, my wife, Martha, and I do."

Bayless smiled. "Will you, please, sir, place the bride's hand in that of the groom?"

Dr. Goodwin laid Breanna's trembling hand in John's. She turned briefly and raised up on tiptoe to kiss the physician's cheek through her veil. Then Goodwin took his place beside Martha, and she slid her hand under his arm.

At the top of the steps, Breanna's eyes glowed with love for John as she looked up at him. He looked back at her, drinking in her beauty, and mouthed, *I love you.*

Pastor Bayless bid the audience be seated and made opening remarks, referring to the first wedding performed by God Himself in the Garden of Eden. He quoted Adam as saying of Eve, "This is now bone of my bones, and flesh of my flesh."

He offered a short prayer, then said that in John 2, the Lord Jesus Christ had been invited to a wedding. Now John and Breanna had invited Him to *their* wedding.

Bayless then spoke briefly of the place of the husband and the place of the wife in the home, according to Ephesians 5.

John and Breanna repeated the marriage vows, followed by the giving of the rings. Then they knelt on the bench while Pastor Walker offered prayer, asking God to bless them as they entered into the bonds of holy matrimony.

To John's surprise, the preacher then said, "Your bride came to me a short time ago, John, and asked if she could say something to you. Breanna..."

The bride turned to her groom and said loud enough so that all could hear, "John, as I become your wife, I want to speak to you those immortal words from the mouth of Ruth. 'Whither thou goest, I will go; and where thou lodgest, I will lodge: thy people shall be my people, and thy God my God.'"

John's eyes misted with tears.

Bayless then said, "John, Breanna...before God and this company, you have solemnly taken your wedding vows. It is with great pleasure that I now pronounce you husband and wife. John, you may kiss your bride."

There were tears in many eyes as John Brockman lifted the veil and took Breanna in his arms. He kissed her tenderly, and said so that only she could hear, "I love you, Mrs. Brockman."

John and Breanna then turned to face the audience, and Dottie placed the bouquet back in Breanna's hands.

"Ladies and gentlemen," said the pastor, "I introduce to you Mr. and Mrs. John Brockman."

The organ played the lively post-ceremony tune, and the bride and groom hurried up the aisle with the wedding party following.

That evening, after the wedding reception in the church fellowship hall, John drove Breanna to their new home in the country. Their friends had decorated the buggy with bright-colored paper streamers and a "Just Married" sign.

The sun had gone down, but its light still glowed in the sky above the jagged mountain peaks.

John stepped from the buggy and went around to help Breanna down.

"Breanna," he said, "thank you for that little surprise in the ceremony."

"Oh, you mean the words from Ruth? I meant every word, darling. Whither thou goest, I will go."

"Well, tomorrow, thou wilt go with me to the honeymoon cabin in the Rockies!"

"Yes, and I'm looking forward to it. Oh, John, I'm so happy!"

"Me, too. Because *you* are now bone of my bones and flesh of my flesh."

"I know. The Lord has been so good to me."

"It will now be my pleasure, Mrs. Brockman, to carry you across the threshold of our new home."

"The pleasure won't be all yours, my husband. There is more pleasure than I can describe when I'm in your arms."

He gathered her up and carried her as tenderly as he would a child. As he looked into her eyes, he said, "I love you with everything that is in me."

⁂

The next morning, John and Breanna were packing to leave on their honeymoon. Breanna had donned her split riding skirt, since they would ride their horses to the cabin in the mountains about six hours away. The day before, Chance and Ebony had been brought to the house from the stable in town and were now in the corral by the barn.

John was tightening a strap on the leather bag he would tie behind Breanna's saddle when they heard a knock at the front door. "I'll go down and see who it is, honey," Breanna said.

John was already on his way toward the hall, and said over his shoulder, "The princess doesn't answer the door. At least, not when the servant is home."

"You're not my servant!" she called after him.

John opened the door to find one of the newer deputy U. S. marshals, Garth Springer.

"Hello, Garth. News about the chief?"

"Not exactly, John. I have a telegram for you that was delivered to our office. Deputy Stone thought you should have it right away, since it's from the White House. He figured it has to do with Chief Duvall's disappearance."

John tore at the envelope and took out the telegram. He heard Breanna coming down the stairs behind him.

Deputy Springer looked past John and said, "Good morning, ma'am."

"Good morning," she echoed, glancing at the telegram in her husband's hand, then focusing on the deputy's face. "I don't think I've met you."

John looked around, "Oh. Honey, this is Deputy Garth Springer. Deputy, my wife, Breanna."

"Glad to meet you, ma'am. I know you folks got married

yesterday, and I'm sorry to bother you, but acting Chief Alex Stone thought John would want this telegram right away."

"No apology needed, Deputy," Breanna said. "What is it, darling?"

John gave her a bleak look and said, "We're going to have to postpone our honeymoon, sweetheart. This telegram is from President Grant."

"Oh?"

"Nobody in the U.S. marshal's office in Phoenix has been able to find a trace of Sol. Mr. Grant wants me to go there and see if I can find him. He's asking that I go immediately."

"Well, if anybody can find him, it'll be *you,* John," said Springer. "Can I tell Deputy Stone you're going?"

"Yes. First stage I can get a seat on."

"That'll make him happy. You want me to wire a reply to President Grant for you?"

"I'd appreciate it. Let me write it out for you."

Moments later, when Springer was riding away, John turned and looked down at Breanna. "I'm sorry, sweetheart, but since it's the president asking, and since it's Sol who's missing, I really feel I have to go."

"Well, darling, I want you to go. I agree with the president that you're the man to find Sol. Besides that, Sol is one of your closest friends. If for no other reason than that, you should be the one to go."

John pulled her close. "See what a wonderful wife you are? Here we are, about to go on our honeymoon, and now I've got to go off and leave you. I'm sorry."

Breanna slid her arms around his neck and looked deeply into his eyes. "Oh, don't be sorry, darling. It won't exactly be your friend's cabin in the Rockies, but we'll still be together."

John squinted at her. "What do you mean?"

"I'm going with you."

"Oh, now wait a minute! This thing could get dangerous, you know. What if some outlaw the chief sent to prison got out and wanted vengeance, so he kidnapped him? Who knows what I might run into? No, you're staying here."

"I can't. I have to go with you. It was one of my vows."

"What?"

"'Whither thou goest, I will go,' remember?"

"But this trip could be dangerous."

"I'm in no danger when I'm with the stranger from a far land. You know, Deuteronomy 29:22."

John squared his jaw. "Breanna, 'whither thou goest, I will go' doesn't take in something like this."

"It does with me."

"Well, by my husbandly authority, I'm telling you that when I climb aboard that stagecoach, you'll be waving goodbye to me."

The sun was lifting off the earth's horizon the next morning as the passengers boarded the Phoenix-bound stage. A woman of sixty and her teenage granddaughter smiled at John Brockman as he offered his hand to help them board. As the girl settled beside her grandmother, she looked past John and said, "You have a very pretty wife, sir."

"Thank you, young lady."

Breanna smiled at him as she took his hand and he helped her board the coach. He gave her a mock scowl, stepped in behind her, and sat down, pulling the door shut.

The older woman said, "The agent told me you're going to Arizona on important government business, sir."

"That's right, ma'am."

To Breanna, she said, "Well, it's nice that you can go with your husband, even when it's important government business."

"Yes, it is," said Breanna. She glanced at John, then looked back at the woman. "I told my husband once, 'Whither thou goest, I will go.' So…here I go!" As she spoke, she looked up at John and flashed him a sparkling smile.

John smiled back weakly, and Breanna winked at him.

20

ON JUNE 9, JOCK HOOD and his four sons sat on the front porch of the sprawling ranch house as the sun was going down. The aroma of hot food drifted from the kitchen through the front door. They knew Hazel Crumpton would soon be calling them to supper.

Billy Hood sat on a rocking chair next to his father, rubbing the arm that was in the sling. Jock frowned as he watched his youngest son. "You hurting, Billy?"

"Yeah," Billy said.

"Someday, kid…someday I'll get even with Brockman for what he did to you."

"And I'll be there to help you, Pa," Harold said.

"Me, too," said Mason and Virgil.

Movement on the desert to the west caught Harold's eye. "Looks like we got company."

Three riders approached, and as they came closer, Mason squinted and said, "It's Cass Beldin."

Jock smiled pleasantly. Two telegraphers worked at the Phoenix Western Union office. Cass Beldin was the one Jock had in his pocket.

The two Bar-H riders escorted Beldin up to the porch, and

Jock excused them to return to their post. He invited Beldin to dismount and join the group.

"How's the shoulder, Billy?" Beldin asked as he topped the steps.

"Not so good."

"Sorry about that. Sure hope it gets better. Jock, I've been out of town a few days...just got back this afternoon. Found out somethin' I thought you'd want to know."

"Sit down and tell me," Jock said, pointing to an empty chair directly in front of him.

Beldin eased onto the chair and removed his hat, then ran a bandanna over his face and forehead. "That there John Brockman who crippled Billy is on his way back to Phoenix this very minute."

"He is?" Jock said. "Tell me about it!"

"Well, he's on his way here to search for Duvall. I saw a copy of a telegram that came from Denver to Cliff Barnes, telling him he would be here on the Flagstaff stage tomorrow."

"All right!" Jock said, swinging a fist through the air in a sign of elation. "It worked!"

"Well, Billy," said Mason, "looks like we'll get vengeance real soon for what that dirty rat did to you!"

Jock laughed. "Like I said before...Brockman's a dead man." He rose to his feet, pulled a wad of currency from his pocket, and peeled off several $100 bills. He handed them to Beldin, who was now standing, and said, "Job well done, Cass. This is just the information I need."

"Thank you, sir. The stage Brockman's on is supposed to arrive in Phoenix about three-thirty tomorrow afternoon."

"We'll, ah...meet the stage before it gets to town," said Jock, grinning.

Beldin swung aboard his horse and rode away, a very happy man.

"Okay," said Jock to his sons, "let's go tell him."

Hazel was coming down the hall from the kitchen as Jock and his sons were moving inside. "Supper's almost ready," she said. "You fellas get washed up."

Jock looked at his boys, and said, "Well, we'll tell him after we eat."

While Jock and his sons were eating, Hazel put food and coffee on a tray and carried it from the kitchen. She returned a while later with the plate and cup empty. "Mr. Hood, his wrists are chafing pretty bad under the ropes," Hazel said as she set the tray on the cupboard. "May I put some salve on them?"

"I guess so," said Jock, wiping the last of his gravy off the plate with a wad of bread. "But wait till we go have a little talk with him."

Hazel watched Jock and his sons pass through the kitchen door and shook her head in disgust.

The Hoods walked down the hallway to one of the spare bedrooms and moved inside, single file, then gathered around the man who lay on the bed with his wrists tied to the bedposts.

"Well, Chief," Jock said, hooking his thumbs in his belt and smiling broadly. "It worked."

Solomon Duvall gave Jock a steely look and said, "You mean John's here looking for me?"

"No, but he's on his way. I'm just glad I learned that you two are the best of friends." Looking around at his sons, he said, "Didn't I tell you boys Brockman would come looking for his old pal if he disappeared?"

"Killing John Brockman is something nobody else has been

able to do," Duvall said. "Even entire gangs. I'm telling you right now, he doesn't kill easy."

Hood laughed. "He's never been up against the Hood family before. We'll get him, Duvall. You can bet your boots on it. John Brockman's grave is practically dug."

Moments later, Jock and his sons gathered in his den, and sat down. "Well, boys, since the stage is supposed to arrive in town at three-thirty, we'll just meet it up north of here about two o'clock."

"Can I go with you, Pa?" Billy asked.

"Best you don't try it. The way the arm and shoulder are hurting you, it'd only get worse."

"But I want to see you kill him."

Jock pondered it a moment. "It's worth adding some pain, just to see him die, eh?"

"Yes, sir."

"Okay, kid. You can go along."

Billy smiled. "It'll be the happiest moment of my life when I see that snake riddled with bullets."

The next morning, Bumble Bee, Arizona's marshal was sweeping the floor of his office when he saw two men ride up in front and dismount. The door was standing wide open, and Dan Thornton noticed the sun flash off the badges of the Texas Rangers.

He leaned the broom against the wall by the door and stepped out to meet them. "Captain Sears and Sergeant Sleppy, I presume."

"You presume correctly," smiled the tall, slender Sears. "And I presume you're Marshal Dan Thornton."

"That's right," Thornton said, shaking hands with both men.

Thornton took them inside, offered them lemonade to drink, and told them that Mark Gray and the other rider rode out of town northward, having said they were going to Flagstaff to visit a friend. He explained that they had told him their ranch was south of Phoenix.

"Well, who knows how much of it was truth?" said Sears. "But you did see them ride north when they left here?"

"They rode north, all right."

"And you haven't seen them since?"

"Nope."

"Okay, Jody," said the captain. "Then you and I will ride north."

When the stagecoach pulled into Flagstaff and slowed to stop at the Wells Fargo office, Breanna was looking out her window. "John," she said over her shoulder, "there's a cavalry unit at the stage office."

John leaned close to her, looked through her window, and said, "If they're here to escort us, it must mean the Apache problem has gotten worse."

The grandmother and granddaughter had left the stage at Tuba City, Arizona, and two men in their forties had boarded in their place. One of the two was peering out his window at the cavalry unit, and said to his friend, "Ralph, I'm sure glad we're getting off here."

"Yeah, me too."

The stage came to a dusty stop. The two men allowed John to help Breanna out first, then emerged to meet friends who had been awaiting their arrival.

While John and Breanna stretched their legs, they saw the driver talking to a cavalryman who wore captain's bars.

Listening, they learned the captain's name was Stuart Manning, and that his lieutenant's name was Royce Robins. There were eight troopers who stood beside their horses nearby. The Apaches were on the warpath, and the cavalrymen were going to escort the stagecoach to Phoenix. Manning and his men were out of Fort Verde, some seventy miles due north of Phoenix.

Only one passenger came out of the office to join the stage. Breanna saw her first. She was well dressed and wore a fancy hat on top of her upsweep hairdo. Her pretty face was overpowdered, her lashes too heavy with mascara, and rouge so thick on her cheeks, she looked unreal.

"Will you look at that?" whispered John, who had just seen her.

Shotgunner Van Hatfield was carrying her luggage out of the office for her.

"We may have us a saloon girl, here, darling," Breanna said.

Driver Ole Scrivner introduced himself to the young woman, who told him her name was Mitzy McLeod. Mitzy was then introduced to John and Breanna.

Before the passengers entered the coach, Captain Manning introduced himself and Lieutenant Robins to the passengers, explaining the danger they might face on the road, and that because of it, they would be escorting them all the way to Phoenix.

Manning looked down at the low-slung gunbelt on John's hip and said, "I trust you know how to use that gun, Mr. Brockman."

"I manage," John said.

"Well, you may have to use it before we get to Phoenix."

"I will if I have to."

"Good. Never hurts to have an extra gun along."

"We've got another gun, too," John advised him. "My wife carries a .36 caliber Navy Colt. And believe me, she knows how to use it."

"Very good," said Manning. "I hope you won't have to use your gun, Mrs. Brockman, but don't hesitate if the Apaches attack. Chief Dogindo is a fierce one, and so are his warriors."

Breanna nodded. "I'll use it if it becomes necessary, Captain."

Mitzy McLeod thanked John with a smile as he helped her board the stage, then he helped Breanna in and climbed in beside her. The stage rolled out of Flagstaff with dust dripping off its wheels like water, the cavalry unit trotting briskly behind. Soon they tipped down a long grade with the mountains around them, bound for Phoenix far to the south.

"You going to Phoenix on business or for pleasure?" Mitzy McLeod asked John and Breanna.

"On business," John told her. "Government business."

"Oh, you work for the federal government? How interesting. What exactly do you do, Mr. Brockman?"

"Well, actually it's secret stuff, Miss Mitzy. I can't tell you any more than that."

"I see," Mitzy said. "It's nice that you can travel with your husband, Mrs. Brockman. Do you always go with him?"

"No. Very seldom." Breanna paused, then asked, "So what's this trip for you?"

"New job. I'm a singer and dancer."

"I see," Breanna said, nodding.

"I'm really excited about it, too. I've only worked in one saloon before. Just the one in Flagstaff...the Bull Moose. But Mr. Morey Higgins, who owns the Silver Slipper in Phoenix, happened to come into the Bull Moose one night a few weeks ago while stopping over on a trip. He saw me dance and heard me sing, and approached me afterward, and—boom!—I was offered a job. You folks acquainted with the Silver Slipper?"

"No, we're not," Breanna said.

"I know it's there," John said, "from having been in Phoenix on numerous occasions, but I don't know anything about it."

"Well," Mitzy said, adjusting her position on the seat, "the Silver Slipper is by far Phoenix's largest saloon and gambling casino. You folks'll have to come and see me dance and hear me sing while you're in town."

Mitzy saw John and Breanna exchange glances. She raised her thinly plucked, painted eyebrows and said, "Did I say something wrong?"

John smiled. "Oh, no. It's just that Breanna and I live in a different world than you. Do you know what a born-again Christian is?"

"Oh...ah...well, I know it's a person who lives sort of a dull life. You know, all wrapped up in religion. When I was growing up back in Philadelphia, we had neighbors like that. Always acted like they were better than us and always preaching hell-fire and brimstone to us. I used to—" Mitzy's hand went to her mouth. "Oh, I'm sorry. You asked if I knew what a born-again Christian is, and here I am spouting off about my neighbors. Of course, you're born-again Christians. That's why you said you live in a different world than I do. I'm sorry. I didn't mean to insult you. I—"

"Please don't feel bad, Mitzy," Breanna said. "You haven't insulted us. John didn't ask you that to upset you. He only wanted to explain why we don't inhabit saloons, dance halls, and casinos."

"Miss Mitzy," said John, "I can't speak for your neighbors, but let me explain about Breanna and me. First, our life isn't dull. It's the most wonderful and exciting life on earth. And we're not all wrapped up in religion. Our lives are wrapped up in a Person...God's Son, the Lord Jesus Christ."

Mitzy blinked. "Didn't Jesus start a religion?"

"Mortal men founded religions. Jesus isn't mortal. He came from heaven and is now back in heaven. He came to give salvation to sinners, which we all are."

"That's right," Breanna said. "Mitzy, we're no better than you. We're simply sinners saved by the grace of God. It's just that when a person really comes to know Jesus, which is to repent of their sin and receive Him into their heart as personal Saviour...He changes their life. He puts a new 'want to' in their heart, and they desire the things of God rather than the things of this world."

"And as for the hell-fire and brimstone," John said, "God's Word does say that unless a person's sins are washed away by the blood of Jesus Christ, they will die in their sins. Since God is holy, He cannot and will not allow sin into heaven. That's why there was a cross of Calvary. Jesus had to shed His blood, die for our sins, and raise Himself from the grave so He could save us.

"Jesus told a very moral man, a teacher of religion in Israel, 'Except a man be born again, he cannot see the kingdom of God.' We don't need religion. We need a spiritual rebirth from the hand of God Himself. We must be born into the family of God, which is a spiritual family. Scripture says of Jesus, 'As many as received him, to them gave he power to become the sons of God, even to them that believe on his name.'"

"You see," said Breanna, "this isn't religion. This is salvation. I have my Bible right here in my purse. Would you let me read some more passages to you concerning salvation?"

Mitzy stiffened, lifting her chin. "Ah...please, ma'am, I'd

rather you didn't. I…I'm really not interested in becoming a Christian. If I had the change that you people have had, it would end my career."

"Probably so," said Breanna, "but the Lord would give you something a whole lot better. But even more important, according to God's Word, if you die without being born again—without your sins cleansed and forgiven—you will spend eternity in hell. Is it worth it?"

"Mrs. Brockman, I don't want to be rude to either of you, but I'd rather not talk about this any more."

"All right," said Breanna, reaching across and patting her hand. "John and I didn't mean to upset you. It's just that we've been on your side of the fence. You haven't been on ours. We want to see you have what we have in Jesus."

Mark Gray and Boone McKeever rode away from the L-Bar-S barn toward the Flagstaff–Phoenix road. Mark had become fidgety again, needing to get away from the same surroundings. This time McKeever had insisted that they not go into a town. They would just ride the hills and forests, or at times, follow the road.

Apache Chief Dogindo knew the approximate time the Wells Fargo stagecoaches ran between Flagstaff and Phoenix. In his mind, it was time to attack another stagecoach, kill the crew and passengers, steal the horses, and burn the coach. White men must learn not to infuriate the Apache. The fact that Gardano and the other warriors were still being held at Fort McFarland had him very angry. White eyes would pay.

Dogindo and twenty-seven fierce-eyed warriors gathered

behind a massive jumble of boulders near the Flagstaff-Phoenix road, some seventy miles north of Phoenix. The boulders surrounded a tall rock formation, except for a narrow passageway on the west side. At the end of the passageway and the base of the towering rock, a tiny spring bubbled up, making a small pool.

The rock formation cast a long shadow at both ends of the day on the rock-strewn sand of the open desert. There were forests some seven or eight miles in either direction, east or west.

Two of the warriors were up on boulders, peering northward as Dogindo and the others stood in the afternoon shade of the rock tower. Suddenly one of them called to his chief that there was a small army escort with the stage.

Dogindo laughed. This was why he had brought so many warriors. They would annihilate the soldier coats and everyone on the stagecoach.

Dogindo sent half of his men farther south along the road, telling them to hide. If the army and stage driver decided to try to race away from the Apaches who attacked them, the second set of warriors would launch a surprise attack on the road ahead of them. Dogindo and his remaining warriors now made their way farther north to attack on horseback from a deep ravine.

Some twenty minutes previously, Captain Terrell Sears and Sergeant Jody Sleppy had trotted northward past the boulder and rock tower, not realizing the Apaches were watching them. Dogindo would not risk his element of surprise by shooting down the two white men.

Unknown to the Apaches, Mark Gray and Boone McKeever were trotting their horses northward about a half-mile south of the spot where the second set of warriors had secluded themselves only moments before.

Sears and Sleppy rode together, discussing what they would do if they did not find Gray by the time they reached Flagstaff. They suddenly saw a roiling dust cloud up ahead, preceded by the stagecoach and several men in blue riding alongside it on horseback.

"Looks like the folks in Phoenix were right, Cap'n," said Jody. "The army must figure to ward off Apaches who might be tempted to attack the stagecoaches."

The coach and its escort were drawing near when suddenly, fourteen Apaches swarmed over the crest of a sandy ravine, whooping and firing their repeater rifles.

Immediately the driver snapped the reins and put the six-up team to a full gallop as the cavalrymen fired back. The shotgunner was blasting away, and gunfire was coming from inside the stage.

Two Apaches peeled off their horses, and one trooper buckled over in the saddle, hanging onto the saddle horn to keep from falling.

"Jody!" shouted Sears. "We'd best join them!"

The Texas Rangers swerved their horses as the stage drew close, and riding beside the cavalry, began firing at the Indians.

Inside the coach, Breanna had Mitzy on the floor while she fired out a window on the right side. John was firing out the left.

Mark Gray and Boone McKeever pulled rein when they saw what was happening up ahead.

"Let's get outta here, Boone!" Gray shouted, and jerked his horse's head around to go the other way. He froze when he saw more than a dozen whooping Apaches thundering toward them.

McKeever swore and said, "Only chance we got is to collect

ourselves with the coach and the army!"

They spurred their mounts, racing toward the oncoming coach and riders.

As Captain Stuart Manning rode alongside the coach, firing his revolver at the Apaches, he saw the second band of warriors coming about a mile and a half away. He shouted to the driver, "Ole! That rock tower up ahead! Pull in there! Our only chance is to take cover!"

Manning shouted the same thing to his men, knowing that at least some of them could hear him. The others, he hoped, would see what they were doing and follow. He winced when he saw a riderless cavalry horse, and at the same time, two more men took Apache bullets and fell to the ground.

The stage and horsemen began to veer toward the rock formation, and Ole Scrivner aimed the coach headlong at the Apache band as they came toward him. The warriors scattered to avoid a collision with the charging vehicle.

Amid the boiling dust and clouds of gunsmoke, Mark Gray and Boone McKeever stayed close to the coach and cavalry. They saw two other riders in civilian clothes, but were unable to make out their faces.

Dogindo hated to see the whites taking refuge in the rocks and boulders, but so many of his men had been shot off their horses, he called for those still in action to pull back. They rode to a spot out of rifle range and watched the stagecoach, followed by the other riders, race around to the west side of the rock tower.

The stagecoach team snorted and blew from the hard ride as Ole Scrivner and Van Hatfield scrambled down from the box. John Brockman quickly helped the two women out.

Captain Manning thundered to a halt and slid from his saddle. He pointed to the narrow passageway that led through the boulders to the base of the rock tower and shouted, "Everybody get in there! Take your horses!"

Ole and Van began unharnessing the team so they could get them to safety.

Captain Terrell Sears and Sergeant Jody Sleppy helped wounded troopers from their saddles. Mark Gray and Boone McKeever rushed into the rock enclosure, leading their horses.

John Brockman watched Breanna helping Mitzy through the passageway, then dashed to a spot where he could see the Apaches gathered at a safe distance, looking on. Captain Manning and Sergeant Hank Durbin drew up beside him.

"What do you make of it, Mr. Brockman?" asked Manning.

"Looks like they're licking their wounds. Do you recognize their leader? It's the guy wearing the red bandanna on the stolen army bay with the white stockings and blaze face. They're all gathered around him."

"Yes. It's Dogindo."

"Dogindo!" John said. "I've heard and read about him!"

"Bloodthirsty," said Durbin. "Heartless and bloodthirsty."

"What do you think they'll do?" John asked.

"Well, we've cut down their number considerably, but I'm sure they still outnumber us."

"I count seventeen of them, Captain," said the sergeant. "The best I could tell, we lost five men back there on the road, and we've got two wounded in the rocks, including Lieutenant Robins. That means we've got three of us in uniform, plus those four men who joined us on the road, Ole and Van, and Mr. Brockman. That's ten."

Suddenly a single Apache rider broke from the group and galloped northwest.

"I figured so," said Manning.

"Going for reinforcements," said John.

"Right. And if you will notice...now Dogindo and the others are spreading out to make sure we don't try to make a getaway."

"We'd be fools to try it," said Manning. "All we can do is take cover here and hope they send a patrol out to find us. I've been in these rocks before. There's a spring in there...unless it's gone dry."

Inside the rock enclosure, Breanna was trying to calm Mitzy. At the same time she saw the Texas Rangers lay the two wounded men in the shade of a huge boulder. The only able-bodied man in uniform in the enclosure was Corporal Benny Eagan.

Eagan drew up, looked at the two wounded men, and said, "I'll see what I can do to help."

Gray and McKeever were some fifty feet away, kneeling at the bubbling spring and small pool, scooping up water and drinking it. Ole and Van were kneeling at the pool opposite them.

Breanna had Mitzy sitting on a rock, and was bending over her, squeezing her shoulders. The girl was trembling and sniffling in terror. Calling over her shoulder, Breanna said to the corporal and the Rangers, "Gentlemen, I'm a Certified Medical Nurse. Give those wounded men some water, and I'll be right there."

"A nurse!" said Benny Eagan. "Ma'am, that's wonderful!"

At the pool, Ole looked at Van and said, "Did you know we were haulin' a nurse?"

"Sure didn't. Hope she can help those two."

Breanna gripped the weeping saloon girl's shoulders hard, and said, "Mitzy, listen to me. The danger is over for the moment. I've got to see about those wounded men."

Mitzy sniffled, wiped tears from her cheeks, and said,

"You...you didn't tell me you're a nurse."

"Just didn't get around to it. Will you help me?"

Mitzy followed Breanna to the wounded men, who were both conscious. Breanna waited till Corporal Eagan and Ranger Jody Sleppy finished giving water to the wounded men from canteens. Then she knelt between them. Mitzy dropped to her knees beside her.

"You're a nurse, ma'am!" said the corporal, who was no more than twenty-two, blond and fair. His face was sunburned. He had taken an Apache bullet in his left shoulder.

"Yes, corporal," she said making a quick estimate of the wound. "I'll have to remove that slug. Don't worry. I've done it before. Your name?"

"Larry Deane."

She smiled. "You hang on, Larry. Let me see about your comrade, here."

When Breanna turned to the other one, she realized it was Lieutenant Robins. His face was pale, and his eyes were glassy. A bullet was in his chest, and it was very close to his heart.

"Lieutenant," she said, "I've got to remove that slug. I won't lie to you. It's in a dangerous spot. I could lose you. I'll leave the decision to you."

"You're a Certified Medical Nurse, didn't you say, Mrs. Brockman?"

"Yes."

"Then please try."

"All right. I have a medical bag in the stagecoach. I'll be right back."

Breanna paused to tell Larry Deane that she would have Mitzy help stay his bleeding while she operated on Lieutenant Robins. With that, she started toward the passageway, but Jody

Sleppy rushed up beside her and said, "I'll get the bag for you, ma'am. Exactly where is it?"

Breanna explained where the black bag was, thanked him, and turned back to her patients. She started giving instructions to Mitzy, who was already doing what she could for Deane.

Terrell Sears stood over the women, marveling at how the blonde had so professionally taken charge of the wounded men.

At the spring and pool, Mark Gray rose to his feet, wiping his mouth, and slowly turned about. "Well, Boone, when it gets dark, you and I will—"

The jolt Gray felt was akin to getting hit by lightning. His heart seemed to freeze in his chest when he recognized the back of Captain Terrell Sears's head. Nothing mattered now but to get away.

Gray slipped his gun from its holster, cocked the hammer, and with Boone McKeever looking on astonished, stepped up behind the Ranger captain and said, "Lookin' for me, Sears?"

Sears spun around. "Gray!" he said. Then he saw the muzzle aimed at his middle.

21

BOONE MCKEEVER RUSHED UP beside Mark Gray, saying, "What're you doin', Mark?"

"Shut up!" Gray said from the side of his mouth. "Don't you see that Texas Ranger badge?"

"Yeah."

"Well, this is the guy I've told you about."

"What's goin' on, fella?" Ole asked.

"None of your business, old man. Get back. All right, Sears, you and I are leavin' here right now." The ex-Texas Ranger's muzzle remained steady on Sears's midsection.

Sears fixed Gray with cold, fearless eyes. "What are you thinking of Gray? Suicide? Have you forgotten those Apaches are still out there?"

"Come dark, we'll slip past 'em," Gray said. Then to the others, "Anybody makes a false move, I'll kill this big shot Texas Ranger."

Breanna saw Jody Sleppy appear at the opening of the passageway, carrying her black medical bag. When he saw what was happening, he laid the bag down and moved so as to remain behind Gray. Slowly, he crept toward him, slipping his revolver from its holster.

"Now, Sears," Gray said, "I want you to reach down real

slow and easy, and drop your gunbelt."

"Mark," said McKeever, "you're gonna take me with you, ain'tcha?"

"Sure."

Sears did not move to touch his gunbelt. "Gray, apparently you don't know much about Indians. They can see in the dark like a cat. We go out there, we're dead. Not just me. You. You and your pal, here."

McKeever was beside Gray and did not see Sleppy, either.

"I'll take my chances," Gray said. "Now, you either drop that gunbelt, or I'll—"

"You'll what?" Sleppy said, pressing his gun muzzle to the back of Gray's neck. "Okay, Mark, give me that gun."

McKeever whirled, cursing and clawing for his gun. Sears's hand was a blur as he drew his weapon and barked, "Hold it!"

McKeever froze with his hand on the gun butt.

"Let's have the gun, mister!" Sears said.

"What's going on here?" came the voice of Captain Stuart Manning as he stomped up stiff-legged.

John Brockman and Sergeant Hank Durbin flanked him.

"Sergeant Sleppy and I were trailing this guy, Captain," said Sears. "His name's Mark Gray. As you can see by our badges, we're Texas Rangers. I'm Captain Terrell Sears. We're from the El Paso office."

"Sergeant Durbin," said Manning, "relieve Mr. Gray of his gun."

While the order was being carried out, Sears stepped to McKeever and took his revolver.

McKeever's gaze drifted to the tall man in black. He gasped, and everybody heard him. Brockman turned and looked at him. "Well, if it isn't Boone McKeever!"

"This someone you know, Mr. Brockman?" asked Manning.

"Yes. I'll explain later, but the man is an outlaw through and through."

"All right," said Manning. Then to Sears, "I'd like to know exactly why you and Sergeant Sleppy have been trailing this Mr. Gray."

Breanna spoke up. "Captain Manning, I'm a Certified Medical Nurse. Your lieutenant, here, is in grave danger. I need to remove the bullet from his chest, and it has to be done now. I'll need my husband to help me. When that's finished, I must remove a bullet from Corporal Deane's shoulder. Could you take these outlaws a little farther away so I can do my work?"

"Mrs. Brockman, I wasn't aware of your medical qualifications, but I'm certainly glad you're here. You and Mr. Brockman go right ahead. We'll move these outlaws to the far side of the enclosure."

Manning sent Benny Eagan and Hank Durbin to keep an eye on the Apaches, then moved away with Sears and Sleppy as they took Gray and McKeever to the other side of the enclosure. There, Sears told Manning the whole story about Gray as Ole and Van listened in.

Mitzy attended to Larry Deane while Breanna administered laudanum to Royce Robins and began the surgery.

As the sun was going down, Corporal Benny Eagan returned and reported to Captain Manning that fifteen more Apache warriors had just come to join Dogindo. Manning took a deep breath and sighed at Eagan's news. Everyone in the enclosure had heard the report.

John Brockman rose from where he had been helping Breanna and stepped to Manning. "Breanna got the bullet out, Captain. She says he's not out of danger, but she would term him stable at this point. Mitzy's helping her remove the bullet from Corporal Deane's shoulder, now."

"Good," said the captain. "I'm so glad your wife is with us."

"Do you think the Apaches will come at us when it gets dark, Captain?" Sears asked.

"It would be a rarity. Most Apaches are afraid to take a chance on dying at night."

"Like the Comanches, are they? Don't want their souls to wander endlessly forever."

"That's it. But I'll have a man on lookout from the top of that tall rock all night. We'll do it in shifts."

"Jody and I will take our turns," said Sears.

"And me, likewise," John said.

"'Preciate that, gentlemen," Manning said.

"But we should be ready at dawn," John said.

"Yes. They'll come at the first ray of sunlight."

Mark Gray and Boone McKeever had been tied hand and foot and were sitting on the ground with their backs against a boulder, listening to every word that was said.

John looked at them. "Captain Manning...Captain Sears...we're going to need every man with a gun in his hand."

Sears frowned. "You don't mean—"

"Yes, sir. Both of them. When those Apaches come, our lone advantage is that we're in these rocks...but only if every gun available is blazing."

"But, Brockman," Sears said, "the first chance Gray gets, he'll shoot Jody and me."

John looked at the prisoners again. "I don't think so, Captain. He knows his own life is on the line. He doesn't have enough bullets in his gun to take out everybody here. To shoot you or Jody would turn all of our guns on him."

"But what if he just decides to shoot us and make a run for it?"

"Be mighty stupid with all those Apaches out there. I'd think Mr. Gray would rather hang with a Texas rope around his neck than be tortured to death Apache-style."

"I agree we need every gun possible to face the attack that's coming in the morning," said Manning, "but I hate to see those two armed."

"I'll say no more," John said, "but you'll wish you had those two with guns in their hands when Dogindo comes at us."

Sears rubbed his chin, looked at Gray and said, "You rather hang in El Paso, or die at the hands of the Apaches?"

"I'd rather take my chances on the noose, thank you."

"What about you, McKeever?" Manning asked. "Mr. Brockman tells me if you live through this, he's going to put you behind bars again. You rather rot in prison or die an inch at a time over an Apache fire pit?"

"I'd take prison over that any day," McKeever said.

"Okay. I'll go ahead and untie you now, and you"ll get your guns back in the morning. But just keep in mind...you're outnumbered here. You take a shot at Captain Sears, Sergeant Sleppy, or anyone else, we'll all shoot you down like cur dogs."

From a nearby arroyo, Jock Hood and his sons had watched the Indians attack the stagecoach and the white people flee into the rock enclosure.

As the sun was setting, he said, "Well, boys, that's all the action for today. Wish it had been us who got to that stagecoach, but at least we'll have the satisfaction of knowing Brockman's dead. Those Apaches aren't gonna let any of them leave there alive. However, we'll come back to this same spot in the morning and watch the execution."

"And I'll love every minute of it, Pa," Billy said. "I want Brockman dead."

The moon arose in the eastern sky, and soon shed its silver light over the desert. The whole sky was shimmering with bright, twinkling stars. There was no wood to build a fire with. The soldiers shared the rations from their saddlebags with everyone else, and they washed it down with spring water.

While they ate, Sears filled everyone else in on Mark Gray, who sat sullenly. When the Ranger captain was finished, Gray said through clenched teeth, "If we get through this Apache ordeal, Sears, you'll never get me to El Paso."

"We'll see about that," Sears said.

John and Breanna sat together with Mitzy beside them. Next to Mitzy lay Corporal Deane, and next to him was Lieutenant Robins, who was sleeping. The laudanum was helping him to rest.

Atop the seventy-foot rock tower, Sergeant Hank Durbin lay flat, watching a small group of Apaches who remained out of rifle range in the moonlight. He knew the others had stationed themselves around the rock enclosure to keep anyone from getting away.

Jody Sleppy, who sat beside his captain, glared at Gray and said, "We'll get you to El Paso, all right, Mark. You can bank on it."

Irritated toward the man who had tarnished his badge, John Brockman said, "Mr. Gray, there's a Scripture that describes your kind. Proverbs 13:2. 'The soul of the transgressors shall eat violence.' You've laid a foundation that assures you, you'll die violently."

"Don't you preach to me, mister!" Gray hissed. "I don't want to hear it!"

"What you really need to hear, Gray," said Brockman, "is that Jesus Christ died on Calvary's cross so you—"

"Shut up!" Gray said. "Shut up! Shut up! Shut up! I don't want to hear it!"

Suddenly Boone McKeever leaped to his feet, stood over John and yelled, "Leave my friend alone, Stranger, or I'll kick your teeth down your scummy throat!"

"Mr. McKeever," Breanna said with a quaver in her voice, "you had best not aggravate my husband. He's one man you don't want to tangle with."

"You butt out, lady!" McKeever said.

John leaped to his feet. "I'll give you three seconds to apologize to my wife."

"Hah! I'm not apologizin' to nobody!"

Brockman's right fist lashed out and caught McKeever square on the mouth. He staggered back, shaking his head, then came at John, cursing him, and swinging a haymaker.

John ducked it and the blow that caught McKeever in the hollow of his jaw lifted him off his feet. He hit the ground on his back and lay still.

"Good for you, Mr. Brockman!" said Corporal Eagan.

"That should take the starch out of him," Manning said.

The group let McKeever lie unconscious, paying him no mind, as they talked about what would come in the morning. Captain Manning tried to encourage them, saying if they could just hold out a day or so, the commandant at the fort would be sending a patrol to find them.

John took Breanna by the hand, lifted her to her feet, and said, "Let's take a little walk out to the stage and back."

Breanna glanced at the wounded men. Robins was still sleeping. Mitzy said, "I'll look after Larry, Mrs. Brockman."

"All right," she said quietly. "And you can call me Breanna."

Mitzy smiled. "All right, Breanna."

Mitzy watched the couple walk away, then sat down beside the wounded corporal.

Larry looked up, smiled, and said, "Miss Mitzy, I've been thinking."

"About what?"

"You."

"Me? What about me?"

"You're too nice a girl to work in a saloon."

"Oh? Well, you really don't know me."

"I'm a good judge of character. You don't belong in a saloon. You should be a wife and mother."

Mitzy was quiet for a moment, then said, "I probably will get married and have children someday. But right now, it's the night life and the gaiety that I want."

"But you might mess your life up so bad that you'll never be a wife or mother."

Mitzy did not reply. She was dabbing at her hair, trying to get it in order.

"Mitzy..."

"Hmm?"

"I'd like to tell you what you really need. I'm a Christian, Mitzy. I know firsthand what it means to have my life changed by Jesus Christ. I used to be—"

"So that's it? We were getting along fine, and now you want to preach to me?"

"I just would like to see you make something of your life,

other than to be a saloon singer and dancer. Let me tell you what real living is. It's a Person."

"Yes, I know. Jesus Christ. Breanna and her husband talked to me about it on the stage."

Larry smiled. "Sure enough? I thought they might be Christians. Well, anyway, Mitzy, would you let me tell you what Jesus did for me?"

"Go ahead."

While others milled about the rock enclosure, Larry Deane gave his testimony to Mitzy McLeod, quoting Scripture as he went along.

John and Breanna reached the stagecoach in the moonlight and sat down on a smooth round rock next to it. He put his arm around her, kissed her soundly, then said, "Some honeymoon, huh?"

Breanna stroked his face and said, "It's not exactly what we planned, but at least we're together."

They kissed again.

All was quiet for a moment, then Breanna said, "You hit that poor man pretty hard, John."

"Poor man, nothing! Nobody talks to my wife like that!"

Breanna smiled, then quickly grew somber. "John...do you think we can hold off those Apaches for another day or two?"

"We have to."

"But can we?"

"With God's help." He drew a breath. "Let's just pray about it right now."

When John and Breanna returned to the others, Benny Eagan was climbing the rock tower to relieve Hank Durbin. Ole Scrivner and Van Hatfield were using buckets from the stagecoach to water all the horses. Terrell Sears and Jody Sleppy were checking the rifles Captain Manning had given them to use.

John went to Manning to discuss the posts for each person when they faced the Apache attack at dawn.

Breanna returned to her patients. Royce Robins was still sleeping, but he seemed to have a slight fever. She hoped he wasn't developing an infection. She turned next to Larry Deane.

"How's this patient doing, Nurse McLeod?" Breanna asked.

"He seems to be fine," Mitzy said.

"Mrs. Brockman," said Larry, "Mitzy tells me you and your husband are Christians."

"Why, yes...we are," Breanna said.

"Well, I am too, ma'am."

"Wonderful, Larry! I'm glad to know that."

"Mitzy says you and Mr. Brockman talked to her about becoming a Christian."

"Yes," Breanna said, setting tender eyes on the girl. "She told us she isn't interested."

"That's what she told me, too."

Breanna patted Mitzy's arm and said, "The Lord loves you, honey. He's brought three of us into your life just today. He's trying to tell you that you need Him. He wants to save you."

Mitzy brushed hair from her eyes, and said, "Well, I guess I'd better go get my patient some water. He's about out."

When dawn was but a hint of light in the eastern sky, John Brockman came down from the rock tower and reported to all that the Apaches were gathering for an attack.

Breanna and Mitzy were placed in the safest spot, on the

sandy ground in an indenture of a huge boulder, where Deane and Robins now lay. Breanna kept her Navy Colt .36 close at hand while she poured cool water on Royce Robins who definitely had a fever. She examined the wound, fearful that infection was setting in. She had a little alcohol with which to treat it, but probably not enough.

When Gray and McKeever were given their guns, they were warned again by Captain Manning that they would be shot down if they turned their guns on Sears, Sleppy, or Brockman.

Each man took the position assigned by Manning, and waited for the attack.

The sun peeked over the eastern horizon, bright and hot, painting the desert with varying hues of deep violet, of pale orange, and streaking the distant mountains with shadow.

Dogindo led his warriors in the attack, then rode the stolen army bay to a safe spot next to a single large boulder to watch the action.

The Apaches attacked from all four sides of the enclosure, guns blazing, yapping like wild dogs. Clouds of gunsmoke drifted on the hot morning air as the sounds of rifle and pistol echoed across the rugged land.

Jock Hood and his sons dismounted in the arroyo and scrambled to the crest where they could watch the action. The hostiles were on foot and on horseback, firing at the men who defended their rock fort.

From where the Hoods lay, they could see three dead Apaches sprawled on the ground, and one who was wounded, crawling for cover.

Billy's eye caught sight of John Brockman high up on one of the boulders. "Look Pa! There's the skunk now!"

"Wish I had a long-range rifle with a telescopic sight," said Jock. "I'd send him to shake hands with the devil right now."

"Don't worry about it," Virgil said. "Those Apaches will get him. They can afford to wait till the guys in the rocks run out of ammunition."

"I'd still like to be the one to kill him," Jock said with a growl.

Breanna's concern for Royce Robins was growing. His temperature was creeping higher. He was conscious, however, and with the guns roaring and the yapping of the Apaches in their ears, Breanna said, "Lieutenant, have you heard what Larry has been talking to Mitzy about?"

Robins licked his lips. "Yes, ma'am."

"If...if we don't make it out of here alive, Lieutenant, will you go to heaven?"

"I'm afraid not, ma'am. I've never repented and received Jesus into my heart."

"You talk like you've heard it before."

"Yes, ma'am. I was raised in a Christian home, but I never got saved. My parents did their best with me, but I just rebelled against the gospel. I've heard it hundreds of times. But..."

"But what?"

"If Jesus will still want to save me, I want Him to."

"Are you willing to come to Him as a lost sinner and ask Him to save you?"

"Yes, ma'am. I sure am."

"Well, Jesus once said, 'Him that cometh to me I will in no wise cast out.' Will He turn you away if you ask Him to save you?"

Robins managed a smile. "I remember that Scripture. No, He won't turn me away."

Mitzy listened as Breanna led Lieutenant Robins to the Lord. When it was done, Robins thanked her. Breanna gave him water and mopped perspiration from his face. He smiled again, and said, "Mrs. Brockman, I've got to make it out of here alive. I want to go home and tell Mama and Papa I got saved. Oh, it will make them so happy!"

Breanna bit her lip. She had little hope that Royce Robins would ever see his parents on this earth again.

"See, Mitzy," said Deane, "it's that simple. Jesus will save you, too, if you'll mean business with Him and ask Him to."

Mitzy dabbed at the sweat of her own brow. "Larry, I'm just not ready to do that."

Suddenly, like something falling out of the sky, Boone McKeever's body hit the ground less than five feet from Mitzy. She jerked and let out a scream, grabbing Larry's hand.

Breanna left Robins to look at McKeever. He was dead. An Apache bullet had hit him in the heart.

Mitzy drew a shaky breath. "Oh, Breanna, is he...?"

"Yes, honey. He's dead."

The girl closed her eyes and screamed. "We're all going to die!" she cried. "We're all going to die!"

Breanna took her in her arms and held her while she wept in terror.

The battle wore on. Captain Manning was the first to see more Apache warriors coming from the south. Without question, Dogindo meant to press the attack until he won.

22

THE WEARY MEN INSIDE THE ROCK enclosure gathered at the pool as twilight stole across the desert. A violet haze still clung to the western sky.

Corporal Benny Eagan was perched on top of the rock pillar, watching the Apaches where they had withdrawn from rifle range only moments ago.

Breanna Brockman knelt over Wells Fargo shotgunner Van Hatfield, who had been creased in the side by an Apache bullet. John Brockman came up, his hair dripping with water, as Breanna examined the wound. "Bad?" he asked.

"Not really," she said. "I'll have to stitch him up a bit, but he'll be able to fight again tomorrow."

"If we have enough ammunition," said Mark Gray, a bitter tone in his voice.

"We're not out yet," Captain Stuart Manning said.

"Don't mind him, Manning," Terrell Sears said. "He's a born pessimist."

Jody Sleppy chuckled. Gray sent him a wicked glare, but the gathering darkness hid it.

"Since we're speaking of ammunition, Captain Manning," said Ole Scrivner, the stage driver, do we actually have enough to last us through another day like today?"

"Smart thing would be to do a count," said Manning, "but I think so."

"Captain Manning," Sleppy said, "you've spoken several times about your commandant sending a patrol to find you. Any idea why they haven't shown up?"

"Only thing I can think of is that every soldier is needed to fight other Apaches."

Sleppy nodded, but said no more.

"So who's gonna bury my friend?" Gray asked.

"We'll let you do it," Manning said. "Mr. Scrivner told me he's got a couple of shovels in the stagecoach. Go pick yourself out one and have at it."

Gray spit in the sand. "Yeah, well maybe I'll just make my way to the stage and keep on goin'."

"You really like flirting with that Apache fire pit, don't you, Mark?" Sears said.

"I'll get the shovel, Cap'n," Sleppy said. "Mark, you pick out a spot for the grave."

"I'd rather bury you."

"Tried that once, didn't you?"

Breanna finished with Hatfield, telling him to take it easy the rest of the evening and no climbing to the top of the tall rock. Hank Durbin told Manning he would do a double shift in Hatfield's place.

Breanna took John by the hand and pulled him toward the other two wounded men. "Darling, I want you to know about Larry and Royce."

"Hmm?"

Mitzy was at her place beside Larry Deane, who was now sitting up with his back against a boulder.

"Hey, Larry, look at you!" John said.

"He's doing much better," said Breanna.

"Well, I guess. What was it you wanted me to know, sweetheart?"

"Tell him, Larry."

"I'm a born-again Christian, Mr. Brockman. Jesus saved me when I was eighteen. A drunken eighteen, I might add."

"Well, praise the Lord!" John said. "I'm glad to hear that!"

Breanna knelt beside Robins, whose face shone with perspiration. "John, Royce was raised in a Christian home, but had always rebelled against the gospel. Today, while all the fighting was going on, he opened his heart to Jesus."

"That's wonderful, Royce. I'm mighty glad for you." Then to Breanna: "How's he doing?"

She glanced at the lieutenant, then looked up at her husband. "He's got some fever. I'm doing everything I can to bring it down."

"Guess we'd better eat, folks," came Manning's voice. "More army rations tonight. Then we'll do a count on the ammunition."

Jody Sleppy appeared with the shovel and handed it to Gray.

Mitzy sat by Larry while they ate. John switched off with Breanna, so that one of them was consistently bathing Royce's face, neck, and wrists with cool water.

While Captains Manning and Scars were eating together, Sleppy eased down beside them, chewing on a piece of hardtack. "Cap'n Manning," he said, "I think one of us should sneak out of here in the dark and get us some help. I was in Arizona a few years ago. I know where Fort Verde is. Your fellow soldiers might be busy with Apaches, but I think if they knew our plight, they'd come on the run."

"Too dangerous, Jody," Manning said. "I know those Apaches. Dogindo's got warriors all around us. Nobody could get through."

"He hasn't got that many. There's got to be open space out there. I'm willing to try it."

"Won't work," Manning said flatly. "You couldn't lead a horse amongst them out there. They'd spot you for sure. And by the time you'd make it to Verde on foot, it'd be too late, anyhow."

"Jody," said Sears. "I appreciate your willingness to hazard yourself for the rest of us, but the captain's right. There's no way you, or anybody else, could make it."

Sleppy rubbed his hands on his pantlegs. "Oh, well, it was worth a try."

John and Breanna were both away from Royce Robins for a few minutes. Robins had fallen asleep.

"Mitzy..." said Larry Deane, as they sat in the dark.

"Yes?"

"I really do like you."

"Thank you, Larry. I...I like you, too," she said, the strain of fear evident in her voice.

"If you'd open your heart to Jesus, He not only would save you and forgive you of all your sins, but He'd give you peace, even in the midst of this horrible situation." Larry laid a hand on hers. "I...I could let myself fall in love with you...if you were a Christian."

Mitzy tossed her head to move some loose strands of hair from her face. "I could have strong feelings toward you, too...if I let myself."

"Guess it can never be, though, huh?"

She waited a few seconds. "Guess not."

⁂

John and Breanna were at the pool. John was filling Lieutenant Robins's canteen, and Breanna was washing the cloths she had used to wipe away his perspiration.

While the water gurgled into the canteen, John looked at Breanna and said, "You were covering for his sake, weren't you?"

"You mean when I said some fever?"

"Yes."

"I was. He's not going to make it, John. I'm sure he's got pneumonia. I'll be surprised if he lives till morning."

John was quiet for a moment, then as he capped the canteen, he said, "You've done everything you could."

"I know. But it's always hard to lose a patient."

"Especially for you, darlin'. You have such a tender heart."

Suddenly from behind them came Mitzy's voice. "Breanna..."

"Yes?"

"It's Lieutenant Robins. He's...he's dead. Larry and I heard him gasping for breath. I rushed to him, but he quit breathing. I told Captain Manning."

John and Breanna hurried to the spot. Manning and all the others were there together...except for Mark Gray, who was digging Boone McKeever's grave, and Benny Fagan, who was still atop the rock pillar.

John had an arm on Breanna's shoulder. "You did everything you could."

She nodded, biting her lips, and blinking at the moisture that had welled up in her eyes. "Praise the Lord he got saved," she said in a choked voice.

"I'll get the other shovel, sir," said Hank Durbin. "We'll go ahead and bury him tonight. Too bad we don't have a bugle so we could blow taps."

"Yeah," said Manning, about to break down. "Too bad."

Breanna heard Mitzy weeping somewhere nearby. She excused herself to John and hurried away. It took a few seconds, but she found her in deep shadows, near the base of a boulder, and took her in her arms.

"Oh, Breanna," Mitzy sobbed. "We're never going to get out of here alive! I know it! I just know it!"

Breanna's reply was cut off by the sound of a galloping horse somewhere outside the rocks. It lasted only seconds, then faded away. She could hear the others talking about it, conjecturing that an Apache was on some kind of errand for Dogindo.

"Mitzy," Breanna said, caressing her cheek, "if God wills it, we'll get out safely. John and I have been pr—"

"She all right?" John said as he drew up.

"Shaken up," said Breanna. "Royce dying, and all. She's afraid we're not going to get out of here alive. I was telling her that if God wills it, we'll live through this. I was about to explain that you and I have been praying hard...but if the Lord sees fit to let us die and come home to Him, that's the way it will be."

John leaned over to look in Mitzy's eyes. "Mitzy, if the Lord should let the Apaches kill us, Breanna and I will go exactly where Royce Robins just went...to heaven. Larry will go there, too. But you won't."

Mitzy began to cry. "Oh, Breanna...Mr. Brockman...I want to be saved!"

Corporal Deane was still sitting up and leaning against the boulder when he saw Mitzy walking toward him between the

Brockmans. As they came within thirty feet or so, the girl bolted to him, dropped to her knees with tears bubbling, and said, "Larry, I just got saved!"

"You did?" he said excitedly.

"Yes, and I'm so happy! My sins are gone! I'm a child of God!"

Larry extended his good arm and wrapped it around her neck, giving her a tight hug. "I'm so glad, Mitzy!"

"She couldn't wait to come and tell you, Larry," John said.

"That's the way it is when a person really gets saved," Breanna said. "They just have to tell it!"

"Captain Manning!" Hank Durbin said. "Jody Sleppy's gone!"

Terrell Sears was with Manning as he hurried to the sergeant, saying, "How do you know he's gone?"

"I was watering the horses, sir, and I couldn't account for his. The horse is gone, and he's nowhere to be found!"

"He's trying to get to Fort Verde and bring help," Manning said for the benefit of the others.

Sears rubbed the back of his neck, drew a deep breath, let it out slowly, and said, "I hope he makes it."

"Brave man," Manning said.

Mark Gray appeared, carrying the shovel. "Brave man or a fool," he said.

"You wouldn't know what a brave man is, Gray," Sears said.

"I'd face you on a quick-draw any day of the week."

"And you'd die, too."

Gray gave him a smug look and returned to his grave-digging.

Manning looked around at the moonlit faces. "Well, folks, Captain Sears and I just finished counting cartridges. We've got enough to keep the Apaches away another day...then we'll be out. I might add, we'll be out of rations in another day, too."

"Then we'd all better hope Jody makes it," said Ole Scrivner.

While Royce Robins's grave was being dug, John and Breanna walked hand-in-hand together through the narrow passageway and sat down again on the rock near the stagecoach. The night lay deep across the desert, and the moonlight was a frozen silver that enhanced the beauty of the winking stars in the great black canopy above.

"Sweetheart," John said, "I want us to pray together again. It's going to take a miracle to get us out of here alive."

"Our God is the God of miracles, darling."

"He is, and we'll pray for Him to work one, but..."

"But what?"

"We know the Lord has a time set for each of us to leave this earth...saved and unsaved."

"Yes."

"If...well, if this should be our time, I want to tell you that these few days we've been husband and wife have been glorious. Sounds funny, considering the fix we're in, but being married to you, even a few days in this world, would be better than being married to someone else for a lifetime."

Tears filled Breanna's eyes. "Oh, John..." She cried softly as she clung to him. When she gained control of her emotions, she looked up at him and said, "I love you, my darling...more than life itself."

They kissed, then bowed their heads in prayer.

⁂

Gray dawn cracked through the night, and the men in the rocks prepared for battle. Larry Deane took a spot, holding a revolver in his good hand, and Van Hatfield positioned himself to fight as usual.

High up on the towering pillar, Sergeant Hank Durbin was preparing to go down to take his position when he saw movement on the ground about a hundred yards east. It was a man. He was stumbling toward the rock enclosure. He fell time and again, but kept getting up and staggering on. Cupping a hand to the side of his mouth, Durbin called down to his leader. "Captain Manning! There's a man on foot, coming toward us from the east!"

Manning was standing with Sears, who followed him as he ran up the side of a boulder to get a look.

"It's Jody!" Sears said. "I'm going after him!"

"No!" Manning said. "The Apaches probably caught him. They'll torture a man till he's at the edge of death, then let him stumble his way back to his comrades. If you go out there, they'll cut you down!"

Nevertheless, Sears slid down the side of the boulder, jumped to the ground, and headed for open country.

"Don't do it, Captain!" Manning shouted.

"I have to! He's one of my men!"

"I can't let him go out there alone," John Brockman said. "He'll need some cover."

"No, John!" Breanna cried. "Please don't go!"

"Can't let him do it alone, honey!" he said, and took off running.

The Apaches did not go after the two men as they ran toward Jody. When they were within about thirty yards of him, Jody stumbled and fell again. This time, he did not get up. When they reached him, they examined him for a few seconds, then John hoisted him over his shoulder and Sears ran beside him as he headed back.

Manning was the first to meet them as they came in, both men panting.

"He's dead," Sears said with a break in his voice.

"They tortured him just like you said, Captain," said John, laying the body on the ground next to a large rock.

"We'll bury him next to Lieutenant Robins," Sears said. "He gave his life to try to get help for us. We'll give him a hero's burial."

At sunup, the Apaches came screeching and yapping, their guns belching fire. Bullets struck rocks, ricocheting and whining away angrily.

From his lofty position in the rocks, John Brockman watched Dogindo lead his men in for the first wave, then ride back out of rifle range to observe the battle from beside the lone boulder. John's eye ran a panorama of the land, taking in the gullies, ravines, and rocky areas that surrounded Dogindo's observation spot.

Suddenly John saw an Apache warrior ride up close to the base of the massive boulders beneath him. The Indian took aim at John and fired a split second after John had ducked back. The bullet splintered rock, showering fragments in three directions. John raised up, fired a shot at the Indian, and ducked back again.

Another bullet hit rock and caromed away whining. The Apache backed his horse up for another shot. John was about to fire again, when he heard a rifle crack off to his right, and the Indian fell from his horse's back. Ole Scrivner waved and smiled. John waved back.

The battle stayed hot and heavy as the sun climbed higher in the sky toward dark clouds coming in from the west. By high noon, the sun was covered.

John thought of their dwindling ammunition and of his conversation with Breanna last night. They had prayed for a miracle. While guns were roaring, the Holy Spirit seemed to say to John's heart, Sometimes I work miracles when My children make an effort to bring about the desired result.

John looked at Dogindo one more time through the rising clouds of gunsmoke. He knew the Apaches worshiped their chiefs, looking on them as demigods. If Dogindo was in the hands of their enemies, they would do nothing to put his life at risk.

John slid down to Ole and shouted above the din, "There's something I have to do!"

"What's that?"

"No time to explain. Just keep firing!"

Ole continued to blast away as John slid into a deep crevice, made his way to the edge of the boulders, and dropped to the ground. An Apache let out a wild yell and galloped toward him bringing up his rifle. John whipped out his gun and fired. The Indian fell off his horse sideways, causing the animal to fall. When it jumped back to a standing position, John leaped on its back, bent low, and gouged its sides for a full gallop. He guided the Indian pony into a deep ravine and rode fast till he knew he was on the far side of the boulder where Dogindo was watching the battle from his horse's back.

Brockman reined the horse to a halt in the ravine, tied it to a bush, and crawled to the crest. He could not see the war chief yet, but he knew he was sitting his horse on the west side of the boulder. John rushed up to the boulder, flattened his back against it, and began to inch his way around to the other side.

He drew up quick when the Apache chief came into view, his back to him. Dogindo's horse bobbed its head and nickered, and John eased back. But Dogindo was intent on the battle.

John drew a deep breath, steeled himself, and crept up behind him. When he was within ten feet, the horse nickered again, pulling his head around. Dogindo glanced over his shoulder and stiffened when he saw the man in black.

But it was too late.

John had him off the horse and cracked him with a blow to the jaw before he could react. Dogindo slumped to the ground. John removed the knife from Dogindo's sheath and threw the revolver he wore on the ground. He then hoisted the limp form over his shoulder and headed back for the ravine.

The sky was becoming black with heavy clouds, and lightning was flashing many miles to the west. The Apaches continued their yapping, and guns continued to roar.

Breanna and Mitzy, crouched low in the enclosure, saw Corporal Benny Eagan dash from his position and say something to his captain, showing him his rifle. Manning shook his head.

"He's out of bullets," Breanna said. "It won't be long till the others are out, too."

Suddenly Mitzy's attention was drawn to the narrow passageway at the west side of the enclosure. "Breanna, look!"

John came charging in on the Indian pony with Dogindo draped in front of him.

Breanna dashed toward him with Mitzy on her heels.

"John," Breanna said, "how—how did you…?"

"No time to explain, sweetheart," he said, and turned to Dogindo, who was starting to come around.

Easing him to the ground, John ripped a part of the Indian's pantleg off and tied his hands behind his back.

"John, what are you going to do?"

"End this battle," he said, smiling at her, then lifted Dogindo to his feet and held him there until his eyes cleared.

The chieftain blinked and looked at John as if he were in a nightmare.

"You understand English, don't you, Dogindo?"

Still somewhat dazed, the chief nodded.

"Okay," said John, pulling his Colt .45 and snapping back the hammer, "you and I are going up on that big boulder over there, where all your warriors can see you. When the firing stops, you're going to tell them all to go home, or I'm going to do something they won't like."

As he spoke, John took a firm grip on one of Dogindo's arms and pushed the muzzle of his revolver up under his chin, making his head bend back. "Breanna," he said, "get somebody's attention and let Captain Manning know what I'm doing."

Lightning split the black sky overhead as the people in the rock formation watched the Apache warriors galloping away at the command of their leader. John Brockman stood with the muzzle of his Colt .45 pressed under Dogindo's chin, until the last warrior vanished from sight.

"You did the right thing, Dogindo," said John, holstering his gun and moving the chief down the side of the boulder. "If you'd refused to tell your men to go home—well, I don't even like to think about it."

When they reached bottom, all but Mark Gray applauded John. To Manning, John said, "I'm turning him over to you, Captain. Main thing now is to get our stage safely to Phoenix. If you'll keep Dogindo under lock and key for a while, I think his people will settle down."

While Brockman was talking to the captain, Mitzy moved up beside Larry Deane and said, "I just want you to know that I don't want to work as a saloon girl anymore. I'm going to get me a respectable job in Phoenix and live in a boarding house. I'll get into a church and wait for the Lord to send me the man I'm supposed to marry."

Larry grinned. "Let me know the address of that boarding house!"

At that moment, lightning cracked through the black sky, and thunder roared. The lightning seemed to tear a giant hole in the clouds, for the rain came down in sheets. Everyone scattered for cover. The wind-driven rain lashed the rock formation, blinding everyone. For ten minutes, it was as though they were standing under a waterfall.

Terrell Sears tried to see through the deluge in search of Mark Gray. There was no sign of him. The Ranger captain ran to the end of the passageway, but both Gray and his horse were gone. Sears shook his head in disbelief and moved back to tell the others.

It rained for about a half hour, then gradually let up. As they prepared to pull out, Manning came to Sears and said, "What are you going to do now?"

"Wire my office from Phoenix and tell them of Jody's death, then go after Gray. I'll track him till I find him…and believe me, I will."

Soon what was left of the army unit was escorting the stage

southward toward Phoenix. They were hardly started when Sergeant Hank Durbin pulled rein and rode to the edge of a ravine.

Manning called for Ole to stop the stage, and trotted over to Durbin, who was off his horse, kneeling beside a dead man. "Looks like the Apaches found some men hiding in here, Captain. There are four more sprawled along the slope, down here."

John Brockman had left the stage and drew up. "What's happened here?" he asked, focusing on the dead man, whose right arm was in a sling.

"Looks like a full-fledged massacre," Manning said.

"Wait a minute!" John said. "I know this one. His name's Billy Hood. His father's supposed to be the biggest rancher in these parts."

"Well, he isn't anymore if he's one of those dead men down there," Durbin said.

"Nothing we can do for them now," Manning said. "Let's move out."

The passengers and crew of the stagecoach and the men on horseback stayed the night in a relay station some twenty miles north of Phoenix and arrived in the town midmorning the next day.

John and Breanna bid Mitzy and Larry good-bye and were happy to know Larry was going to court her. When the cavalrymen were gone, John and Breanna booked the next stage for Denver, which would leave the following morning at nine-thirty, then took a room at the nearest hotel.

John took Breanna to a nearby café, and after they had

enjoyed a good meal, he told her he would take her back to the hotel, then go to the U.S. marshal's office to see if there was any word about Chief Duvall.

"I'll just go over there with you," she said. "Then we can go to the hotel."

John agreed. They were about to head that way when Captain Sears rode up on his horse. They discussed their adventure, then Sears told them he would be heading back north to see if he could pick up Mark Gray's trail. John told him they were leaving on the nine-thirty stage in the morning. Sears said he'd be riding out about that time and would stop and tell them good-bye.

When the Brockmans walked into the U.S. marshal's office, they were both shocked to see the silver-haired Duvall sitting in front of the desk, talking to Cliff Barnes.

"Well, look who's here!" said the chief, rising to his feet. "John and Breanna! Cliff told me John was supposed to be showing up here, but Washington didn't say anything about Breanna. I assume you went ahead with the wedding?"

The reunion was sweet. Duvall told them of having been kidnapped by Jock Hood and his sons, and why. John told him of finding five dead men, of which one was definitely Billy Hood.

Duvall said it had to be them. They had all gone to find the stagecoach John was on. It was Hazel Crumpton, Hood's housekeeper, who had set Sol free just that morning. She had been against his captivity all along, and was willing to face Hood when he came home to learn she had let him go.

And John and Breanna were pleased to learn that Duvall was booked on tomorrow morning's stage for Denver.

✦

The next morning, John, Breanna, and Sol were about to board the stage when Captain Sears rode up. He dismounted, and John introduced him to Sol.

After chatting a few minutes, Sears said, "Well, maybe our paths will cross again someday."

"I hope so. You take care, Captain," John said.

Sears was just turning to mount his horse when a sharp voice from behind him said, "Sears!"

The captain turned around to see Mark Gray standing in the middle of the street, his hand hovering over his holstered gun. John and Breanna were almost as stunned to see him as Sears was.

Sears tensed and moved toward Gray.

"Hold it right there, Sears!" Gray barked, the fingers twitching on his gun hand.

"I figured you'd be running," said Sears, stopping some forty feet from him.

"I was, but...I had to come back. I've lived too long wanting to put you down. Go for your gun."

"You can't out-draw me, Mark. Drop your gunbelt. You're under arrest."

"We'll see about that!" Gray said, his hand darting downward.

It was over in less than a heartbeat. Mark Gray lay dead in the sun-bleached street.

Tiny wisps of smoke trailed from the muzzle of Sears's gun as he moved to the body and looked down, a satisfied expression on his face. "Jody was right, Mark. I did have the edge on you. And the Bible was right too: 'The soul of the transgressors shall eat violence.'"

23

THE DENVER-BOUND STAGECOACH rolled out of Phoenix and started up a long hill. The six-up team pressed hard into the harness, their muscles bunching and the soft dirt flying in yellow clouds.

John and Breanna Brockman sat across from Chief U.S. Marshal Solomon Duvall, and two elderly men, who promptly went to sleep.

"Well, I'm glad this episode is over," sighed Duvall. "Tom Wall is going to prison. There are two new deputies on their way from Kansas City, and Cliff Barnes is permanent head of the Phoenix office."

"Nice to have things wrap up smoothly, isn't it?" John said.

Duvall nodded. "But, of course, the thing I don't like about it all is that I missed your wedding."

"We missed having you there, too," said Breanna.

"Well, at least I'm glad Matt stepped in and took my place."

"He's a prince," John said with conviction.

Breanna set concerned eyes on Duvall. "You look tired, Chief."

Duvall smiled. "There's a reason for that, my dear," he said, removing his hat and running splayed fingers through his thick mop of silver hair. "I am tired."

"Well," said John, "a good rest when you get home, and you'll be up and at 'em like always."

Duvall dropped his hat back on his head. "Not this time, John. I'm afraid this body of mine is telling me I can't do it anymore. I've been thinking about retiring for several months. It took this ordeal to convince me it's time to turn in my badge."

"You don't mean it," John said, frowning.

"Yes, I do. The time has come. I'm getting too old for the job."

John looked at Breanna. "Do you have anything in your medical bag that would stimulate him to stay with it another twenty years?"

The chief laughed. "Twenty years! You're a dreamer, Mr. Stranger Man."

John laughed, then said, "Seriously, Sol…I know you have to do what you have to do. It's just hard to picture that office without you in it, and that badge without you behind it."

"Well, time changes everything except God and His Word, John."

"Can't argue with that."

Duvall rubbed his tired eyes. "When we get to Denver, I'll wire Washington and give them the details about what happened in Arizona, including John Brockman's brave deed in capturing Dogindo. And in the same wire, I'll officially submit my resignation. I'll stay on, of course, till Washington can find a replacement."

Four days later, Breanna was dusting furniture in her parlor when she looked out the window and saw John ride up on

Ebony and dismount at the front porch. She went to the door to meet him.

When he stepped inside, she said, "Well?"

"All set! My friend in Central City wired me right back. The cabin in the mountains will be waiting for us. We'll leave first thing in the morning."

Breanna threw the dust cloth in the air, wrapped her arms around his neck, and said, "Oh, praise the Lord! At last, we're going to have our honeymoon!"

The next morning, John had Ebony and Chance saddled and at the front porch, and was tying small pieces of luggage behind the saddles. Breanna came out the door, smiling happily, wearing one of her split riding skirts. "Oh, darling, isn't it wonderful? I'll have you all to myself for ten whole days."

Even as she spoke, Breanna saw a rider come trotting from the road toward the house. "Oh, no. I wonder what this is."

John turned and recognized Harley Withers, one of Western Union's messengers at the Denver office. "Must be a telegram for one of us."

Harley pulled rein and smiled. "Good morning, John...Miss Breanna. Telegram for the head of the house."

"Oh," said John, winking at Harley. "It's for you, Breanna!"

"Funny, Mr. Brockman," Breanna said. "Real funny!"

John signed for the telegram, thanked Harley, and watched him ride away. He opened the envelope, and Breanna stood on the porch while he began reading it. "Who's it from, John?"

"The president," he said without looking up.

"The president of what?"

"Of the United States." John lowered the yellow sheet of

paper and set his steel-gray eyes on her. "He wants me to become chief U.S. marshal of the western district in Sol's place."

"He does?"

"That's what it says right here."

Breanna thought on it a moment, then said, "John, we both agreed that when we married, neither of us would travel as much as we've been doing. I'll work at the hospital and at Dr. Goodwin's office more. And we agreed that you wouldn't be gone so much."

"Well, we've certainly prayed about it enough. It strikes me that this must be the Lord's answer for what I should do, sweetheart."

"Sure seems so." Breanna smiled. "Oh, John, I'll be so proud to see you behind that desk and wearing the chief U.S. marshal's badge!"

John pulled at an ear. "Well, now, I'll have to work out a deal with Mr. Grant. Since I don't need the salary, I'll ask him to give me an assistant who can handle the desk work when I go after outlaws. The assistant can have my salary."

Breanna was studying him.

"Breanna, you know I can't sit behind a desk all the time! I've got to feel the heat of the sun and have the wind in my face once in a while! I've got to do my part to make the West a decent place to live for good, law-abiding people."

Breanna laughed. "I understand, darling," she said, moving down the steps and into his arms. "And I'm sure President Grant will understand, too."

John kissed the tip of her nose. "I won't plan any long stretches, you understand, but this man would rather ride a horse than a desk."

"Of course," she said, raising up on her tiptoes to kiss his lips. "How soon does he want you to take the position?"

"He uses the word *immediately.*"

Breanna's countenance fell. "But John…our honeymoon."

"Nothing's going to keep us from that. Chief Duvall can handle the job for another ten days. I'll wire the president that I'll take the job if he'll accept me on my terms, and if he'll wait till we get back from our honeymoon. Okay, darlin'? I'm going to that cabin. How about you?"

Breanna laughed, kissed him again, and said, "Of course I'm going. Didn't I say at the altar, 'Whither thou goest, I will go'?"

Other Compelling Stories by
Al Lacy

Books in the Battles of Destiny series:

☞ *A Promise Unbroken*

Two couples battle jealousy and racial hatred amidst a war that would cripple America. From a prosperous Virginia plantation to a grim jail cell outside Lynchburg, follow the dramatic story of a love that could not be destroyed.

☞ *A Heart Divided*

Ryan McGraw—leader of the Confederate Sharpshooters—is nursed back to health by beautiful army nurse Dixie Quade. Their romance would survive the perils of war, but can it withstand the reappearance of a past love?

☞ *Beloved Enemy*

Young Jenny Jordan covers for her father's Confederate spy missions. But as she grows closer to Union soldier Buck Brownell, Jenny finds herself torn between devotion to the South and her feelings for the man she is forbidden to love.

☞ *Shadowed Memories*

Critically wounded on the field of battle and haunted by amnesia, one man struggles to regain his strength and the memories that have slipped away from him.

☞ *Joy from Ashes*

Major Layne Dalton made it through the horrors of the battle of Fredericksburg, but can he rise above his hatred toward the Heglund brothers who brutalized his wife and killed his unborn son?

☞ *Season of Valor*

Captain Shane Donovan was heroic in battle. Can he summon the courage to face the dark tragedy unfolding back home in Maine?

Books in the Battles of Destiny series (cont.):

☞ *Wings of the Wind*

God brings a young doctor and a nursing student together in this story of the Battle of Antietam.

Books in the Journeys of the Stranger series:

☞ *Legacy*

Can John Stranger bring Clay Austin back to the right side of the law...and restore the code of honor shared by the woman he loves?

☞ *Silent Abduction*

The mysterious man in black fights to defend a small town targeted by cattle rustlers and to rescue a young woman and child held captive by a local Indian tribe.

☞ *Blizzard*

When three murderers slated for hanging escape from the Colorado Territorial Prison, young U.S. Marshal Ridge Holloway and the mysterious John Stranger join together to track down the infamous convicts.

☞ *Tears of the Sun*

When John Stranger arrives in Apache Junction, Arizona, he finds himself caught up in a bitter war between sworn enemies: the Tonto Apaches and the Arizona Zunis.

☞ *Circle of Fire*

John Stranger must clear his name of the crimes committed by another mysterious—and murderous—"stranger" who has adopted his identity.

☞ *Quiet Thunder*

A Sioux warrior and a white army captain have been blood brothers since childhood. But when the two meet on the battlefield, which will win out—love or duty?

Books in the Journeys of the Stranger series (cont.):

☞ *Snow Ghost*

John Stranger must unravel the mystery of a murderer who appears to have come back from the grave to avenge his execution.

Books in the Angel of Mercy series:

☞ *A Promise for Breanna*

The man who broke Breanna's heart is back. But this time, he's after her life.

☞ *Faithful Heart*

Breanna and her sister Dottie find themselves in a desperate struggle to save a man they love, but can no longer trust.

☞ *Captive Set Free*

No one leaves Morgan's labor camp alive. Not even Breanna Baylor.

☞ *A Dream Fulfilled*

A tender story about one woman's healing from heartbreak and the fulfillment of her dreams.

Books in the Hannah of Fort Bridger series (co-authored with JoAnna Lacy):

☞ *Under the Distant Sky*

Follow the Cooper family as they travel West from Missouri in pursuit of their dream of a new life on the Wyoming frontier.

☞ *Consider the Lilies*

Will Hannah Cooper and her children learn to trust God to provide when tragedy threatens to destroy their dream?

Available at your local Christian bookstore

Printed in the United States
by Baker & Taylor Publisher Services